D1544271

LARK ASCENDING

LARK ASCENDING

By

MAZO DE LA ROCHE

BOSTON

LITTLE, BROWN, AND COMPANY

1932

THE ATLANTIC MONTHLY PRESS BOOKS
ARE PUBLISHED BY
LITTLE, RROWN, AND COMPANY
IN ASSOCIATION WITH
THE ATLANTIC MONTHLY COMPANY

FOR EMILY WATERS
*remembering a lucky voyage
from Naples to London*

LARK ASCENDING

CHAPTER I

THE wind rushed through the street with the savage playfulness peculiar to a wind from the sea. It swept between the wooden buildings of the seaside resort as though in search of some definite damage it might do to prove its malice. But the weather-beaten boards were inured to its attacks, the wicket gates accustomed to be shaken almost off their hinges, and all loose and fragile projections had long ago been blown away. So there was little for it to do but whip the shirts and long drawers that writhed on the lines, whirl sheets of newspaper along the deserted road, and blow the picture young Diego Palmas was painting off its easel. It fell paint side down, on the long grass that grew between sidewalk and road, and when he picked it up, he found a dusty nettle plastered across the glimpse of tossing sea, between two pinkish-yellow houses, that was its subject.

He looked at it ruefully. His face was of that strongly marked, swarthy variety which so lends itself to the expression of emotion that a look of annoyance is translated into a forbidding scowl, a rueful glance into an expression of dark despair. So now an observer would have felt real pity for him, when all he was thinking was, "Oh, hell, I'll get stung!"

He gingerly caught the rough stem of the nettle between finger and thumb and drew it off the canvas, drawing with it a blue door, a yellow hitching post, and a green wave. He cast all these together into the dust of the road and put his finger in his mouth. The stinging sensation made him pull his mouth down at the corners, enlarge his eyes, and draw his eyebrows up on his forehead. Instantly his expression became one of tragedy. The imaginary observer might now be almost moved to tears.

But no one saw him. He folded up his easel, wiped his brushes on a bit of rag, and collected the other implements of his art. Then he crossed the road and turned into the deserted main street, all his movements being of such extreme indolence that it seemed doubtful if he had an objective, and, if he had, if he would ever reach it. He was strongly built; he was nineteen years old; he wore a black beret, a gray sweater coat over a faded shirt, open at the throat, and dirty white duck trousers on which there were stains of paint.

The main street bore evidence that the tourist season was over. The shop where souvenirs were sold was already closed. The shop that advertised clam chowder, lobster salad, and blueberry pie was closing. The last waitress stood in the doorway, her short skirt blown above her knees, inhaling the salt air with a feeling of vagabond freedom. She had an eye for the young artist as he slouched past her, and he returned her look with a glance half humorous, half surly. He moved on, looking in every window as he passed, though he could have told you, with his eyes shut, what was in each of them. The sausages, the round steaks, the boiling pieces that had lately taken the place of sirloin roasts, lamb chops, and chickens, in the butcher's window. The bathing suits, bathing caps, berets, and sweaters that had been rejected by the summer colony, in the drygoods store. The picture postcards, the brightly colored magazines, the boxes of chocolates, now noticeably specked by flies, in the stationer's. Saltport, which lent herself but grudgingly to her summer season, was now withdrawing into her natural state of reserve and suspicion toward the outside world, preparing for her long winter of icy gales without, and conversations in slow nasal voices, beside red-hot stoves, within.

Those who looked out through the open doors of their stores and saw young Diego Palmas go by did not look after him with resentment as a belated summer artist, but with an intense and possessive interest, for he was one of them, in spite of his name, his foreign face, and his beret, and they wondered what he and that mother of his would do next, now that his father was gone.

He was conscious in every nerve of the eyes watching him from shop doors and from between the curtains of windows above the shops. All Saltport was watching him and his mother. They were the only people of real interest in the place. He threw a glance of proud suspicion at the windows as he passed beneath.

At a corner where the street descended steeply to

the beach there stood a tea house painted black and
orange, outside which a row of little tables were set.
He remembered how, only a few weeks ago, the tables
were crowded with people at this hour and how many
heads had turned to look at him as he slowly passed
by, resting his sombre eyes with the same look of
proud suspicion on them.

On the corner opposite the gayly painted tea house
stood a shabby weather-beaten building, on the
ground floor of which was the one drug store of the
little town.   The sign, almost illegible, read, "Purley
Bond, Prescription Druggist."   In the window stood
two large glass jars containing a green liquid, and,
scattered about them, a display of kodaks, film spools,
tins of talcum, rolls of fly paper, boxes of candy, beach
balls, and bottles of patent medicine.   The window
was framed in glaring advertisements of different
brands of cigarettes and dentifrice.   Inside the store
other highly glazed tin and cardboard signs, the
bright expanse of a soda fountain, and the glass cases
containing cigarettes and chocolates almost obliterated the section given over to drugs, which looked,
by comparison, dingy and depressing.   Yet in this
dark and depressing corner the only dignity of the
place was exhibited.   Between the old-fashioned
green bottles in the window and the dark phials on
these shelves there was an affinity, a bond of mournful
pride in the past, when a chemist had not needed to
degrade his profession in order to get custom.

Diego, easel and canvas in hand, sauntered in and,
finding no one behind the counter, peered into the

corner enclosed behind frosted glass where prescriptions were filled. It was so dim in there that he could just make out the figure of a man tilted back in a chair with his feet raised against a paper-littered desk. A blue veil of smoke was stretched above his head, and in one hand he held the bowl of a short, curved pipe.

"Hullo, Diego," he said, without taking the pipe from his mouth, "what have you been up to? Painting, eh? I should think it was pretty windy."

"It was," growled the youth. "It blew the darned picture right off the easel and it got a nettle on it. Look here" — and he held the picture in front of the man's face.

"I can't see it in this light." He stretched a long arm to reach a switch, and in an instant he was exposed to view in the glare of a strong unshaded electric lamp. In it his rather coarse hair looked almost white, but in reality there was not a white hair on his untidy head. It was so pale a yellow as to be almost silver, and his rough eyebrows, and even his eyelashes, were the same. With pale eyes, a delicate skin or weak features, he might have been an anæmic-looking fellow indeed, but he had none of these. His eyes, not large, yet well shaped, were a vivid and flower-like blue; his flat, shaven cheeks, on which a coarse beard was barely subjected, showed a sunburnt sandy color; his features were strong and well cut.

He gripped his pipe in his teeth and, with the hand that had held the bowl, took the picture from Diego.

He blew out his breath when he saw the devastation caused by the nettle. "It certainly disarranged things," he said sympathetically. "It'll take you some time to fix it up." He now held the picture at arm's length and knitted his blond brows critically. "It looks as though it might have had the making of a good one in it, too. It's funny how your pictures never look real good till you work them up at home. They've got the promise. Yet they're sort of slovenly, as if you just slapped the color on — always the right color, too — and did n't care a hang for form. But when they're finished they're first rate, and I'll not be surprised if you make a name for yourself."

Diego watched him with an expression half amused, half sulky. He did not trouble himself about conversation. He let other people do the talking while he, with an aloofness almost feline, accepted or rejected what was said. Now he accepted this remark of Purley Bond's in silent acquiescence.

Bond laid the painting on the desk and puffed at his pipe. "It's a good thing that New York artist takes an interest in you," he said. "If it had n't been for him your father would never have agreed to your studying art."

"Yes," agreed Diego, contemptuously "He'd have made a baker of me, like himself."

"Oh, I don't know about that. He was ambitious for you, all right, when you were a little boy. I've heard him talk of putting you through for a civil engineer. You must n't forget that he was one when he married your mother. It was only when his health broke down that he went in for baking."

"What a business to go in for!" Diego shrugged a heavy young shoulder in a manner he had picked up from the New York artist.

"Well, he had to do something that he could keep warm at. He'd a wife to support." The last sentence was uttered in a lower tone, almost as though to himself.

Diego laughed. "He kept warm all right! Sweat was always running off him. Seems to me I was brought up in an oven. Raised — like a cake! And now my mother's doing it. . . . It makes me sick!"

"Yes, it's pretty bad for her. But — Josie does a good deal, does n't she?"

"Well," — Diego scowled, — "she ought to, I guess! She's always had her living off us!"

Purley Bond laughed in his turn. "Josie has certainly earned anything she has had from your family. She's been standing behind that counter almost as long as she could see over it! And it would have taken a pretty smart person to fool her on the change, even then."

Diego picked up his artist's paraphernalia.

Bond knocked out his pipe and got up. He was not very fond of Diego, but he did not want him to leave just yet — not until he had spoken again of Diego's mother, whom he loved. He said: —

"Don't go without something to drink. You like this kind of slop, don't you? It's the last week of the season for it, thank God! What'll you have?"

He had led the way into the store and he now stood behind the polished soda fountain, revealed as a well-built man of thirty-five, in a dark tweed suit.

"Pineapple ice-cream soda," said Diego, laconically. There was a hissing, a gurgling, a spurting. A ball of ice cream was taken from a tin container and dropped into the frothing glass in its nickel holder. Diego set his easel against the counter and laid his picture on it. He sat himself on one of the high stools and watched the mixing of the confection with absorbed interest. "Thanks," he muttered, and introduced two straws between his full red lips.

Bond stood looking down at him, wondering what went on in that black head beneath the beret. He allowed him a long undisturbed pull at the straw, then he said: —

"If only your mother could sell the business and you could begin to make something, it would n't be so bad. But she 'll scarcely be able to sell at the end of the season."

"The bakery 's always busy," grumbled Diego, fishing for the ice cream with a spoon.

"But she and Josie must n't wear themselves out. What with nursing your father through last winter . . . then his death . . . and the tourist season on top of that   . she 's had the devil of a time."

"I 'll say she has! Her nerves won't hold out much longer. She 's in for a breakdown or something. You 'd better come in to-night and have a talk. She told me to tell you." He gave a sly look into Bond's face as he said the last words.

Bond replied imperturbably: "Very well, I will. Tell her to expect me about eight. Are you going straight home?"

"No, I'm going down to the studio to put my things away."

"Decent of Mr. Selby to let you share it with him, isn't it?"

"It's just as much to his advantage as mine. I look after it for him — see that it isn't interfered with. Shut it in the fall and open it up in the spring. Josie's down there this afternoon putting away the bedding."

Josie! Always Josie, thought Bond. He said: "But you've a good deal to be grateful to him for, just the same. He persuaded your father to let you study art and then he gave you lessons for nothing. I call that pretty decent of him. What does he think of you?"

Diego again shrugged his massive shoulders. "Oh, he thinks I'm a genius. Well, — " he added self-consciously, — "he thinks like you do — that I work in a queer sort of way. He can't make me out." He gave a little laugh and again picked up his things.

A small boy entered and laid a coin on the counter. "Pleh, I wah a bohhle o' cahor oil," he said.

Bond got the castor oil and began wrapping it up. "Has Mamie got the stomach ache again?" he asked.

"Yeh. Eah hoo muh rhuburb."

Diego asked, when the child had gone, "Say, Purley, what makes so many folks here talk like that?"

Bond drew down the corners of his mouth in a

grimace of mingled resignation and disgust. "In-bred. That's what's the matter. We've married and intermarried till we haven't palates enough to go round. Nothing but the summer people coming and going makes any stir here. And that's only on the surface. Be thankful you're all there, Diego!"

"Well, I've different blood in me, anyway."

"Yes, you certainly have." Purley Bond looked at him speculatively. "A queer mixture. A strain of Portuguese in your dad. A dash of Indian in your mother. No wonder you're an oddity, Diego."

"Am I an oddity?" He wanted to hear that he was different from other Saltporters.

"Do you ever look at yourself in the glass?"

Diego looked gratified. "Mother's different, too."

"Yes. She's different." Again he spoke in a muffled tone, as though the image of her produced a hush in his being.

Diego went on, "Well, I'm not going to stay here and intermarry and get kids with cleft palates, you can bet!"

Bond smiled grimly. "Wait till you're grown up yourself before you begin to worry. I'll come along to-night and talk things over."

A customer came in and Diego, with a nod of half-sulky friendliness, went out.

His big limbs were weary of stillness. He had stood before his easel most of the afternoon, he had sat on the stool in the drug store. Now he wanted to run, but he was cumbered by his wet picture, the easel, and the box containing his palette, brushes, and paints. He went in a heavy jog trot down the steep little side street that led between the tea house and the drug store, to the sea.

A change had taken place while he was indoors. The hazy yellow sunshine of the September afternoon had deepened to the dense still light that comes before sundown. Every object was intensely visible in the light, as though magnified. The wind had fallen, but the dark blue waves still shouldered each other carelessly as they climbed the beach. Gulls romping above them swam along the dying wind with tenuous cries.

At the foot of the street Diego turned and began to climb the shell-encrusted rocks that circled the harbor. He made for a large square wooden building — a barn that had been converted into a studio. Windows had been cut in it, the shutters of which and the door had been painted a bright blue in imitation of doors and gates not uncommon in the village, relics of Portuguese sailors who had once settled here. An old iron lamp hung above the doorway, and a brass knocker in the shape of a ship was fixed to a panel. Diego lifted the old-fashioned latch and closed the door softly behind him.

The ground floor of the barn had been converted into a dining room, with a kitchen at one end separated from it by a screen. The shutters were closed and the room dim. He mounted the closed-in stairway and reached the large living room above without having been heard by the girl who stood looking out of the window across the harbor.

Cautiously he laid the things he carried on the table and glided up behind her. He put a hand on each of her hips, then put his head beside hers, his chin resting on her shoulder. She gave a cry of fright and turned so that her face touched his, their eyes close together.

"Jimmy!" she cried. "How you frightened me! You 're a perfect brute! You think it 's funny, don't you? But I don't see anything funny in it — sneaking up that way and sticking your black face over my shoulder."

"Are n't you polite! If people knew what a temper you have they would n't always be saying what a nice quiet little thing Josie Froward is."

She had turned pale with fright. Now her color, of a flower-petal freshness, came back into her cheeks. She was a thin fanciful girl of medium height, gray eyes, mouse-brown hair, vivid only in the color of her cheeks. She carried herself with an air of stubborn courage as though she were in the habit of undertaking more than her strength was equal to, and even carrying it through. She was morbidly afraid of strangers, of sudden noises and starts, but she was not afraid of Diego. They had been in the house together since she had come, a little girl of thirteen, an orphaned cousin of his mother's. She called Diego "Jimmy."

She had sprung back from him, facing about, so that he was able to watch the delicate bright color return to her cheek, her gray eyes widen in anger, in a way that had always pleased him. She had a queer beauty at these moments in spite of her extreme thinness and irregularity of feature. The fact that he could make her look like this gave him a sweet sense of power. He watched her paling, quivering, flaming, as an indolent cat might watch a fluttering bird — interested in a puzzled, feline, lazy way. His stillness fascinated her, as her fluttering interested him. When he was in the room she could never keep her eyes off him. If he raised his hand to pass it through his dense, black hair, that gesture was as mysterious, as strange to her, as the play of moonlight. If he rose out of the waves when they were bathing, it was as though some strange sea god rose and stretched himself. Yet he was not a young god to her. She was contemptuous of his talent. She despised his sloth. She had always been ready, eager, to exert herself beyond her strength. He must be goaded to any activity beyond what his healthy body craved. Yet his fascination for her was renewed with the freshness of each new day.

He looked about the room, saw the piled-up quilts and blankets on the couch that was used as a bed.

"No wonder you 're frightened," he said. "You 've been doing nothing. Have n't got the bedclothes put away. Yes — and been drinking coffee! I see the coffeepot and milk pitcher. Oh, what a nice, quiet, energetic girl Josie Froward is! However would you get on without her, Mrs. Palmas?"

"You dare sneer at me!" she cried. "How much have you done this afternoon? Come — let 's see your old picture!"

"Now," he said, holding it in front of her, "what do you think of that?"

She looked, drew back, bent forward. "Why — why — what is it? I can't make it out! It looks like the bit of sea between Thornton's and Fred Taylor's, but — what 's happened? My God, what a mess it is!"

"New Art," said Diego, bending to look over the top of the picture at its wet scarred surface. "Study in the Nude. Emaciated nude girl hanging out clothes in back yard — high wind — sea beyond — I think it 's great!"

"You can't bluff me! It 's been on the ground. I see dirt sticking to it. . . ." She looked intently at the picture with mounting interest. "Oh, what a pity, because there 's something good in it. Why, you can feel the wind! It 's full of movement." She took the picture from him and studied it. "Jimmy, how could you have been so stupid as to let it fall?"

"The wind blew it off my easel. It was a regular gale. Do you think anything can be done with it?"

"I don't know. You 'd better try to-morrow." Her tone was challenging.

"You know I won't try again. Have a go at it yourself."

She repeated in a tense voice: "What a pity you dropped it! It 's so seldom you do anything worth while!"

"You always say the same thing. For my part — I don't care what becomes of it. Here — give it to me! I 'll throw it on the rubbish heap."

She knew he was capable of this. "Don't be an idiot! I'll see what I can do. But, upon my word, it's good, Jimmy!" She carried the picture across and held it beneath one, on a similar note, of those that covered the wall — half-finished studies left by the artist who owned the studio. "Look — it's better than this one of Mr. Selby's! But it's like everything you paint — there's something wrong with it."

"Till you take it in hand, eh? You've conceit enough for the two of us. I hate conceited girls."

"And I hate flabby men — and flabby pictures!"

But she looked enviously at the picture as she held it against the wall. He had the ability to create and she knew she did not have it. But she had the power to interpret what he created. She could take his form-less, ill-judged creations and build them up, coax them into a kind of serenity, so that they satisfied the senses, not tormented them. Josie loved painting as Diego did not. She had conquered her shyness sufficiently to come secretly with Diego to Mr. Selby for lessons. She had got up at dawn, she had worked into the night, in order to find time for this secret expression of her being. All she did she kept hidden in her attic room where no one went but herself. But it was over the pictures which she and Diego had painted together that she exulted. He got all the credit for these. No one knew that she had put a brush to them. These were the pictures that puzzled Mr. Selby. Under his eye Diego showed only a chaotic, primitive promise. Away from him Diego painted things that made him stare. He scarcely gave a second thought to Josie.

She had a slight, fanciful talent, to be sure, but he found the girl more interesting than her work. There was something in her mingled shyness and hardness; the detached, fanciful look in her eyes; her beautiful color that paled and flamed, — in a town where sallowness was the usual thing, — which attracted those who met her. But so few met her. Lately she refused to attend to the shop. She preferred to burn her cheeks and redden her hands baking endless cakes, pies, and loaves of bread. To Diego's father she had given more of her inner self than to anyone else. They had talked together by the hour while they kneaded, stirred, spiced, and iced in the heat of the big range. He had been a man quite apart in the narrow, conventional community. He had been regarded with suspicion because he was an agnostic. Strange books by writers like Edward Carpenter and Winwood Reade had been propped on a shelf above the baking board while he worked. He had read a paragraph, thumped the dough, and expounded his convictions to Josie Froward. Now that he was gone, that part of her mind that had been open to him was closed. She gave herself up to her fancies, to her painting, to her fascinated watching of Diego. She did the baking in a kind of feverish dream.

Between the baker and his son there had been no understanding. The strain of Portuguese from one side, the strain of Indian from the other, had merged in Diego, making him a foreigner to his father. He was an exotic. He did not belong to the bakeshop.

He did not belong to Saltport. He belonged only to his mother and to himself. . . .

Josie stood holding the picture against the wall, drinking in its strange, clumsy beauty; wondering what it was that he could do and she could not; itching for a brush in her hand, itching to make the attempt to drag it up from its chaos in a crescendo of beauty. Sometimes she could do this, sometimes not. What would be her luck this time? Everything Diego did so fascinated her that she could not look at the marred spot caused by the nettle without seeing something of Diego in it.

He went and threw himself on the couch, pushing aside the piled-up quilts and extending himself on his back in a feline way, like a dark, glowing-eyed cat.

"Josie," he said softly, "come and sit beside me and tell me what you are going to do with the picture."

"Oh, I don't know. . . . I must go first and stand where you stood and get it inside me." That was what she did with his pictures. She stood in the place he had stood, absorbing what he had seen, trying with all the power in her to translate his fierce primitive efforts into serenity. Then she would go back to her attic room and spend her happiest hours complementing his work.

"What 's the use," she said, "of talking it over with you? You would n't understand." But she came and sat beside him on the couch.

"Josie," he repeated in a coaxing tone like a spoiled child, "tell me things. . . ."

"What sort of things?" she asked, surprised.

"Oh, nice things."

"I 'd like to know what nice things I could tell you!"

"Tell me why you are always staring at me."

"I don't stare at you." And she looked down intently at him.

"You 're staring now!"

She turned her eyes away and her color brightened.

"Tell me why you can't look at me the way you look at other people."

"I can."

"You can't."

This was the way they had gone on as children.

"Do it, then."

She drew her eyes from where they had been resting on the picture and tried to force them into a cool detached contemplation of him as he lay on the couch.

He peered up into her eyes. "That 's no good! That 's not the way you look at other people."

"I don't want to look at you." She shut her eyes.

"You look better with them shut," he said. He began to stroke her thin arm with long gentle strokes. She had on a sleeveless pull-over and her arms were burned brown by the sun, but her hands, from being much in the dough, were strangely white in contrast.

"I don't like your hands," he said. "They make me think of the bakery. I hate it. But I like you, Josie. Honestly I do. Let 's kiss. . . ."

They had never kissed except when they had been forced to, as children, to make up a quarrel.

"No," she cried fiercely, and opened her eyes wide. But she could not stop him. He drew her down beside him and kissed her twice at random, first on the ear, then on the cheek. Then he deliberately kissed her a third time, on the mouth.

Filled with surprise they lay there close together, the light from the skylight falling down on them, big September clouds touched with the red of sunset passing above. The ropes by which the skylight was manipulated dangled overhead. The smell of paint, which they both loved, hung in the air. The waves pushed their way with gurgling noises among the rocks beneath. Gulls cried, now thinly and far away, now so close as to seem almost in the room. The two lay still under this wave of strange new intimacy, scarcely thinking, astonished by the difference a putting out of two arms, a drawing close, a breathing as one being could make.

She pushed him from her. He relaxed his arms and she got up. She passed her hand over the arm he had stroked, turning her face away from him. He lay staring up at the clouds sailing above the skylight.

"I must come back and finish up here to-morrow," she said rather gaspingly. "There 's no time to do it to-night. It 's nearly supper time! Let 's go and buy a lobster to take home."

"All right," he agreed, rising to his feet in one movement. She found herself staring at him, and turned angrily away. She emptied the grounds from the coffeepot and rinsed it. He sauntered to a large zinc-lined box containing clay for modeling, lifted the lid

and dug out a handful.   He began carelessly rolling it
between his palms, shaping it.

"Dough," he said, "this is my dough.   Better than
your old dough in the bakery."

"It 's not my dough," she answered angrily.   "It 's
yours."

"Dad did n't leave it to me, he left it to Fay" — he
called his mother Fay.   "It 's hers, if you like, but it 's
nothing to me. . . . Look, Josie, I 'm going to do a
head of you.   This is what you 're like!"   And he
began to mould roughly a head that soon showed a
grotesque likeness to hers.

She stood watching him, looking sidewise, her head
and gray eyes slanting, sneering at his essay in sculpture,
yet fascinated.   The movements of his hands had an
almost cruel fascination for her — strange that they
had stroked her arm — strange that he had kissed her
after all these years of living in the house together. . . .

The sun was gone when they ran along the beach to
the lobster house, but every wave still held a golden
halo on its crest.   The fishermen standing with bent
legs in their dories rowed themselves home.   Gulls followed the dories, screaming and fascinated by the moving silver of the filled nets.

The lobster house was hot and steamy.   The floor
was wet, with scarlet claws and feelers strewn on it.
In one vat live lobsters strove heavily to mount each
other's backs.   In another stewed their fellows.   The
boy and girl chose one.

They stood close together. They wanted to feel the
excitement, the comfort, of nearness.   They were two

adventurers, bound for strange experiences. Life was opening out before them — sweet, rather overpowering. Diego caught Josie's fingers and held them tightly. It would be hard to say whether this was a gesture protective or clinging. What he perhaps felt was that all these scenes they were so accustomed to would soon be a part of their past, and that his future was like one of his own pictures — strange, indefinite, even chaotic. Perhaps Josie would take it in hand, translate it into a serenity lucid to the world — and even to himself.

CHAPTER II

AT THE time when Josie and Diego were running along the beach toward the lobster house, Purley Bond was walking in the direction of his home. He had a good swinging walk and he liked the outdoor movement after so many hours in his close, poorly lighted store. He had grown up with the intention of being a doctor, like his father and his grandfather before him, but after six months at a medical college he had changed his mind and taken a course in chemistry. The horrors of the dissecting room, the sights he had seen in hospitals, were more than he could endure. The messiness, the anguish, affected his nerves. He could not sleep or eat. It was useless for his father to tell him that he would get accustomed to it. He said he would rather become a fisherman or break stones on the road than be a doctor. His disappointed father gave in, and he took his degree from a pharmaceutical college. Now sometimes he was driven to wish that his father had been harder with him, or that he had hardened himself. He was not made for an indoor life, and the pressure of times which forced him into the selling of chocolates, magazines, and cigarettes made him angry and irritable.

The Bonds had been one of the most respected families of Saltport. Purley Bond wondered sometimes if it was in him that the family was to run to seed. The men of his family had prospered in their profession, they had married into other respected families. They had built a fine house and kept it up well. They had had children. Now he was thirty-six. He was going back, rather than forward, financially. He was in love and had been in love for years with Fay Palmas. Could he afford to marry her? Would she have him? Her husband had been dead for seven months. How soon could he decently ask her? Did he really want her disturbing presence in his house? Had he, in truth, the making of a bachelor in him? These questions occupied him as he strode down the street.

He unlatched the gate in the ornamental picket fence painted white, passed through the high clipped hedge, and heard the gate click softly behind him. Inside was a cold, almost frosty shade, for the hedge shut out the afternoon sun and evening came early to the house. His grandfather had planted the hedge; in his father's time it had been kept below the level of the fence, but for several years now he had encouraged the privacy it gave and allowed it to shut out, with its dense glossy leaves, not only the gaze of the passer-by, but the sun and air. The front windows of the ground floor looked into it. The windows of the upper stories peered distrustfully over it. The brass plate with the name of both his father and his grandfather — Frederick Bond, M.D. — shone on the door. It was a beautiful door, he thought, deeply set and arched, and, like the rest of the house, was painted a pure and smoothly finished white. He had been too sentimental to remove the brass plate. The brass knocker and doorknob would have looked lonely without it. The large flat front of the house, with its many windows, its pillared porch, stood to him for what was admirable in his life. The interior of the house was getting shabby, but the white paint of the exterior was never long allowed to need renewing.

He lingered for a moment to look at the border of dahlias and salvia, wondering how long the frost would spare their brightness. They needed more sun. But he could not bring himself to have the hedge cut.

He unlocked the door and went into the hall. A thick quietness shrouded the house and it had an un-used smell, though the Finnish woman who came in to work for him kept it clean and in order. She had left his evening meal on the table — cold corned beef, pickles, catsup, potato salad, a covered dish of corn on the cob, and a large slice of pumpkin pie with a mound of whipped cream on it. The coffee percolator was bubbling on the side table.

He was not at all intimidated by the sight of this re-past. His New England digestion was inured to such ordeals, quite able to cope with them. To-night, however, he did not know what he ate. He left half the food untouched. His stomach must go unfilled because his mind was overflowing with the problems of those who lived at the bakery. Diego had said that his mother was ready for a nervous breakdown. And no wonder! To have kept the business going, with only the help of Josie, through the tourist season, after the long months of nursing, after the years of disappointment, was enough to wear down the nerves of any woman. Even a strong woman like Fay Palmas.

He thought of what her life had been. A disappointment. A bitter disappointment. How old was she now? She must be thirty-eight. Thirty-eight — and the mother of that big fellow of nineteen! Close work, that! She had been the only child of John Elwood, the principal of the high school. He was the close friend of Dr. Bond and, like him, a member of one of Saltport's most respected families. Religious, expecting others to be as high-minded, as honorable as themselves. Yet the Elwoods were not quite the equal of the Bonds. They had something to live down. The Bonds might have washed all their linen in public and not even clouded the water. For their ancestor, who had crossed the Atlantic from Yorkshire, was a Presbyterian minister, and his descendants had lived, without noticeable deviation, according to the precepts of the Shorter Catechism.

But it was said that the first Elwood had been nothing more or less than an old pirate. He had owned a sloop and in it he had harried foreign vessels up and down the coast. He had thought as little of taking their lives as their gold. He had lived, with his half-naked family, in a log house on a rocky promontory. Retribution had never touched him. He had buried his spoils under the house and, when he had acquired what was in those days a fortune, he had clothed his children, bought respectable black for himself (his wife had died from the strain of being the wife of a pirate), and become a Baptist. Something picturesque

and adventurous in that faith had attracted him.   The
Baptist minister of the day had immersed him in the
water of a near-by creek, and he had emerged a new
man.   He had educated his youngest son for the min-
istry and, before he died, had sat in a front pew — a
rugged, weather-beaten figure — and heard the young
minister preach his first sermon, the text being the
Tenth Commandment.   It was through the bounty
of this son that the present Baptist Church had been
built, the prettiest church in Saltport, surrounded by
a garden and ornamental trees.   But the son of this
minister had given a jolt to the family's upward prog-
ress.   He had been a missionary and, on a mission to
the Indians of Hudson's Bay, he had fallen in love with
and married a handsome Indian girl.   All Saltport
had been shocked when he brought her home, but he
had reared an exemplary family from her.   Fay
Palmas, his great-granddaughter, was the last of the
Elwoods in the district.   She had been the darling of
her father, the schoolmaster.   His own school had
not been good enough for her, and he had sent her
to Boston to a young ladies' seminary where she
would get not only a refined education, but a train-
ing for her lovely voice.   She had just returned from
there — eighteen years old and striking-looking —
when she met young Palmas, ten years her senior,
a civil engineer.   They had fallen in love and been
married that summer.   Through his profession she
had hoped to escape from Saltport and see something
of the world, but her hopes came to nothing.   Within
the year she gave birth to Diego (she had named him

Diego against the will of both families), and, before he could run about, Palmas had been taken with inflammation of the lungs, from exposure, and forced to give up his profession. Her father could not help them, for he had lost all his money by investing in the Saltport fisheries, already doomed by Gloucester's ascendancy. The civil engineer had become a baker, and there she had been caught, a prisoner in the bakery, for seventeen years.

Purley Bond and she had played together as children, but they had seen little of each other in the years following. He had been installed in his drug store for two years before he had given her a second thought. Then one night he had himself taken some medicine to the Palmas house for Diego, ill of a serious complaint. He and she had talked together in the sitting room behind the shop. They had not sat. He had watched her swaying up and down the tiny room — lithe, swarthy, anguished for her child. She magnified his sufferings, thought him dying. Bond had tried unsuccessfully to soothe her.

The next evening he had called to ask after the child. She had taken him into the sitting room again. This time she had caught his hand and led him. She was wild with joy and gratitude. Her darling was better. He was almost well. She gave Bond — not his father, the doctor — the credit. From the moment he had entered the house Diego had improved. Virtue had gone from him into the child. From him into her. There was a kind of noble simplicity in her — as in a primitive Indian. Anything seemed possible to her.

From that time she gave him a sort of proud homage.
She went often to the drug store to ask his advice —
to get strength from him, she said.

Strength she took from him — the strength to resist
her. During the years since he had thought of no
other woman. He did not know what were her feelings toward him. Not a word of love had passed
between them.

He, the lonely druggist, living alone. . . . She, the
widow of a bookish baker, Indian blood arching her
nose, her nostrils, her eyelids, making her hair black
and strong, though her father and her father's father
had shown no trace of its sultry flow. . . . Diego, her
dark son, with his chaotic talent, his dramatic face that
exaggerated his indolent emotions, his Portuguese blood
that crept out of the past to mingle with her Indian.
. . . Josie Froward, her cousin on her mother's side, —
pure blood of the Pilgrim Fathers there, — with her
bright changing color, her secrecy, her ironic devotion
to mother and son. Purley Bond brooded on this
group of four, their intermingled relations that were
drawing closer together, as he bit the yellow kernels of
corn from the cob with his strong teeth.

He walked about the parlor, furnished just as his
mother had left it. She had kept to the style of the
old New England parlors. There were ladder-backed
chairs, a mahogany secretary, old glass bottles on the
mantelpiece, and a spinning wheel by the unused
hearth. He walked through his father's surgery, kept
just as he had left it, still retaining its smell of a surgery,
lined with out-of-date medical books. He climbed

the stair with its spindled banister and wandered through the bedrooms. Faintly musty, spotlessly clean, with framed texts on the walls. He tried to picture Fay Palmas in this house and could not. Strange that the heat, the sweet sticky smell of the bakery, was a more convincing background for her than the old-fashioned austerity of this house.

He looked at his father's large gold watch which he carried and saw that it was time to go to the bakery.

He felt excited and nervous as he always did when he knew that he was going to be with her. Yet once in her presence he was reserved, almost irritatingly stolid towards her.

A large bright moon hung above the whiteness of the street. The houses in the best streets were all clearly white, the intense, delicate shadows of elm-boughs laid against their whiteness. Dead leaves had been burned in the gardens that day, and the teasing odor of smoke still hung in the air. The air was so clear with coming frost that it seemed to crackle in the moonlight.

His steps rang out, for he was the only one on the street. Yellow squares showed against the drawn blinds. From one house came the sound of a cottage organ playing a hymn tune. Saltport submitted to her tourist season as to a necessary evil, but she was now her unchanged self again. The cottages of her summer colony, their grotesque or sentimental names painted above their doors, were boarded up for the winter. The rocky point known as Wolfskin Neck,

disfigured by them, was now deserted.   Motor loads of
holiday makers seeking the "picturesque and quaint"
no longer filled the steamy restaurants to devour
"chicken dinners" and clam chowder.   Saltport had
dropped them all like a dingy carnival garment.

He climbed the hill to the bakery, mounted decor-
ously the six steps which led to the door, and rang.
Josie opened it.   She drew back almost behind it, said
good-evening in her quick, rather breathless way, and
asked him to go through to the sitting room.   The
shop was unlighted, but he saw the glimmer of the
glass cases and the pallid shapes of a mound of loaves.
Fay Palmas and her son were in the sitting room.   Josie
passed through a narrow hallway behind and went to
her room.

Fay Palmas took Bond's coat and hat from him.   She
was as tall as he, and, as their hands touched and their
eyes met, a shining net of intimacy was thrown about
them.   They were caught in it and stared startled
into each other's eyes, scarcely conscious of the presence of Diego.

He lolled on a sofa, smiling calculatingly at them.
He said: "It's a good thing you've come, Purley.   We
were just beginning to quarrel."

"What about?"

"You."

"Oh, we were not!" said Fay Palmas.   "We were
just — I was just saying that you would come to the
rescue — Diego, that you would not."

"With advice, of course," said Diego.   "We did n't
mean money."

"Scarcely," added Fay. "No one in Saltport has any money to spare."

"But the market is glutted with good advice," went on Diego. "Everybody that comes into the bakery to buy a loaf hands back a large slab of advice. They all seem to think that Fay and I are going to make fools of ourselves now that Father's gone."

Bond stood, with his hand on the back of the chair she had placed for him, looking from one to the other under his frowning yellow brows, trying to understand them. They were so disconcertingly candid, yet behind the candor lay something — if not exactly devious, still very different from his own straightforwardness.

"Do sit down," said Fay Palmas, and touched him persuasively on the arm.

He sat down obediently, following her with his eyes as she moved to a seat beside her son.

Though she spent her days indoors, she moved beautifully, with a strong swift suppleness unlike Diego's feline grace. There was something animal about them both, but in her it was the strong-boned lightness of the deer. In him the muscular softness of the cat tribe. Yet they were alike, Bond thought, in their swarthiness, the dark flash of their eyes, their concentration on their own needs.

Diego's needs did not particularly interest him. The desires of Fay Palmas fired his own. He sat staring dumbly at her poised upright on the end of the sofa, backed by shelves filled with the books of her schoolmaster father. They were all he had left to her.

"What's it all about?" Bond got out at last. "Had an offer for the business?"

Diego and Fay Palmas looked at each other, then turned to him smiling. "Yes," she said, "there was a man here to-day. It's the first promising offer we've had." There was a flicker of excitement in her eyes.

"How much?" Bond's tone was almost surly. How glad she seemed at escaping from Saltport — her old life!

"When the mortgage is paid off I would have fifteen hundred dollars left." She looked defiantly at him.

"H'm — and how long do you think that will keep you?"

"It will give us a start — somewhere."

"But, Mrs. Palmas" — he always called her stiffly by her married name, though he had pulled her black pigtails as a little girl. "You must remember that there are three of you and that Diego should not throw up his art studies, especially when he is taught for nothing here."

"I'll sell some things! Pa's books, for instance."

Bond uttered a grim sound. "No one would give you twenty-five dollars for those books."

"Why, Purley," — she called him by his Christian name, with a sliding caress on the *r*, — "I think I have several first editions!"

"First editions of *what*?"

"Oh, I don't know exactly. That *Ivanhoe* looks old." She indicated a battered book on the table. Evidently she had been mustering her resources. "There's a fortune in first editions."

He picked up the book.   "Philadelphia, 1857," he read from the title-page.

"Well, that 's terribly old, is n't it?"

He looked at her with irritation and compassion in his blue eyes.   "Now see here, Mrs. Palmas, you 've got to be more practical.   Eighteen fifty-seven is young for *Ivanhoe*.   It 's no more old than Diego is old."

"He 's my first edition," she laughed, "and a valuable one — to me!"   She laid her hand on the boy's knee. So lightly did she turn from her disappointment. "However, there are other books."

"I 'll look them over and see if there 's anything promising.   But I wish you would tell me just what it is you think of doing when you leave Saltport."

"Now you 're trying to corner me."

"How can I advise you when I don't know what 's in your mind?"

"And we have other means," she parried.   "Josie will be twenty-one in January.   She gets a thousand dollars then — inherited from the estate of her grandfather."   She spoke grandiloquently, her bright eyes flickering into his.

"An heiress, eh?   Poor little Josie!"

"You need n't say *poor* about her," put in Diego. "She 's able to look after herself."

"What I mean is," said Fay Palmas, "she 'll not be dependent.   A thousand dollars would keep Josie for a long while."

"Yes — if she stayed in Saltport!   It would keep her for a couple of years.   But when the money is gone

what can she and you do for a living?   You know how
to do — only one thing."   He did not like to say "bake
bread and cakes."

"We don't care!"   She got up and began to walk
about the room.   "We 've got to get out of this town!
Our people have been here for generations.   We 're
stale!   Do you think I want to see these two children
stay here and marry here?"

"Not palates enough to go round," mumbled Diego,
and he mimicked: "Pleh, I wah a bohhle o' cahor oil."

His mother frowned at him.   "This is a serious
matter. . . . Oh — if only I had n't lost my voice!
I 'd make money for all of us!   I 'd go out into the
world and sing!   I 'd make a name for myself."

The two men watched her as she moved with a dis-
traught air in the restricted space.   Bond, pitying but
embarrassed by the demonstration.   Diego with an
inscrutable, half-sulky smile.

She stopped in front of Bond.   "You know that I
had a wonderful voice, Purley!   It was a glorious
voice, was n't it?   You 've heard me sing, have n't
you?"   Her brilliant eyes blazed down into his.

His looked steadily back, but his lip quivered.   Yes,
he had heard her sing in a concert in the Town Hall and
at a Presbyterian Social, years ago.   He had no music
in him.   He had known the voice was good, — high,
clear, passionate, — but he remembered only her standing there on the platform, above everyone else, where
she always was in his mind.

"Oh, how I could sing!" she went on.   "I could sing
like a bird.   Terazzi, the singing master from Boston,

heard me . . . a voice like a lark, he said. He was
mad to teach me, but — I was a fool. I gave up my
young life to baking bread — "

"Oh, no, no," interrupted Bond, too much pained.
"Your husband baked the bread."

"I baked it in spirit! I sacrificed myself to lumps
of dough. . . . Think of it! And I was always in
by the heat and out again into the draft of the shop.
Half the time I had my throat inflamed. And now
this last winter and spring — this summer — have finished it. . . . That 's true, is n't it, Diego? Tell him
the truth. Don't spare me."

Diego looked at her stupidly.

"Tell him that my voice is gone!"

Diego still stared, unable to bring himself to speak.
Both men were unhappy, but Fay Palmas was not unhappy, in spite of her tragic attitude. She had an audience. The exhilaration of throwing off old bonds gave
her a sense of power. She swept away from them, then
turned and faced them, and raised her arm in a dramatic
gesture. She began to sing: —

> "Way down upon de Swanee River —
>   Far, far away,
>   Dere's where my heart am turning ever —
>   Dere 's where de old folks stay . . ."

Her voice swung, in a strong plangent swing: —

> "All de world am sad and dreary,
>   Ev'rywhere I roam,
>   Oh, darkies, how my heart grows weary — "

The sweet notes grew husky, faltered, broke.   She stared fixedly at Bond.   There was a moment's dead silence.   Then, pursing her relaxed lips, she finished the last bars in a limpid whistle.

Diego slanted his head toward Bond.   He had an expression of childlike pride.

"She always does that," he said.   "Her voice goes — then she finishes in a whistle.   It 's funny.   She never lets it just die down.   She always finishes in a whistle."

Bond searched his mind for something to say, in praise, in comfort, he knew not what.   But he could find nothing.   He pulled at his lip.   He had a vision of her, standing on a platform, the world at her feet.

"I think if she could get away from this place," said Diego, "her voice would soon come back to her."   He looked calculatingly at Bond.

Fay Palmas gave a short laugh.   She was suddenly quite calm, though flushed.   She went to the bookshelves and took out a book.

"Now here 's another," she said, carrying it to Bond, "that must be pretty old.   What do you think?"

He accepted it with great relief.   The singing, her emotion, had been a strain on him.   He examined the dog-eared copy of *Huckleberry Finn*.   "This looks more promising.   It may be worth something.   May I take it and show it to a fellow I know who buys old books?"   He had no hope of it, but he wanted to say something to comfort her.

She went and threw up a window.   "How hot it is in here!   I feel as though I should suffocate!"

"Now that's not good for your voice, you know," said Bond. "That air is frosty."

"I don't care," she said indifferently. "It does n't matter about my voice."

Again the two men stared at her in discomfort. Frosty air, smelling of the sea, swept like a wave into the room. Diego shivered and drew one of the sofa cushions on top of him. Instantly Fay Palmas closed the window.

"I wish," she said, "that Josie would come down and make us some coffee. No one can make coffee like she can. Whatever she does in her room for hours at a time I can't imagine."

"Let her have a little peace, can't you?" said Diego. He was thinking that Josie might be working on his picture.

Bond thought his tone was rude. He threw him an angry glance. Fay went to the foot of the stairs and called loudly: —

"Josie! Josie! Come down and make us some coffee. Purley thinks you're very queer to go off like that."

But Josie took her own time. Every now and again Fay Palmas looked impatiently toward the stairway. She wanted the coffee so badly she could think of nothing else. She could not talk. She looked almost stupidly at the two men, as though she wondered what they could find to say. At last Diego rolled himself in one supple movement to his feet. "I'll go and get her," he said. As he passed behind his mother's chair he stroked the back of her neck with his hand.　She caught at it, wanting to press it against her neck, but he was gone.

Bond looked after him, trying to imagine what it had been like to touch the brown rounded neck, to have laid his hand for an instant just beneath the dark hair that sprung, strong and yet fine, and was coiled firmly in an unfashionable way that became her. He wished that Diego had not left them.　It was too disturbing, too strange, to be left alone with her. His heart began to pound uncomfortably.　He wished that he could see her as she was, clarify his romantic conception of her, but no — everything about her was strange and beautiful to him.　He could no more see her reasonably than he could control the beating of his heart.

She was looking at him, a little puzzled.　She said, "It 's good of you to try and help me, Purley."

"I wish I could help you."

"Why, you do!　You certainly do!　Coming here to-night.　And giving me good advice."

"Advice!　As though you 'd take my advice!"

"But I will."　She hooked her arm over the back of her chair and bent her head toward him almost meekly.

"Then I advise you to wait for a better offer for the business."

"I 've promised Diego to accept this."

"I see. . . .　Well — I 'll miss you."

"You 're the only person in this hateful town I mind leaving."

"Then — why leave me?"

She knit her brows, trying to make him out.

"You might marry me." His voice came from his pounding heart — rather thick and husky.

"You 're not in earnest!"

"I 'm in dead earnest."

"Oh, I could n't think of that — just yet!"

"But you 'll think about it — after a little?"

"Oh — I don't know. . . . You 've given me a mighty big surprise." She had gone pale.

"I 'd no intention of asking you to-night. I suppose it 's too soon to be decent."

"It is n't that. . . . It 's only that I want to feel free for a spell. . . . I sort of want to spread my wings."

"I 'll miss you terribly."

"Oh, Purley, you are kind!" She put her hand on his. Perhaps it was the coldness of his that made hers feel so feverishly hot.

He sat rigid, looking down at their two hands.

"I know I should n't have spoken," he said, with a stubborn desire to blame himself.

"I 'm glad you did. Because — because — I 'd a kind of feeling you despised me."

"Despised you!"

"Well — for going on about my voice and getting up in the air over things. You 're so sensible."

Diego found Josie, just as he had expected, standing before an easel on which was propped his picture, with an expression of complete absorption.

"You 're to come down and make coffee," he said from the doorway.

She backed away a little from the picture, still staring at it, ignoring him.

"Have you been doing anything to it?" he asked, coming up behind her.

"Idiot! Could I do anything in this light?" The attic room was lighted by a kerosene lamp with a somewhat smoky chimney. The light from this showed the walls covered with pictures, finished and unfinished, all the work of Diego, excepting one which hung by the dressing table, a head of him in oils, an indifferent likeness, by herself. It showed, too, the bed covered by a bright silk patchwork quilt, the patches joined by black featherstitching. The window, under the sloping roof, looked out across the harbor, black save for a quietly rocking light or two and the intermittent beam of the lighthouse.

He looked over her shoulder at the picture on the easel. "Come on down, Josie, and make the coffee."

"Let someone else make it. I don't want to go down when Purley Bond's there."

"Don't worry. He'll never notice you! He just sits staring at Fay."

Josie made a contemptuous sound with her lips. "People make me sick! I'm going to stay up here."

"You won't get any coffee."

"I don't want any. . . . I wish you'd leave me alone." She turned and looked at him, and continued to look with something of the same absorption that she had given his picture.

"Well," he said ironically, "do you think you can do anything with me in this light?"

Her cheeks flamed bright and angry.

"Now you're getting a pretty color," he jeered. "What will they think if you go down looking like that? See here — I'll tone it down for you!"

He picked up a brush and a palette and squeezed a worm of white paint from a tube on to it. She did not realize what he was going to do until he came toward her, brush in hand. She drew back against the wall, but he caught her, pinning her arms to her sides. They struggled silently. Then he mastered her, held her tight while he painted a white spot on each of her cheeks, covering the red. She stared up into his eyes, her mouth compressed, making no sound, feeling the smooth stroke of the brush on her cheeks, the press of his strong body against hers.

He drew back and looked at her. He said: "Now you look nice and ladylike. Let's go down."

She went to the looking-glass, gave her face one furious look, then marched to the stairway. He followed her, laughing softly to himself.

The kettle was always on the range. It sat there singing now as if cheerfully ready for any emergency. With a set face Josie went about making the coffee. Diego lounged in the doorway watching her.

When she appeared in the sitting room carrying the tray, Fay Palmas screamed at the sight of her. "Good heavens, Josie! Have you gone crazy?"

"Diego did it," answered Josie, sullenly. "I had no time to take it off if you were to get your coffee."

Fay laughed loudly and threw a mischievous look at Diego. Bond stirred his coffee with a feeling of dislike for the girl.   He felt that she was proud of what Diego had done to her, that she was showing off.

"You look a perfect little clown," said Fay.   "I'm sure Purley's disgusted with you."   She got up and went into the bakeshop.   She took a pumpkin pie from the case.   "Get that bowl of whipped cream, Josie," she called.

When the large slice of pie, topped by a mound of whipped cream, was set in front of Bond, he seemed to remember having seen something like it before. Why, it was only a couple of hours since he had eaten a similar slice, probably from the same oven.   But he meekly took the fork given him by Josie and set about devouring it.

"How do you like it?" asked Fay.

"It's mighty good," he answered.   "Did you make it?"

"I?   No — Josie.   I suppose it's good.   But you get tired of sweet things when you smell them all day. I hear that the French don't eat pie.   I guess that is one reason why I'm going to Paris."

A mouthful of pie crust was stuck motionless in Bond's throat.   Then he bolted it.

"Paris!" he exclaimed.   "You're not in earnest!"

She laughed at his astonishment.   There was an intimate note in her laughter that separated them from the others.   "Yes.   Paris.   Why not?"

"Well, I suppose it's no more expensive than Boston — "

"Me go to Boston?   Half the people in Boston have heard of Palmas's Bakery."

Bond scarcely agreed with this, but he would not belittle the bakery to her. He said, "Well, then, why not try New York?"

"Not if I know it! I have five cousins and a sister-in-law there. Everyone we met would hear about the bakery."

"I don't believe they would. New York's a pretty big place. And if they did — what would be the difference? There's no disgrace in being a baker. And Diego's artist friend would be useful. He'd introduce him to other artists."

Her anger flamed intimately against him as her laughter had sounded intimately. "Yes — and tell every one of them that we kept a bakery! No — my husband was an engineer when I married him — my father was the principal of the school — Josie's father was — well — Josie's father never seemed to settle down to anything. But he was always a gentleman. Good heavens, Josie, I wish you'd take that paint off your face! You look like a clown."

The girl sat in a corner invincible, drinking coffee. Diego lay like a spoiled child, half asleep on the sofa. His half-shut eyes rested on Josie's face. He had a feeling of sleepy power.

"I see what you mean," said Bond, gravely. "What I don't see is how you're going to live for any length of time in a city like Paris. It will take quite a lot of money to get you over there, and I should think it would be a bad place to be poor in."

"We're willing to risk it. We want to live. We don't care if there is danger in it. And I have faith in us. I don't believe anything can hold us down. Diego has genius. Mr. Selby is a grudging sort of man, but I made him acknowledge that. I just pestered him till he did." She clasped her long slender fingers together and looked beseechingly at Bond. "You do understand, don't you? I'm thinking about my voice. A complete change and rest may bring it back. A singing teacher told me that this summer. Perhaps you'll live to see me having a great success in Paris. And even if I don't — we'll be living — living dangerously! That's what we want — isn't it, children?"

A great compassion for her moved Bond to his depths. She had had an awful life. She was calling those others "children" when she herself was more of a child than they. Three children setting out on a risky adventure. And he envied them, too. Wished that he might be going with them to Paris. Supposing that she had accepted him . . .

"Then it was all settled," he said, "before I came. You didn't really want my advice at all."

"Purley, don't throw that up to me! I just wanted to get you here to tell you about it. You're the only one we have to talk things over with."

Bond turned to Diego. "You're the man of the family. You'll have to look after these two."

Josie gave a sneering laugh. Bond turned and looked sharply at her. She was sitting looking straight before her, the grotesque painted spots on her cheeks shining white. She did not look as though she had uttered a sound.

Bond said to Fay Palmas: "It 's the money that I 'm worrying about. We must see if we can get you more money to start out on."

An idea had come into his head, but he did not tell them that night what it was.

CHAPTER III

JOSIE FROWARD could talk fluently enough when she
was alone with Fay Palmas. Then she was freed from
the shyness that hedged her in when she was with
strangers. She was free also from the necessity of
watching Diego, paying him the homage of watch-
fulness and female sneers. She and Fay talked for
hours, interrupting each other, chiming in on each
other, but always developing one theme, like chimes
in a steeple. High on a hill the bakeshop stood with
its flight of steps leading to the door. They would
hear someone mount the steps, the bell inside the shop
door would jangle, and their talk cease. Josie would
wipe her hands and go in behind the counter looking
into the eyes of the customer with her inquiring,
rather hostile, look. She would carefully place the
fresh, warm purchase in a paper bag, ring the cash register, and hurry back to chime in with the talk. The
two exulted over their impending freedom. They
honestly mourned for the dead baker, yet they could
not have borne to have had him back and become his
prisoners.

The October gales (once that Indian summer was
by) lashed the sea, strewed jellyfish and starfish on
the beach, and drove flecks of foam and dead leaves
through the street. And all in bright sunshine. There

was not a cloudy day. All foretold excitement and
more excitement. And, unsubstantial as the dead
leaves, feckless as the foam, gossip scurried through
Saltport. . . . What were those Palmases up to?
For Josie was included under that name. The doubtful glamour that always hung about them was in-
tensified. The townspeople, sallow, sharp-featured,
with eyes as blue as their summer sea, sought to pierce
the soul of young Diego with one glance as he slouched
by them on the street, his dark brow exposed beneath
his beret, a lazy, contemptuous smile curving his lips.
For the Palmas family were scornful of their neigh-
bors, even while they detested the imperfections of
each other. Fay Palmas had never forgiven her husband for becoming a baker, yet she thought him the
most intellectual man in Saltport. He had despised
what he had considered her lack of intellect, yet he
had thought her above all other women of the town.
Josie was constantly chafed by Fay and Diego, but
put them on a pedestal. Diego felt that he and his
family were the subject of envious gossip. Now that
the summer colony was gone he had no friend except
Purley Bond. Not a day passed but Diego spent an
hour or more in the drug store discussing plans for
the future with Bond. The soda-water fountain and
its appurtenances had been put out of sight, and
Bond had settled down to a long season of dignified
repose. The bathing caps, beach balls, fly powder,
and picture postcards had been taken from the window, and only the large glass jars filled with green
fluid, that had entranced Diego as a child, remained.

He could no longer treat Diego to ice-cream soda, but gave him acid drops and cigarettes instead, for he liked his visits. He led him on to talk about Fay. He cherished any remark of hers repeated by her son, sat alone in his dark corner with his pipe, brooding on it, turning it over in his mind, being either encouraged or troubled by it.

Gossip was beginning to connect his name with Fay's, for, though he always went to the bakery at night, there was always some person to see him and pass the word on. His neighbor heard his gate click and saw him go out. Someone passed him on the street, lingered in a convenient shadow, and saw him go in. What sort of stepfather would he make to Diego? Or was it perhaps Josie he was after? In their anxiety to discover the truth they bought more cakes and pies than ever before, though there was no doubt that the quality had gone down since the death of Palmas. And not only that — neither Josie nor Fay any longer cared. In spirit they were already removed from Saltport.

Then a great disappointment came. The prospective buyer of the business faded away and was not heard from again. No other appeared in his place. Still they were not discouraged. They advertised the business in the Boston papers and put a sign in the window. They hated the sight of the shop and resented the very customers who came to buy.

Fay and Josie made two visits to Boston, leaving Diego to look after the shop. They left what they thought an ample supply for two days (they had reached the point where they no longer minded their bread and cakes being a little stale), but it was not nearly enough. Their customers, hearing that Diego was in charge, thought he might be more communicative than the women and flocked like curious birds to the bakery.

Diego rather enjoyed the unusual situation. He lounged against the counter, cigarette in mouth, handing out what was asked for and accepting what was given for it with a nonchalant air. To every purchaser he gave, as a sort of premium, some cryptic remark about a flat in Paris, an art course in Rome, or a houseboat on the Thames. He said whatever came into his head and, between customers, lay on his back on the sofa in the sitting room nursing the cat. Certainly, thought Saltport, the Palmases were going to the dogs.

Fay and Josie bought new clothes in Boston — the sort of things they had seen in fashion papers but had never worn. They looked so striking when they appeared at the Baptist Church in these that the usher all but showed them into the stranger's pew. They were poor churchgoers, but they went twice that Sunday, Josie sneering at herself for doing it, but carried away by Fay's exuberance.

Bond did not go to church, but he called the next evening. Fay, in a black crêpe de Chine dress, received him, opening the door of the shop herself and letting him in. She had asked the assistant in a Boston shop for a "simple black dinner dress — not too expensive." The price of it had terrified her, but she had bought it.   The price of the little black dress that the assistant had tried on Josie had terrified Josie so that she had almost screamed, but Fay had bought it without the flicker of an eyelash.   Old acquisitive pirate blood was surging in her.   The trickle of acquisitive Indian blood stung her into the decking of her body and Josie's.   She was too generous ever to want anything the girl could not have.

"Oh, Fay," Josie had said, half laughing, half crying, when they were back in their own house, "you must be crazy!"

"There 's nothing extravagant in it," answered Fay. "We can't expect to be noticed in Paris if we dress as we dress here.   And I should just like these Saltporters to see us in style before we go."

"But how can we go if no one buys the business?"

"I 'll find a buyer.   And if I can't, Purley Bond will.   He 'd like nothing so well as to help us."

"What about marrying him, Fay?"

But Fay shook her head.   "No, I must be free — spread my wings first.   Of course — if nothing else . . ."

Josie felt sorry, somehow, for Purley Bond.   Was Fay going to keep him in reserve — a last resort? The image of him came before her mind, his well-shaped, tow-colored head; his eyes, of a tender blue, under their rough blond brows.   He was too good for that. . . .   She said rather sharply: —

"You hate yourself, don't you?"

But Fay was not offended.   Nothing could offend her in those October days.

The next time they went to Boston she and Josie had their photographs taken. The large "studio" sort, in enormous folders, by the most expensive photographer. Fay told him that they were New Yorkers who had taken a house in Saltport for the sake of her son's health. She had scarcely uttered the words when a superstitious fear overtook her. What if she should bring some terrible illness to Diego! Illness could be induced by thought, — it was mental; she'd heard that, — and there might be an inherited tendency to lung trouble from his father. She hastily repeated the remark, using the word "daughter" instead of "son," and looked apologetically but firmly at Josie, who returned the look with startled resentment. It was contemptible of Fay so readily to wish an evil on her for the sake of sparing Diego!

What captivated the photographer was how Fay had managed to have a daughter as old as Josie. Josie was twenty-one, but a look of intensity made her seem older. Fay was thirty-eight and scarcely looked more than thirty. The photographs were perfect. Every pose was so good that Fay must order a finished example of each. This so brought up the cost that, when the bill came in, Josie again almost screamed.

Fay placed the five photographs of herself on the table in front of Bond. He was to choose one for himself. Josie had refused even to allow him to see hers.

He sat hunched above the pictures, his fingers clutching his hair, baffled by the problem. He studied each pose with hungry eyes, noting the line of her

neck in this, the curve of her side in that, the strange
likeness and haunting unlikeness brought out by the
camera. Fay did not hurry him. She would have
joyfully spent the evening hanging over the photographs with him, aiding his indecision. . . . Josie
and Diego sat side by side on the haircloth sofa, looking on.

At last Bond chose one, with a desperate final twist
of his yellow hair. He took it home, but within the
week he visited Boston and bought the other four
for himself. One of Josie's photographs was shown
in the window. He lingered, scarcely interested, to
look at it for a moment.

Diego viewed these extravagances with some resentment, especially since he had no part in them. To
be sure, presents were brought to him, but these were
a new supply of paints and a wrist watch which
seemed to indicate that time was flying and that he
ought to get to work. He showed his resentment on
the second occasion by locking up the bakery and
going duck shooting with Bond.

When Fay and Josie came home, more than half
the supply they had left in the bakery remained.
They were aghast. What had happened?

"The natural thing," answered Diego. He was
lolling on the sofa eating a banana. He held it by
the stalk, peeling it all the way down so that it tot-
tered and seemed about to fall on him. The two
women regarded him in speechless irritation as he
took a large mouthful. When he had swallowed it
he said: —

"The folks here are getting tired of you gallivant-ing. They know you 're not interested in the busi-ness. And there 's that 'For Sale' card in the window. They 're going to the Model to buy." The Model Bakery did a second-rate trade near the railway sta-tion. He finished the banana, slid the skin across the linoleum under the sofa, and turned his face to the wall.

It was a chastened pair of adventuresses who re-moved the stale bread and cake from the cases and stayed up half the night baking fresh. After that there were no more trips to Boston. Winter de-scended on them.

Diego still nursed his feeling of resentment against the others. He sat hunched by the stove in the sitting room reading novels from the lending library, or he sat with Bond in the dim drug store listening while Bond talked. He, too, was a patron of the library and borrowed a book or two of travels each week. He talked about these to Diego, telling of the strange customs of foreign countries and sketching out trips he would like to make. One night he took Diego home with him to supper. It was the first time the boy had been in Bond's house, and to him it seemed austerely beautiful, quite different from the houses of the summer colony which had been his standard of the artistic and beautiful. He wondered what it would be like to have a house all to one's self and no bakery in front of it — just a nice quiet drug store on the main street where there were few cus-tomers to bother one and unlimited supplies of cigarettes and ice-cream soda. He rather envied Bond and told him so.

"Oh, don't envy me," said Bond. "I'm a lonely sort of fellow. I've no one to care about me."

"And I don't suppose you care about anyone," probed Diego.

"Not many."

"Well, you're lucky not to have two women watching everything you do, like I have. Of course, a wife's all right. I'm not saying anything against a wife. I'll probably marry myself when I'm twenty-five or thirty. But a mother and a cousin, who thinks herself superior, make a fellow feel like a little boy. It's sort of boring."

"Perhaps a wife would make one feel like that too."

"Well, I wouldn't stand any nonsense from a wife. . . . But Josie's always watching me. Does n't seem able to stop watching me if I'm in the room." He spoke with a certain complacency.

"She's a queer girl. I certainly don't interest her. She seldom looks in my direction."

Diego began to laugh loudly. Then he told Bond what had happened on the day of the duck shooting. Bond laughed too, but when he went to bed that night he was filled with anger at the thought of Fay, tired out after her journey, greeted by cases of unsold cakes, staying up half the night to bake fresh ones. He felt a swift anger against Diego. The thought of Fay baking for the stupid clowns of Saltport disgusted him. He must and would help her to free herself from her bondage. For two months now the

idea of selling his own business had been in his head.
Why should he rust for the remainder of his days
in Saltport? If Fay left, it would be intolerable.
He knew that he could rent his house for the summer at a good rental. Suddenly he discovered that
he was sick and tired, not only of the soda fountain
and all that it stood for, but of drugs, prescriptions, and everything that had to do with his life in
Saltport. Everything and everybody but Fay Palmas. . . . He would never tire of being near her.
He also sent an advertisement to a Boston paper.

There was a heavy snowfall that winter, and in
February a great storm of wind and sleet came off
the sea. It froze again and the sun appeared, showing
Saltport as a port of salt indeed, glittering like Sodom,
cursed in whiteness and yet grown proud.

Diego glided along the back passage into the shop.
It was empty, as he knew. It was the dinner hour
and Fay was laying the table. Josie had run up to
her room. He opened the cash register, where he
had seen his mother put the monthly payment of a
hotel, which she supplied with bread, an hour before.
It had come into his mind that morning that it was
his turn to have a trip into Boston. It was against
his mood of resentment to ask his mother for money.
He would take it, — after all, it was as much his as
hers, — but he would take it without being seen, and
when she discovered the loss let her say what she would
— it was his turn now. She and Josie had had their
fling. He never had two cents to rub together. . . .

But just as he slid the drawer of the register into

place, Fay caught him. That faint Indian strain in
her made her wary of every sound. He had listened
to her singing as she set the dishes out, had heard her
voice break and the tune carried on in a clear sweet
whistle, had thought the moment safe. But under
cover of the whistle she had come upon him, and
caught his wrist and held it. She drew her lips from
her fine teeth and stared into his eyes without
speaking.

"Let me go!" he snarled, struggling, but she held
him fast.

"You little thief!" she enunciated hissingly.

He raised his voice and shouted.

"It 's as much mine as yours!"

"To think that I 'd raise a *thief!*"

"I 'm taking my own."

"Then why did you sneak about it?"

He gave a roar like a young bull and pulled himself
away. The money was scattered over the floor.
Josie came running down the stairs to find mother and
son facing each other like enemies.

An old woman, a gossip, was cautiously ascending
the icy steps to the bakery. Diego threw open the
door to her with a grand gesture and she entered, walking, as she had often dreamed she was doing, on a
pathway of strewn bank notes. The shop bell
clanged. He gave a fierce, tragic, despairing look
over his shoulder at his mother, then flung himself
out of the door and slithered down the glittering
steps.

Josie ate dinner alone.   Fay lay upstairs on her bed,
weeping.   Josie ate in a kind of haze and sat afterward
smoking one cigarette after another, brooding on
Diego.   Twice she was interrupted to serve customers, but she came back, lighted another cigarette,
and again sank into thought.   She despised Diego for
what he had done.   If he had boldly demanded the
money of Fay, she would have admired him.   But,
after all, he was a boy and they had treated him rather
badly.   His tragic expression haunted her.   What
was he doing now?   She lived over again the time in
the studio when he had kissed her, held her in his arms.
She had seen each separate hair of his brows and lashes,
he had been so close.   She rose, stretched out the
arm that he had stroked, to its fullest extent, then
dropped it to her side.   She looked about the untidy
dining room with hatred.   Upstairs Fay began to cry
loudly, like a child, but Josie sullenly collected the
dishes and washed them between interruptions from
customers.   After a while she carried a cup of coffee
to Fay, who drank it thirstily and moaned: —

"He will never come back!   Oh, he will never
come back!"

But Josie knew quite well that Fay was not really
frightened.   Yet when a blue shadow of evening fell
at four o'clock she had a sudden pang of fear herself.
She went to the telephone and called up Purley Bond.
No — he had not seen Diego.   She had been cooking
doughnuts.   She was hot and tired as she climbed the
stairs to Fay's room.   She found her sleeping in the

twilight, her dark hair lying across the pillow, even hanging dramatically over the side of the bed to the floor.   She woke when Josie came in.

"Has he come back?" she asked instantly.

"No.   I 've baked the doughnuts."

Fay sat up with a wild look.   "As though I wanted to hear about doughnuts!   My God, it 's nearly dark! Why did you let me sleep like this?"   She got up and began to coil her hair.

"You stay and mind the shop," said Josie.   "I 'll go and find him."

"Did you telephone Purley?"

"He 's not been there."

The shop bell clanged.   Fay said: "We must n't let anyone know there 's anything wrong.   I 'll go down while you look for him."

Although it had been twilight in the house, the sea and the ice heaped up on the beach were red in the sunset as Josie ran down the sloping street toward the studio.   A remembrance had come to her, filling her with horror, of how Diego had once said that the rafters in the studio would be convenient to hang one's self from.   He had got a rope and thrown it across one as though in preparation for such a deed, and she had paid his teasing the homage of screaming and pretended fright — just as he had expected.   That had been a year ago.   But might not the thought have remained in his mind?   She felt that he was strange, unaccountable, beyond her understanding.

In the untrampled snow of the little side street one set of footprints was easily discovered.   She followed them, placing her own feet in the pure blue-white depth of each. They led to the door of the studio. But none led away. She opened the door softly and went inside. There was a dead dark chill there and she could see heel marks of snow on the stairs. She called in a shrill, trembling voice: —

"Diego! Are you up there?"

There was no answer. Terror seized her and she hurried out of the studio, closing the door behind her. She went through the snow to the beach and stared up at the windows. Two gulls were flying above the skylight, crying and peering down at it as though to see what was inside. The waves made a crunching sound against the broken ice.

She ran up the steep street, not following the tracks now, but ploughing through the snow to her knees. She ran along the main street to the drug store and presented herself before Bond, in his dark corner, with a blanched face.

"Come with me to the studio!" she said, trembling all over. "Diego has done something to himself in there!"

Bond switched on the light. He had dropped asleep over a book of travel. Now he blinked under the glare and his pale yellow hair looked white.

"What 's he done?"

"I don't know. Something awful, I 'm sure. He and Fay quarreled and he burst out of the shop, looking black. I went into the studio and called, but he did n't answer. There are some gulls flying over the skylight as if there was something queer inside."

Bond got his hat and they hurried together to the studio. She had come upon him so suddenly and so distractedly that she had him almost as frightened as herself.

The snow on the steep side street lay in violet shadow, but the ice-covered rocks below the studio shone with a brighter radiance. The sun had disappeared, but the western clouds still discovered his power and spread it on the sea and rocks, giving the impression of a newly created world. Bond and Josie, snow to the knees, went into the studio, she clutching his sleeve as they climbed the stairs.

Above, it was almost dark except for a red splash of light that revealed a half-finished study in the nude. A gust of fresh air icier than the dead chill of the room below met them. As they cautiously advanced they saw that the skylight was open and above it hovered the gulls crying loudly, their wings reddened by the afterglow.

Bond struck a match with a hand that trembled a little — there was a genuine sense of horror in the room — and looked about. . . . Diego was lying on the couch with all the quilts and blankets Josie had carefully folded away heaped on top of him. He was sound asleep. They bent over him and heard his comfortable breathing, smelled the odor of moth balls from the blankets. . . .

"Well, if this is n't the limit!" said Bond. "He ought to be horsewhipped!" He dragged the bedclothes off him and shook him. "Wake up, you young scoundrel! I should think you 'd be ashamed!

You 've got your mother and Josie almost scared to death!"

"Not me!" cried Josie angrily, as he sat up and rubbed his eyes. "Fay was, poor thing! But not me! I knew it was just bluff!" Her fascinated eyes were fixed on his face, on his fingers, as he rubbed his heavy eyelids. She felt the warmth of him come out to her from under the heavy quilts.

"I don't know what it was all about," said Bond, with an unreasoning feeling of compassion for Diego, "but he might have caught his death of cold. I 'd better send around a dose of something for him."

Diego got up and began to manipulate the rope that controlled the skylight. It closed with a noise that sent the gulls off screaming.

"What were they after?" asked Bond, staring up.

"I opened it to let in the sun. Then I threw them some stale rolls that were here." He shivered audibly. "I'd rather have them about me than women."

"Nevertheless, home 's the place for you, my boy," said Bond, "and go straight to bed. Josie, you come with me and I 'll give you a dose for him."

Again they climbed the snowy incline to the main street and separated there, Diego, bare-headed, going with a loose jog trot toward the bakery.

"He 's a queer boy," said Bond, as they hurried along the deserted street, their steps crunching the packed snow.

"I hate Jimmy sometimes," answered Josie, in a husky voice. "He 's so damned inhuman. He 's just like a cruel glossy cat. He cares for no one but himself. He purrs when he gets what he wants and when he does n't get what he wants he lopes off to some dark hole and hides!"

"Well, there 's nothing very cruel about that, is there?" commented Bond.

"Oh, you don't understand. He 's got an overpowering sort of personality. . . . Then he and Fay had an awful scrap. They talked at the tops of their voices and old Mrs. Bell was just coming in and saw the money lying all over the floor."

"So it was about money!"

She answered only by a small suffocated sound, and when they were in the light of the drug store he saw that she was crying. He brought her something in a small glass.

"Here," he said, his blue eyes kind, "drink this. It will steady you."

But she turned her head away and would not touch it. She began to sob loudly. Bond took his father's watch from his pocket and looked at it. Time to close — and safer too, with Josie in this state. He locked the door and led her to his own corner. He was really distressed. He tried to force her to take the brandy. But she would not touch it. She caught his arm in her hands and held it. Her face was hidden against his shoulder. Bond was amazed, for she had always been distant with him. He looked down at her and saw the lovely color flushing her cheek. Gently he took the little red knitted hat from her head and stroked her fine hair comfortingly. "Now,

Josie — now, Josie," he repeated, as though soothing a child.

She raised her face to his. Her eyes were wet, her lips looked hot and were trembling from sobs.

"Kiss me," she breathed. "Kiss me . . ." Her hands left his arm and were clasped behind his neck.

He could not believe it possible he would be so moved. He held her to him and kissed her — not once, but again and again. They stood together then, locked in each other's arms, silent and motionless. They heard someone come to the door, try it and go away, the footsteps crunching on the packed snow.

At last she gave a deep sigh and withdrew herself. She took her hat from his hand and pulled it on her head well over the eyes. She picked up the glass then and drank the brandy.

"Good girl," he said. "You 'll feel better now."

He turned away embarrassed and began to prepare something for Diego.

"I suppose you think I 'm a queer girl," she said.

"No. You were just feeling overwrought. It was quite natural for you to . . ."

"I just had to! I could n't help myself. I did n't mean anything — particular — "

He agitated the mixture he was preparing. "I know. I just happened to be on the spot."

"You need n't think," she said, quickly, "that I would have done that to anyone."

"I 'm glad to hear that."

"For your sake — or mine?"

"Well — for both our sakes — "

"Why?"

"I 'd like us to be friends.   You 've never been very friendly with me."

"What about to-night?"

He gave her an amused look.   "You 'll be angry if I tell you what I think about that."

"I swear I won't!   Tell me — please!"

"Better not."

"You must!"

"Very well.   I think you were pretending to yourself that I was Diego."

Her color flamed, but she said quietly: "I daresay you 're right. . . . I 'm as silly about him as you are about Fay."

She had given better than she had got.   Bond almost dropped the bottle.   "Well — that was a mean one," he said.

"I did n't intend to be mean.   I just want you to know that we 're in the same boat."

"And might as well pull together, eh?"

"I 'll help you, if I can."

Bond was much embarrassed.   He fidgeted with the things on his desk to hide it.

"I guess I 'll go," said Josie.

He took up his hat.   "I 'll go with you as far as the door and see how he is.   That was a terrible thing for him to do."

"Better than hanging, though."

At the door of the bakery she said: "You wait here

and I 'll run in and see if they 've made it up. Perhaps Fay will want to speak to you."

In a few minutes she was back.

"She says to come in. They 're sitting on the sofa together. As thick as thieves. What a pair! We do all the worrying."

They went in.

"Hello, Purley!" called out Fay when she heard his step in the shop. "Come right in! I want you to look at Diego and see if you think I ought to get a doctor. He seems kind of feverish."

She and her son were sitting pressed close together on the sofa. Their resemblance, not often noticeable, was at the moment striking. They both were flushed, with eyes bright, and under the eyes the skin was brownish dark. Their dark thick hair was ruffled.

Bond felt his pulse, Fay looking up at him with what, he suddenly thought, was a look of animal trust. Diego's hand hung limp from his, like a child's.

"How is he?"

"His pulse is a little quick. He ought to get to bed. I 'll come in the morning and take his temperature."

"Want my supper first," muttered Diego, in a surly, sick-boy voice. "Nothing to eat since breakfast."

"For pity's sake, Josie, get us something to eat!" exclaimed Fay. "We 're starving! Purley 's to stay and eat with us. Don't you say a word against it, Purley!"

Josie laid a new yellow and white check cloth on

the table and set it with the best dishes. It was the first time Bond had taken a meal with them. She was so excited by the presence of a guest that she took twice as long as usual in preparing the meal. It was laid in the sitting room so that Diego need not leave the heat which Fay had created by filling the self-feeder to the lid.

"What are you giving us, Josie?" asked Fay. "Let 's see — ham and eggs, fried potatoes — that 's all right." She drew Josie aside. "What 's to finish on?"

"Canned peaches," answered Josie, "and cocoanut cake. There are two pies left in the case — mince and pumpkin. Which will you have?"

"Which would you like?" Fay asked of Bond with a happy intimate look.

"Let Diego choose," answered Bond a little grimly. "It 's his party."

"Punkin!" shouted Diego.

The four who were to have so many meals together sat down.

Fay had had the table moved beside the sofa so that Diego might not be caused the exertion of crossing the room. He sat up tousle-headed beside it, beaming with satisfaction. Bond had his back against the stove and his rather pale skin soon glowed a deep pink. Fay had coiled up her hair so rapidly that it was now of itself uncoiling and curled like a snake ready to spring, on her shoulder. She was oblivious of everything but her relief of spirit. She praised everything Josie had done. She pressed Bond to eat to repletion.

She hung over Diego, reached out her dark-skinned shapely hand to stroke his hair, all but fed him.

With their cigarettes they drank large cups of coffee golden tan with thick cream.

Bond, accustomed to eating alone, experienced a feeling of boyish hilarity in the closeness of this group. He found himself talking fluently about the travel books he had read. He found himself wanting to tell them of his plan for selling the drug business which his father, with so many cautious ponderings, had bought for him. All the while he talked of France and Italy and Algiers he was thinking how astonished they would be if they knew what was in his mind. Then, almost before he knew it, the words slipped out and the half-formed idea loomed like an accomplished fact. It was a fact, he said recklessly, he had advertised the business in a Boston paper.

The other three were in a mood in which nothing surprised them. It seemed the natural thing that Bond should sell out and join them in their adventure.

"We 'll say that you are my brother," said Fay. "And so prevent any gossip."

He did not object even to that.

"I 'll tell you what we 'll do," he said. "We 'll take a Mediterranean cruise and get off at Monaco. Then we can make our way to Paris taking our own time."

"How heavenly," said Fay, stroking Diego's hand. "If only someone will come along and buy us out!"

Someone did. Before the New Year, both the drug store and the bakery had been disposed of and their passages were booked on a foreign cruiser.

CHAPTER IV

THE four people, of such diverse temperaments, who sailed in the New Year for France now saw the Atlantic in an entirely different aspect from the one to which they were accustomed. They had been born and had lived all their lives within sight, sound, and smell of it. The prosperity of Saltport depended on it. It was like a great dancing bear secured by the iron chain of the shore. It might rage and roar all the winter, but in summer it danced for the summer colony, and Saltport passed the hat. But it was a new experience to see it in mid-ocean from the heaving deck of a liner. If it was, in truth, a dancing bear, they were now no more than the fleas on its shaggy back.

Their new situation affected them according to their individual characters. Fay Palmas, the oldest of the quartette, responded in a spirit the most temerarious and childlike. Even as she lay seasick in her berth, wondering if the ship would ever right herself after the last roll, she felt a wild joy in her escape from what she looked back on as years of hateful bondage. She had ceased to love her husband from the time of Diego's birth. She had always been conscious that he had been criticizing her, and she abhorred criticism. Now she thrust the remembrance of his aproned figure, his floury arms, his ascetic face, out of her mind forever. She stretched her arms toward the Old World with the rapturous hope that spurred early explorers on toward the New.

From the day she appeared on deck in her long black fur-trimmed coat, she was the subject of speculation among the other passengers. Her height, her long, swinging walk, her swarthy skin, arched brows, and brilliant eyes made her singular. She had an air at once naïve and reckless. She was eager to investigate every part of the ship, from engine room to captain's bridge. She studied the maps on the walls of the promenade deck. She read the ship's newspaper from end to end, and when she came upon an item from Massachusetts she wondered if she had ever lived there. She had never before dressed for dinner, but after she had done it half-a-dozen times she wondered how people could eat without dressing — how they could stomach dinner at noon. She had no shyness, but pushed her way to the front at the afternoon horse racing, learned how to place her money, and from then on usually backed a lucky horse. Luck was with her, she felt. She won a pool on the day's run. She learned to play deck tennis and won a prize at that. In playing it her chief aim was to hurl the rubber ring in her opponent's face. What she liked best was the long breezy walk the length of the promenade deck with Diego at her side (she was aware that he set off her looks) and Bond and Josie close behind. She talked and laughed, even though Diego made scarcely any reply, and threw laughing remarks over her shoulder to the other two, conscious that their group was an object of interest. She tried to drop her New England drawl and imitated in turn the accents of various people on board whom she admired. Sometimes she hurried up to Bond and began talking to him like a Southerner — calling him "Pully." Sometimes she imitated quite successfully, for an hour or more, the grave unhurried accents of a Harvard professor. She was not above trying out the peculiar tones of the Detroiter. But after an evening spent in the company of a young Chicagoan, a Rhodes Scholar at Oxford, she settled down to imitate the fine frenzy of his accent alone. She was trying to absorb in haste what life had so long denied her.

Bond reminded himself of this when he felt irritated by her. But indeed any irritation he felt was so slight as to be almost negligible. He was filled with pride in her adaptability, her power, like that of a bright-colored flower to unfold in the first warmth of the sun. His reaction to the change was an almost unbelief in himself. Was it possible that he, Purley Bond, after all those years in the dim drug store at Saltport, was here, sailing on the ocean in the company of his beloved? The letter of credit he carried in his pocket represented to him his only link with his life as a chemist. Sometimes he felt himself poised in mid-air, between the two continents, as though nipped up by some great finger and thumb for the pleasure of a mysterious power. His happiest moments were far from those which Fay enjoyed. His nature was retiring and he disliked being stared at. He thought of himself as lanky, tow-headed, and rather unattractive. But as they neared the African coast and the nights grew warmer and he and she hung in the darkness together over the ship's side, watching the snowy unfolding of the wake, he had a feeling of profound and almost frightening bliss. He had regarded her so long with love from a distance that to be isolated close beside her like this, the music of the orchestra coming muted to them, made him wish for nothing beyond this moment.

He had never seen her in evening clothes before, and the gleam of her breast or arm beneath her cloak filled him with a strange joy. All day he looked forward to this hour. If he was cheated of it his disappointment was deep. Then he would find Josie and talk to her of his love for Fay. A new relationship was now established between them. For the first time in their lives they enjoyed the pleasure of a confidential friend of the opposite sex. Sometimes, in talking to Josie, he forgot for the time his preoccupation with Fay. He liked to watch the color come and go in her mobile face, the pupils of her gray eyes enlarge when she was moved. He had thought of her as shy, rigid, self-centred. He found her almost cruelly frank; sensitive to every contact. And they had so many dislikes in common! That drew them together in a gibing, fun-making closeness. They gave ridiculous names to the people who amused or disgusted them, and began to have secret jokes together. They even made fun, a little, of Fay. Bond

did it in a spirit of bravado, to show Josie that he was
not slavish in his adoration. But he hated himself
for it afterward. He preferred to make fun of the
people Fay imitated.

To Josie the immensity, the power of the sea, discovered from its heaving bosom, was terrible and
beautiful. She resented the floating hotel atmosphere of the ship and wished that she might have
crossed on a schooner, an ocean tramp. She hated
the daily newspaper, the pretty page boys in their
smart liveries, the games, the prize-givings, the men
in plus-fours, the women who changed their clothes
three times a day, the dogs on leads, the spoiled, bold-
eyed children. Most of all she hated Diego for taking to the life on board as a duck to water.

But she liked Bond and this new comradeship with
him. She liked the way he walked, the way he
looked at her out of his blue eyes. She liked his long,
nervous, well-kept hands and his long sensitive upper
lip. Sometimes she said amusing things about Fay
just to see this lip quiver, half laughing, half tighten-
ing in anger.

"Listen," she said, as they sat, swathed in rugs on
their deck chairs. Fay, farther along, was talking
with an almost featureless-faced lady from Philadelphia.

"It was my first visit home in years," the Philadel-
phian was saying, "and how sadly it has all changed!
When I was a girl my family could know almost anyone in society. Now one never knows whom one
may be introduced to there. The strangest people

are breaking in and actually being received. Many
of the perfectly magnificent old homes have gone into
the hands of very queer people. My own old home
included."

"Oh, yes, that's going on all over now," said Fay.
"I suppose you notice it in Boston, too."

"Oh, yes, we notice it terribly. So many queer
Irish creeping into society. . . ."

"I suppose you are like myself and don't often go
back."

"Well, I've had to be at home a good lot lately on
account of family ties. But I guess it will be years
before we go back again."

"Ah, the more one lives abroad the harder it is to
go back! What did you say your name is? We used
to know a good many Boston families. We have
connections there. A cousin of mine married one of
the Lowells."

"I don't suppose you'd be acquainted with my
husband's family. He was a Spanish gentleman.
Awfully poor, of course, but proud. You know
what Spaniards are like."

"I adore Spaniards! I spent many years traveling
in Spain when my husband was living. It's a second home to me. I suppose you know it well."

"No, I've never been there, I'm sorry to say.
Don't you think my son looks sort of Spanish?"

"I do indeed. A fascinating boy. But you should
never tell anyone he is your son. You look just like
brother and sister. And you're such a *contrast* to
your own brother."

Fay slid an apprehensive glance toward Bond.   He
had not liked the deception at all, thought it quite
unnecessary, but Fay seemed to feel safer when bul-
warked by fiction.   She answered: —

"I favor my mother's family.   There was a kind
of disgrace away back a hundred years or so.   An
Indian princess, they say.   We never talk about it,
but those things have a way of coming out generations after."

"How *fascinating!*"

"Well, it is sort of romantic.   But it's better to
be pure American, don't you think?"

"My dear, is there such a thing?   I doubt it!
What did you say your maiden name was?   I used
to go to so many dances in Boston when I was a girl.
I may have danced with your father."

"I was an Elwood," answered Fay, rather haughtily.

Bond grasped Josie by the wrist.   "I'm going to
be sick if I stay here," he muttered.   "Let's go for
a walk."

As they strode, arm in arm, against the wind on
an upper deck, Bond thought, "Oh, my darling, why
do you humiliate me by talking like such a little
fool?"   To Josie he said: "We seem to be leaving our
past behind us."

"It'll keep us busy living up to Fay," answered
Josie.

"I think she'll get over this sort of thing when she
gets off the boat, don't you?"

"Why should she?   She's only begun.   She's having the time of her life.   And Diego's just as bad.

He does n't talk much, but he gives the impression of being in with the Art set both winter and summer. As for you, Fay tells everyone that you 're an analytical chemist and a scientist."

"Good Lord!" said Bond, horrified. "I 'll be glad when we land."

Diego did not trouble himself much with the subtleties of their position, but he followed where his mother led and accepted the pleasures the day offered without thought of the future, beyond the hope that Paris would be as good fun as this. He had never been so happy. The sulky look was seldom on his face now. He made friends with all sorts of people, sought among the passengers for a substitute for Mr. Selby, the artist. But there was no older artist on board to take him under his wing in Paris. However, he found many who promised to take him under their wing for flights of a different sort. He was proud of his mother and Josie. He wished Josie would not look at him with that searching, fascinated look of hers, but he supposed he would have to go through his life bearing that, or until one of them married. Sometimes he wondered if she loved him. If she did she had a strange way of showing it — never seeming really to approve of him, always gibing. Lying in his berth, he sometimes remembered how he had kissed her, held her in his arms on the couch in the studio, and thought that one day he might do it again. . . .

At last they lay off Teneriffe.

The island rose before them in summer sunshine.

It was the first warm day and the passengers appeared in summer clothes. Fay did not accompany the others on the trip ashore. She had got up with a headache. Unless she kept quiet, it might develop into a day of misery. Reluctantly she gave up the excursion.

But an hour of sitting in a deck chair in a shady corner, with closed eyes, brought relief. Her brain, eased of the pressure of pain, became alive to the various sounds of the ship. Farther along sailors were washing down the deck, cleaning windows, laughing, shouting and singing in French, just as though there were not a passenger on board. She wondered if they had forgotten her. She knew they had seen her, as they trooped past her chair, for they had given her curious glances from their bold French eyes. Head throbbing as it was, she had looked back at them with curiosity, noticed how free and unrepressed and bold they seemed.

A trim young officer strolled by, letting his eyes rest for a moment on her reclining white figure. He said good-morning in a pleasant light-toned voice and passed on, stopping to watch the sailors heave something with ropes over the side. She wondered what they were doing and whether the young officer spoke English. Her head felt smoothed out, relaxed, and a faint sense of exhilaration made her smile. She would lie where she was, resting all the day, be refreshed and strong when the others came back tired out. The steeps of Teneriffe rose olive green in the sunlight. The little town had taken in all these strange voyagers and still seemed to sleep.

Then there came to her ears a commotion from the other side of the ship. Voices raised, bumpings, chuggings, barkings. She realized that this was but the crescendo of a medley of sounds she had subconsciously been listening to for some time. She got out of her chair and crossed the deck.

She almost gasped with astonishment at what she saw far below, close to the ship's side. A black little tug which had been towing one of the three bumboats that lay alongside was still straining and puffing in the attempt to bring it into line. Another bumboat, this with its own engine beneath a grotesque erection of boards, was being insinuated into the most desirable position and, by its intrusion, pushing aside the one already attached by ropes to the ship. From them had been unloaded a supply of the small sweet bananas of the island, but there still remained baskets and canvas-covered bundles of goods which the owners hoped to sell to the returned excursionists. Besides these goods, the boats were strewn with baskets, boxes, coils of rope, and oddments of what looked to Fay mere junk. In and out among these ran small dogs, one to each boat, hysterically barking in emulation of the outpouring of rage, invective, and despair from their owners. Canaries in cruelly small wooden cages fluttered against their bars, terrified by the hubbub. A choppy sea set the bumboats thumping against each other, and now and again a clear

green wave slid across their decks, leaving deposited
on the boards scraps of bread and lettuce leaves
thrown from the ship's kitchen.   Half a score of heads
were stuck through the portholes of the kitchen,
and laughing adjurations in French were added to the
harsh Spanish outcry.

Fay's attention became centred on the two boats at
grips in a dispute of which she scarcely understood
the meaning.   But she saw clearly enough the rage
into which the antagonists were swept.   Up and
down their heaving decks they strode raising their
hands to heaven, shaking their fists, distorting their
features into masks of tragedy.   One was a short full-
faced man with powerful shoulders, long arms, and
short legs.   From under his protruding black moustache came such bellows and outcries as Fay had never
heard before.   His woolly-coated dog leaped about
him, its four feet never all on the deck at once.   The
other man was old, rather tall and with fine features.
His rage was divided between the black-moustached
one and a young man at the helm of his own boat.
After launching insults at the one, that made him
beat his breast in frenzy, he would turn and, with
upraised arm above the helmsman, call down the
wrath of heaven upon him for not having been first
at the ship's side.   His dog, an old pure-bred pug
whose appearance in this situation might well be a
mystery, saw all the horror of their position eye to
eye with his master.   First toward the other boat,
then toward the young man at the wheel he turned
his wrinkled muzzle, barking without pause.

The brilliant blue of sky and sea, the bright-colored shirts of the men, and the mounds of gay fruit, the tossing wave-washed decks of the bumboats far below, at first only amused and delighted Fay Palmas. She leaned over the side, looking down until she felt dizzy. She walked away, took a turn around the deck, came back, and it was still going on. Sometimes the owner of the first boat took a hand in the quarrel. Once all three poured out their anger at the young man at the helm. It was then that she began to notice him particularly.

He had been drooping over the wheel in an attitude of dejection, but now he turned and faced them, his arm upraised in a flourish of self-defense. He shouted at them in a voice and accent oddly different. She noticed the slender elegance of his body, — he was bare to the waist, — his cameo-like, Grecian features, his long bronze-colored hair. Once she had given her attention to him she scarcely looked at the others, but watched his every move, wished that he would raise his voice again. Suddenly she felt limp and tired from the excitement of it all. The young officer came and stood by her and talked laughingly of the scene below. Not infrequently, he said, this sort of thing happened. Did he know who the young man was? No, he had not seen him before, but probably he was the old man's son. But he was so handsome, was n't he? Did she think so? But, of course, these barbarians were often quite good-looking — especially the women. He complacently stroked his gold-laced sleeve.

While they had talked the uproar had suddenly ceased. There was silence below now except for the sound of the waves and the quiet thumping of the boats against the side. The dogs had thrown themselves down exhausted, with hanging tongues. A canary ventured a trill of song. From a kitchen porthole a roll was tossed to the man with the large moustache. He caught it dexterously. Caught at, but missed, a piece of cooked meat which fell on the deck near his dog, who snapped it up and again fell back exhausted. There was laughter from the porthole and this time the piece of meat was caught. He was animal-like, repulsive, Fay thought, and turned her eyes to the other boat. The old man was squatting on his haunches, in a dejected attitude. The young man stood alone in the bow, as though to catch the breeze on his bare chest. He raised his eyes and looked at her. She looked back and again had that feeling of weakness, but this time it was connected with him, as though he had taken something from her. A roll was thrown from the porthole towards him, but he made no effort to catch it and, as it slid near him, kicked it away disdainfully into the sea.

The luncheon gong sounded. . . . Fay Palmas and an elderly man, who had been ill most of the way across, were the only passengers in the dining room. A swarm of stewards, like hovering bees, moved about them. The man, enjoying his first meal, tried to draw her into conversation, but she could give her mind to nothing but thoughts of the scene she had just witnessed. If only she could find out the history of the thin, proud young boatman! It was romantic, she was sure. Quite possibly tragic.

She recalled his attitudes, each one of which had displayed his naked brown torso and sensitively modeled head to advantage, as the unconscious posings of a wild creature. If she had not been there no one would have given a second glance at him, except in hatred or derision.

After lunch she turned at once toward her former position on the deck. On the way she discovered that a closed-in space at the stern had been given over to the natives for the exhibition of their wares. There they were spread out on the floor: shawls, brightly embroidered; vivid kimonos; necklets of beads; pyjamas with gold dragons on the breast; table linen; boxes of Spanish cigars and cigarettes. Canaries twittered timidly in the tiny cages, and a red and green parrot sulked, muffled on his perch.

Behind each exhibit squatted a swarthy patient figure. Hours must pass before the return of the excursionists, yet all was prepared, as for a feast. Hopeful, patient, resigned to waiting, they squatted in apparent amity. Quite near her Fay saw the old man of the conflict, a thin spiral of cigarette smoke above his head, his hands palm upward on his knees. But she could not discover Black Moustache or the young man.

Once she was seen, a dozen dark hands beckoned to her or held out beads or birds or embroideries to tempt her. She slipped away and turned along the sunny deserted deck, glittering in its clean freshness.

She looked over the side and saw the flat boats, deserted except for the dogs that lay sleeping in the hot sun.

Then she saw a man walking ahead of her far down the deck. It was Black Moustache, his bullet head bare, his ragged trousers reaching just below the knees. She had never seen such a walk. He moved so pridefully on his high padded instep that he seemed made of India rubber, ready at any moment to bound into the air.

He walked a short distance, staring intently at some object hidden from her by a projection of the smoking room. He wheeled abruptly and retraced his buoyant steps, facing her. But he did not see her. He continued to gaze in the same direction, with a belligerent, conquering expression. His face was dark red and beaded with sweat as a result of his frenzy. His eyes had a glazed look.

Fay was half afraid of him there on the lonely deck, but curiosity overcame her. She went nearer, then passed him, looking in her turn into the corner formed by the projection. She saw curled up there the object of her speculations, fast asleep.

He was half-naked. He was in an attitude of exhaustion, his head almost touching his knees. She saw his beautiful hands hanging limply, his long lashes, the patch of tawny beard in front of his ears. His smooth-shaven face was like a face she had once seen on an old coin. Again she had that feeling of weakness, as though something had gone out from her.

She walked past him, then returned, meeting Black Moustache as before. He glanced timidly at her and, after they had passed and met again, he went on down the deck and, stretching himself in the full heat of the sun, lay down like a child, tired out. She had never seen people at all like these. They excited her, for they were of a different world. How glad she was that she had not gone on the excursion!

The young man had become conscious of her eyes on him. He opened his own and looked up at her, startled. He rose quickly and faced her, as though defiantly. He looked about, as though for a way of escape, then frowned, tossed the hair out of his eyes, and returned her stare.

"I must go," he said in broken English. "I have no right here. I was asleep."

"It's too bad I woke you," she said. "It certainly was mean of me to stare at you. But that man down there acted so queerly. I thought he was going to start another fight perhaps — and I felt sort of nervous." She laughed a little, showing her white teeth.

He glanced contemptuously at Black Moustache, now himself fast asleep. "I'm not afraid of him," he said. "He is all wind. He knows I would as soon slit him up with a knife as not."

She laughed again, this time more loudly. She was excited, felt that she had stepped into a new dangerous world.

"But you speak English!" she said. "You gave me a big surprise when you began to talk so that I could understand."

He raised his brows. "Oh, yes — I have been in England. I speak English — not badly."

"But you live here — on this island?"

"Live here?" he repeated with a shrug of distaste. "No, I do not live here. I stay here — yes, a little while. But I am not one of these people. Ignorant, contemptible, filthy peasants!"

She longed to ask him what he was, but only said: "It must be hard for you then — living like this."

"Yes — it is very hard. But then — life is hard. For some of us."

"You came from far off?" She found herself imitating his tone, his way of speaking.

"I come from Sicily." He compressed his lips and gave her a searching look as though he would find out what sort of woman she was. Then he added, "I am of a noble Sicilian family. I have lost everything. There is nothing left for me to do but live among ignorant, contemptible, filthy peasants." Now he looked proudly past her, out towards the open sea.

With a secret dalliance of the mind she pictured him as her lover, they two driven to these islands by cruel disaster, she also with barely enough rags to cover her. She looked down over her smart summer clothes and thought of them as rags — her own feet bare. Even he, a Sicilian, would be surprised, she thought, if he could see the length and darkness of her hair.

"Must you stay here?" she asked. "Can't you get away?"

"I am reduced," he answered, "to these rags. This

medal on my neck which keeps me from to drown.
This ring on my finger which keeps in my mind that
I am Montleone." He held up his hand, supple, with
rounded fingers, yet strong. The antique ring suited
it well.

"Would it be rude of me to ask what happened?"
She spoke simply, like a child.

"You also have known great trouble," he said, his
eyes again searching her face.

"I have known little else." There was more than
a suggestion of his tragic pride in her tone.

Quick sympathy softened his clear-cut face. "I
am sorry. It is good of you then to spare time for
my trouble. . . . We will talk of it no more."

"Yes, yes," she said, eagerly. "Please tell me more
of yourself! It is better for me to forget my own
trouble."

"Are you married?" he asked abruptly.

She raised her hand that wore a wedding ring, in a
gesture clearly reflected from his as he had shown his
ring. "My husband is dead," she said gently.

"Ah, that is part of your trouble! But not
all . . ."

"I have lost a beautiful voice. . . . I can say
beautiful — now that it is gone."

"That is a great loss. But you are yourself beautiful. You should be happy in that."

Fay Palmas had never been told that she was beautiful, though in secret she thought so. She felt that
at this moment, for the first time in her thirty-eight
years, she was really living. To think that, if she had

gone on the excursion, this erotic moment would have glided by uncaptured!

"My beauty is nothing to me," she said. "I would gladly have been hideous if I could have kept my voice."

"It will come back — in Sicily!" he said, and smiled at her.

Again she had that feeling of his power, her own weakness. She shook her head.

"I am not going to Sicily."

"Not going to Sicily! Ah, but you must! You were born for Sicily. The moment I see you I say to myself — 'She goes to Sicilia — my Sicilia!' "

"No, I am not going to Sicilia," — she pronounced it as he had, — "I am getting off at Monaco. Then going on to Paris." As she said these words she had a feeling of acute melancholy.

He took a step nearer. He came so close that she saw the separate hairs of the dark down on his chest, she smelled the warm, salt-water freshness of his body.

"Not to Monaco! You must not go to Monaco! You will never become happy there. And Paris — even worse! It is in these places that I lose everything. I gamble and I lose everything. Ah, but they are fatal places for you!"

"But I do not gamble." She had a vision of herself haggard-eyed before the gaming table, losing, with a weary yet gallant smile, all the proceeds from the sale of the bakery. "But, of course, I may gamble when I get there — who knows?"

"I know. . . . You will not go. I beg that you will not go! You will go to Sicilia and I will tell you where my old home is. And you will wander about its garden and perhaps meet my spirit there. I shall be thinking of you — seeing you in my garden. Even while I work for these ignorant, brutal, and filthy peasants I shall see you in my garden — walking beautiful among the flowers!"

She pitied him from the bottom of her heart. She pitied herself for having to leave him here, having to go on to Majorca and Monaco — take shore excursions under the direction of a paid guide. Oh, to see his garden in Sicily — to be led about the garden walks by him! She said: —

"But if you still have your own home, why don't you go back to it?"

"It is not mine now. My father left me only debts. The war ruined us. I went to Monaco with that little I had from selling my mother's jewels to see if I could win back our house. But instead I lost the little I had. I should have blown my brains out then, but the idea came to me to seek this peaceful island — and think about life — try to find out its meaning — and face it. But I find no peace here. It is horrible and I long to get away. But my last money is stolen from me. Even my clothes are stolen. I am reduced to nakedness and to work for these people. They know I am noble and hate me for it. I am a Sicilian and they hate me for that. I shall not see my home again, but if I could think that you — " he half turned away, then again faced her with an imploring gesture. "I wish you would not go to Monaco. You will not like it there. It is not your sort of place. You will not find your voice there and you will lose something that makes you beautiful."

She looked about her bewildered, almost frightened. Was it really she, Fay Palmas, standing on this deck, being urged by this half-naked stranger to go to his island, his garden? And not only that, but feeling that she must obey him?

"But what can I say," she said haltingly, "to the others? You see, I am not alone. I have my cousin, and my son, and — a friend, with me."

A shadow crossed his face. "I am sorry for that. I want you to be alone — except for me . . ."

She put her hands on the polished brass railing to steady herself.

"That is an odd way to talk to a stranger," she said.

"You are not a stranger. From the moment I looked up and saw you far above on the deck, I thought, 'That beautiful woman is not a stranger. She has taken this voyage and I have come to Teneriffe so we may meet again.'"

"But we had not met before."

He did not answer. He laid his hand on the brass railing beside hers, smiled at their two hands, then his slipped over hers and covered it. They stood so a moment in the bright sunlight without speaking. Then she moved her hand away.

"All this is very strange to me, anyway," she said, a little shakily.

"Now but listen — " he said. "It is so easy to

change your plans — when you have money!   Your
friends will do what you want.   I am sure of that.
Your little boy — ”

"He is nineteen.   He is taller than you."

"Impossible!   You are not yet thirty!"

"Thirty-eight."

He dismissed her years with a shrug.   "You are a
girl.   It will be the same when you are fifty.   The
friend you speak of is a man?”

"Yes.   He's an analyst.   Interested in science.
An old friend of the family."

"There is much to interest a scientist in Sicily.
Much to analyze.   Why should he go to Monaco or
Paris?   Oh, you can do with them what you will!
My instinct tells me that.   If only I could go with
you to Tramontana!   So much I should like to show
you the place where I once live!”

She began to walk up and down, twisting her
fingers together, as was her way when excited.   What
was she to do?   Go away and leave him here, among
these half-savage people, to end his young life in
suicide perhaps?   Or, if not that, to wander from
one foreign place to another, earning scarcely enough
to keep soul and that beautiful body together?   She
could give him money.   But would he take it?   And,
if he did, would she ever see him again?   It was
scarcely likely.   They would drift apart, and all the
romance and beauty towards which her desires had
struggled, like plants that had never flowered, would
be swept away.   She would never see him again!
She took the shining brass railing in her two hands

and, supporting herself by it, swayed from side to
side, trying to produce in her being some primordial
rhythm to direct her.　He went and leaned over the
side, his back to her, as though conscious of her struggle, throwing himself on her mercy, but in no way
influencing her by look or word.

But to stay here with him — how could she do
that?　And to take him with her — what could she
say to the others?　They would think she was crazy
if she picked up a half-naked boatman and made him
one of their party.　But — her thoughts ran on, as she
swayed from side to side — why need they know?
He might come on board as a passenger picked up at
Teneriffe, quite independent of them.　She knew she
could persuade them — well, it would amount to in-
sisting — that they should go to Sicily instead of
France.　A primitive determination not to allow
conventions to deprive her of this romantic escape
from the tameness of ordinary relations tightened her
nerves.　She felt capable of flying across the windy
expanse of the Mediterranean with the Sicilian, as
an eagle with its mate.　"I am part Indian," she
thought.　"This is what it must have felt like to be
an Indian woman in the savage old days.　I am afraid
of nothing, nothing."

She turned to him.　"I must tell you," she said,
"that I am part red Indian."

He looked at her contemplatively across his shoulder, a shy, almost dreamy look.　"That does not surprise me," he said.　"I knew you had wild blood in
you.　You are not like other women."

"And my son has Portuguese blood."

"Ah, I hate the Portuguese," he returned calmly.

"But you will not hate Diego. He is such a darling boy."

"I shall never see him."

She came to his side and said in a hurried tone: —

"You must come with us. I cannot leave you here — like this. Please don't say no! I want you to come."

He said, scarcely above a whisper: "I have no money. I must stay here, but — I am glad you would like to have me."

"We can easily arrange that. I can lend you some. I have plenty." He must be made to feel that money was nothing to her, that she was offering him help out of a whim for her own pleasure, if he chose to think that. Or from pure kindness of heart.

He gave her a look of such trust as a child might give. "You are very kind. But how can I go with you even if you lend me money? I have no clothes but these so ragged ones. Also a jersey on the shore. You cannot take me with you so." He looked helplessly down at his smooth brown torso.

She was reckless now that she saw consent in his eyes. She would do anything to have her own way. She said: —

"That is nothing. I will give you some of my son's clothes. Have you a passport?"

"Yes. It too is on shore."

"Now listen! I will go down to my son's cabin and get you some clothes and a suitcase to carry them in. So you need not appear without baggage. Then, when the other passengers come back, you must come too. You will simply be returning to Sicily from a stay here. There will be no trouble about getting a cabin. The ship is not two-thirds full."

Again he gave her that trusting look. He would confide himself to her, do just as she said. She was rich, powerful, sent by a beneficent Providence to rescue him. . . .

She rummaged through Diego's cabin almost too excited to know what she was doing. Her cheeks had never burned more hotly in front of the oven than they did standing in front of Diego's wardrobe tearing out and replacing one garment after another, suddenly conscious that Diego was much the broader of the two, suddenly afraid of what Diego would say when he discovered some of his best clothes missing. She dared not take his evening things. Even to clothe a Sicilian noble she dared not do that! Montleone would have to wear a lounge suit at dinner. Other men, who were traveling alone, did that sometimes. She had seen two in the dining saloon and rather disapproved.

She dragged one of Diego's three new suitcases from under his berth and ruthlessly took sufficient of his clothes to do Montleone until more could be bought for him. Then she went to her own cabin and, from the bottom of her trunk, took out the beaded bag containing her money. She had traveler's checks, but he must have the cash — enough to buy his ticket to Messina to begin with. She could give

him more later, if necessary. She made a rough cal-
culation, then folded the notes and put them in a
pocket of one of the suits, so that she might not have
the embarrassment of handing them to him.

She looked at her reflection in the glass. No wonder he had called her beautiful! Her eyes were glowing, her cheeks the loveliest red, under the brown.

Black Moustache had disappeared when she returned. Montleone stood with folded arms in the
corner where he had lain sleeping. She put the suitcase into his hand and said, not looking at him: —

"In a pocket of the gray suit you will find enough
to buy your ticket."

He took the suitcase from her, but set it down.

"I do not see how I can do this," he said gravely.
"It is too much. Do you not know that I may be
an impostor and never show myself again to you?"

She was going to say, "I trust you," but changed her
mind and said instead: "You must come back or not,
just as you like. I have done what it pleased me to
do." Again her tone, her bearing, reflected the grave
simplicity of his.

He took her hand and raised it to his lips. Her
hand, the hand of Fay Palmas of Saltport, was kissed
by a Sicilian of ancient lineage. . . . When he had
gone she stood in the corner where he had stood, her
arms folded across her breast.

But she began to worry as to how he would get the
suitcase past the officials and into his boat. She hurried to the side and was just in time to see him placing it, completely hidden under a piece of native

embroidery, in the stern of a skiff attached to the barge. Apparently he had made satisfactory explanation to the old man, for they were talking together amiably and it was he who untied the painter and gave the skiff a push outward.

She watched him row away, the oars flashing like steady beating wings, taking him back to the unknown island, his unknown life there. Ah, if she might fly with him unseen — discover the place he had come from and what his life there had been! Perhaps there was a girl there who cared for him — who would cry bitterly when he left. But — would he leave? Would he return to the ship? "He will come back," she repeated to herself. "He will — he will — something in me that never fails me tells me that he will."

She was too restless to remain long in one spot, though she arranged herself on her deck chair with a magazine and a determination to be indolent. She lay with her head turned sideways against the back of the chair, the magazine in her lap, savoring the delight of being alone. She realized suddenly that she had never had any privacy in her life. She had gone from the young ladies' seminary straight into marriage. Soon she was with child. Then a baby to care for. A sick husband. Then the seventeen years in the bakery, its little hot rooms, her husband's constant, irritating presence, the flow of petty customers, the clanging of the shop bell, Josie always at her side.

But here, on this magic deck, she was alone, alone. More alone than if the ship had been moving, out at sea. For on one side lay Teneriffe, a mountain fastness, its peaks turning to purple against the late afternoon sky. On the other, the ocean, tranquilly lapping against the ship's side, dreaming under the shadows of gulls. The officers or stewards who passed her were no more than shadows. No one here to remind her of Saltport.

But she could not remain quiet for long.

An idea came to her. She rose and went to the closed-in part of the deck where the natives of the island were displaying their wares. She strolled about, looking at the embroideries, and asking a question now and then about Montleone. They could speak little English, but she found out that he had been three months at Teneriffe. That he was proud, though no more than a beggar, that he was dangerous too, and had once tried to kill one of them, and might have been killed himself but for the women who interceded for him.

She bought herself a white silk shawl embroidered with red roses. She bought bright pyjamas for Diego, a necklace of carved beads for Josie, and a box of cigars for Bond. They returned just at sundown, tired and cold, for a chill wind had sprung up. She watched them from the stairs overlooking the gangway, holding her breath for the reappearance of Montleone.

He came with the last of the excursionists, carrying Diego's suitcase, looking swallowed up in Diego's suit. She scarcely knew what she was saying to the others. She laughed when they said they were half-frozen. She looked pained when they said they had had a delightful time. All the while she was staring past them at Montleone, making his way toward the deck. She lingered, terrified by what she thought was a look of suspicion on the face of the purser. She saw Montleone produce his passport, the officials confer together, a page boy dart forward and snatch the suitcase, bending under its weight as he led the way to a cabin. She could not help it — she burst into song as she ascended the stairs with the crowd, not noticing how they stared. On the top step, and the top note, her voice broke and she finished the tune in her clear sweet whistle. Josie kept as far from her as possible, hoping that people would not remember that they were of the same party.

They received their presents with less gratitude than she had expected. She was a little subdued as she followed Josie to the cabin they shared.

Josie was washing her face and hands when Diego threw open the door. His expression was tragic.

"They 're a pretty lot on this boat," he said. "Someone has been in my cabin and swiped a suitcase and a lot of clothes."

Fay was sitting on the side of her bed smoking a cigarette. She blinked at him through the smoke, feeling, for the first time in her life, afraid of him.

Josie lifted her wet face and glowered at him. "Jimmy, you make me sick! Why did n't you see that your cabin was locked?"

"It was locked! It was locked when I came back. It was someone on this rotten boat!"

Fay rose and took him by the arm. "Let us go together and investigate," she said soothingly.

When they were in his cabin she smiled at him in an appealing way that she could, in spite of the dominating cast of her features. She said: —

"You're my darling sweetheart little son, aren't you?"

Diego returned her look sullenly.

"This is no time for baby talk," he said.

She put her long arms around his neck. "Oh, my precious little baby boy!" she insisted.

Diego drooped against her warmly for a moment, then he said, disengaging himself: —

"That's all right, Mum, but it won't bring back my things. I'm going to make a fuss, I can tell you!"

"Sh," she said. "Don't raise your voice like that! Listen, Diego! I gave your things away. To a poor Sicilian count who had lost his own clothes."

He stared at her stupidly. "I want them back," he said.

"But you can't have them back! He's got them on."

"How do you know?"

"I saw him in them. Your gray suit with the blue and white shirt and the blue knitted tie."

"Well, he hasn't got my suitcase on. I want it back anyway!"

Again she took him in her arms, attempting to suffocate his natural resentment with love. This infuriated him.

He jerked himself away and bawled, "Where is he? Just let me at him! I'll have my clothes back or know the reason why!"

Josie put her head in at the door.

"I can hear you right across in my cabin," she said. "Do you want to disgrace us all, Jimmy?"

"Come in here and shut that door," he ordered.

"Whatever is the matter?" she asked, closing the door behind her.

"Fay's been and given away a lot of my best clothes, and a suitcase, to some Italian count! By hell — if I can once lay my hands — "

"Stop it this minute!" commanded his mother. "I bought the things, and if I want to give them away, I will!"

"Once before," said Diego, "you drove me to desperation, and you'll do it again." He made for the door, but they both caught him and held him.

"Leave me alone with him, Josie," said Fay. "He'll be perfectly reasonable once he understands the situation."

But Josie clung to his arm for a moment longer, looking in his face, fascinated by its expression, that always seemed to mean more than it did.

When he and Fay were alone she held up the new pyjamas before him.

"Are n't they sweet?" she asked.

But he turned his face away. "I want my gray suit and my shirt and my tie," he reiterated.

She laughed gayly. "You shall have them back and new, better ones as well. Just wait till you meet this count, darling! I have only lent him your things. You see, he was in a shipwreck and that was how he lost his. He will be delighted to repay you twice over when we get to Sicilia."

"Sicilia," repeated Diego, stupidly. "Is that in France?"

"No, little angel-face, that's just a different way of pronouncing Sicily. It's an island lying to the south of Italy. Italy is shaped like a boot and Sicily is a football right at the toe of the boot." She spoke in a kind, explanatory tone, but her eyes, fixed on his, sought to subdue him.

"I 've heard all that before," he said, "and I want to go to France."

"But you can't. I arranged this afternoon for us to go to Sicily."

"By God, I 'll see Purley about this! We 'll see if we 're going to be led around by the nose like two dumb-bells!"

"We 'll go and find Purley," she said, taking his hand, "and tell him about it together. He 'll understand. There 's far more to interest a scientist in Sicily than in France."

Diego made a gesture as if trying to free himself from a feather pillow that was smothering him.

"Druggist," he growled. "Drugs — patent medicine — ice-cream soda — Gosh, I wish I had one!"

"You shall! I 'll order one to be made for you to-night. . . . Now let us find Purley and tell him all about it."

They found Bond on deck. A small crowd was

collected watching a youth dive for coins. The boat
from which he dived was rowed by a young full-
blooded Negro, black as jet. The youth, beautifully
built, had Spanish features. He crouched, hugging
himself, for it had turned very cold, grinning up at
the passengers, calling to them in Spanish to throw
him a coin.

A silver quarter sped through the air and had
scarcely touched the water when he was after it, his
dripping body flashing like a leaping fish.

He rose, struck out toward the boat, clambered
into it, throwing the coin on the bottom, and again
grinning expectantly up at the crowd.

Another coin fell and could be seen settling in the
green depths before he espied it. He was after it,
kicking like a frog down below. He was scarcely at
the surface when another flash of silver touched the
water at some distance.

He had them both. He climbed into his boat and
spat them out on the bottom, tossed back his wet
streaming hair, and again raised his face, grinning but
with chattering teeth, toward the deck.

It was superb, Fay thought. Every time his body
described a graceful arc, she saw hers flashing alongside; flashing, diving, securing the coin, climbing into
the boat, her long wet hair to her knees, like a mer-
maid's. . . . She pressed to the front and threw him
a quarter. Back in his boat he smiled at her and
waved his hand. She threw another, aiming so that
it fell at his feet and need not be dived for. This
time he kissed his hand to her.

She saw Montleone standing on the edge of the crowd watching her every movement. . . . She would show him that money was nothing to her — or something to be tossed away. Then he would feel no embarrassment at accepting help from her.

Coin followed coin from her outstretched arm. The diver crouched, laughing up at her. The other passengers had ceased to throw him anything, leaving the way free to her.

Bond stood watching her, a smile half tender, half sardonic, on his face. With every quarter thrown he saw a dozen doughnuts, two dozen cookies, or a couple of loaves of bread hit the water. How poor Palmas had sweated in that bakeshop!

Diego came scowling to his side.

"Fay's gone crazy," he said. "First she gave most of my clothes to a naked Italian. Now she's throwing our money to a naked Spaniard. Can't you stop her?"

"The ship's getting ready to sail," said Bond. "That will put a stop to it."

A hoarse whistle sounded deafeningly. A shudder ran through the ship.

Josie joined them. "Did you see how Fay was showing off?" she demanded. "I could have screamed."

"You might scream," said Diego, "if she'd given your clothes away."

"I don't understand," said Bond. "Whose clothes to who?"

"Mine," answered Diego, "to that guy over there.

I spotted him right away in my gray suit and blue shirt and knitted tie. They're two sizes too large for him. He's got my brogues on too, and a pair of my best socks."

Montleone saw them looking at him and a dark flush overspread his face.

A moment more and Fay brought him up to them and introduced him. "Conte Gian Montleone — Mr. Bond — Miss Froward — my son, Diego Palmas."

The four bowed gravely to each other. The quartette was now a quintette.

CHAPTER V

FAY PALMAS was at once conscious of a new power and a new weakness in herself, with the coming of Montleone. She felt power to change the circumstances that surrounded her, to create a new life — after all those years of being hedged in, helpless to free herself from the forces that had trapped her. With his coming came this new sense of power. She had forced Diego and Bond and Josie to give way, to accept him into their circle. She had changed their destination from France to Sicily. She felt her spirit expanding in the companionship of a man so different from any she had ever known. Yet there was also this weakness — the feeling that what he gave with his lips he took away with his eyes. His lips paid her homage, but his eyes, from which looked out the secret of an old civilization, made her feel weak as a flower under the Mediterranean sun.

Montleone at once became a noticeable figure on board, in spite of the ill-fitting suit. And he did not wear that for long. In Algiers he went to a fine French shop and bought well-cut English clothes. None of the others guessed that they had been bought with Fay's money. He returned Diego's things to him and intimated that he had been able to communicate with his own bankers.

He was a delightful companion. In spite of his youth he seemed to have been everywhere, to speak every language. He took them into strange wine shops in Casablanca. He took them to the native quarter in Algiers — through the narrow seething strangeness of the Rue du Chameau, the Rue des Janissairis, the Rue Ben–Ali. He bribed the guide to allow the women to go into a Mosque which smelled as though fresh air had not entered it for a thousand years. Fay stood transfixed, seeing herself laving her hands and feet among the other worshipers, prostrating herself, raising her arms to the domed roof. Diego saw only the moving richness of the colors. Josie, breathing quickly, lost all consciousness of self. Bond held his breath and thought of the disinfectants in his drug store.

Veiled figures, hooded figures, wild-looking young men from the desert, carrying staffs, jostled them in the streets. They were surrounded by little girls with great eyes, filthy rags, and dirty hair, who pawed them imploringly. Montleone stood laughing among them, not seeming to mind their dirt, putting sweets and copper coins into their shapely little paws.

They drank strong sweet coffee in a native restaurant. They had lunch in an English hotel in a garden overlooking the town. It was better than any number of travel books, yet Bond felt strangely out of it, flat and disappointed. He had pictured these excursions with himself as leader, always at Fay's side, listening to her excited laughter, her naïve comments on it all. He had thought they would be drawn closer in these foreign lands, but they were farther apart. He was the fifth, the odd one, the outsider.

It was the same at every place the ship stopped. Montleone took the party in hand, did with it what he willed. And Fay seemed to delight in submitting to him. That was the hardest to bear. And yet Bond liked him. When they were alone together he liked him very much.

The impression of one foreign place after another was laid on Bond's mind, not with the clear-cut freshness of new experiences, but all blurred by this sense of disappointment. Yet he did not regret what he had done in selling out his business and coming with Fay. Perhaps something would happen when they left the ship to bring him near to her again. He hated the ship.

They were to spend two days in Naples before going on to Messina. Bond decided that he would stay in a hotel. He would see more of Naples and less of Montleone. At the last moment Diego declared his intention of joining him. He too was sick of the ship.

"And I'm sick of that Italian," he said, throwing open the French window of their room and stepping on to the balcony. "He's always on the spot. He always knows just what to say about everything. I think we were better off when we were by ourselves, don't you, Purley?"

Bond stepped out on the balcony beside him. "Well, I must say that I've felt out of sorts these days," he answered. He had not wanted Diego with him, but, now that he was there, he found his presence rather soothing.   Diego was so natural, so altogether himself wherever he went.

"He's so finished, so hard.   He's like an alabaster statue," went on Diego.   "He makes me feel like a charcoal drawing.   What's he make you feel like, Purley?"

"A murderer," answered Bond, curtly.

"But I can't help sort of liking him."

"Neither can I."

They stood on the balcony together looking down on the bay that stretched in changeful blueness to the gold-misted horizon.   Capri raised a golden shoulder from its depths.   A dozen small white sails moved like blown flower petals across its surface.   Vesuvius, clothed by the sunset in a jeweled robe, reared her proud plume and forgot her rages.   From the shadow of the Castel dell' Ovo three racing shells, manned by young Neapolitans, shot into the open.   Their cox-swains shouted to them in musical tones; athletic bodies shone like bronze.   Two soldiers in long capes and plumed hats stopped by the balustrade to watch them.   A friar passed by, his bare red heels showing at each step beneath his dark robe.   A little boy selling chestnuts cried his wares in a sweet melting treble. Horse cabs clattered by.   Hysterical motor horns sounded gaspingly.   Diego leaned far across the bal-cony and had a glimpse of the funnel of the ship.

"There they are," he said, in a tone of satisfaction, "and here we are.   I'm mighty glad you thought of doing this, Purley. I think it's great. I'd like to stay here for a while and paint."

Bond did not answer. He sat perched on the railing of the balcony, pipe in mouth, absorbed in the scene below. He had known it would be different from Massachusetts, but he had not imagined how different. He too saw the ship's funnels and was glad to be separated from Fay Palmas for a space. Perhaps at this distance he would be able to clarify his vision of her, see her as she was. This was what he never had been able to do.

But her face was clear enough. Everywhere he looked he saw it — burning bright in the sunset; dark and tragical against the blue sky; laughing in the water; looking slantwise over the shoulder of Capri.

Diego was saying, "This place suits me. I could live here forever. I don't care if we never go back to Saltport."

"You must do a lot of painting while you are over here."

"Montleone says the scenery around his place is wonderful."

"Hmph . . ."

"I wish I knew what that little beggar with a basket on his head is chanting."

"Roast chestnuts."

"And what that fat old friar is thinking about."

"About God."

"And the fellows in the capes."

"Mussolini."

"And the boys rowing."

"Aphrodite."

Diego stared at him contemplatively.   "And you, Purley."

"Oh, I think about my drug store."

"Gosh, you 're a practical fellow!"

They became silent again, absorbing the sights and sounds below.   Diego heard a slight sharp sound near him and turned his head.   He was surprised to see that the balcony of the room adjoining was occupied. The girl sitting there had dropped her scissors.   She bent, picked them up, and began carefully cutting her nails.

Diego looked quickly at Bond, who obviously did not see her.   He looked back at the girl, full of curiosity.   She was so unusual, so absorbed in what she was doing.   In her bright-colored negligee, perched on her balcony, she was like a gay-plumed bird in its cage, hung there on the sunny wall.

He could see the side of her face, its healthy pallor, its shortness, its high cheek bones.   He could see the bare, exquisitely rounded arm, the hand with spread fingers and red-tinted nails.   He could see the small sharp scissors snipping.   Her hair was cut short, of a pale bronze, and so curly that no hairdresser could set it in waves.

She sat slumped in her chair in an attitude of the most complete abandon to herself.   She looked as comfortable as a snake or a toad or a low-growing bushy plant.   She snipped at her reddened nails with the concentration of a cat washing its paws.   Diego

felt in her something akin to himself. He leaned
against the railing of the balcony possessing himself of
every detail of her presence. He even strained his
ears to hear the snip of the scissors.

A regiment of *bersaglieri* passed below, headed by a
band. The shrill music subdued all other sounds except the tramp of feet. They wheeled, crossed the
bridge to the Castel dell' Ovo, and disappeared into
the barracks. Once more the shouts of the coxswain,
the cry of the chestnut vendor, and the gasp of the
motor horns were heard. She had put her chin on
the iron railing and was looking over it into the street.

Bond had gone back into the bedroom without
having noticed her. He said from there: —

"What about going for a walk? I'd like to see
something of the back streets before dinner."

Diego looked at him stupidly from the balcony.

"I'm tired," he said. "I think I'll stay here."

He saw that, at the sound of his voice, she had
turned her head and glanced at him.

"Tired!" echoed Bond, irritably. "What have you
done to make you tired?"

Diego did not answer. He just sat looking
through the doorway with the still expression that so
maddened Josie.

"Well," said Bond, more relieved than disappointed, "I'll go off by myself then." He got his
hat, and in a moment Diego heard the door shut behind him.

He turned with a pleased look toward the other
balcony. The girl was now polishing her nails with

a pink buffer.   She had turned in her chair so that
she faced him.   Her lips were parted, showing an even
rim of white teeth, but she did not raise her eyes.

Diego took out a cigarette and lighted it.   The
breeze wafted the first puff of smoke across to her
like a message.   It disappeared against her body as
though absorbed by it.   Should he speak?   Or just
force her to look up, draw her eyes by the magnetism
of his?

A door in the room behind her slammed.   Steps
sounded and a man spoke from the threshold of the
balcony.   She raised her face with what seemed to
Diego a bored expression and, without answering,
went into the room.

He sat there, sulky, disappointed.   Late afternoon
had turned suddenly to evening.   The water of the
bay was shadowed by a cloud.   The little boats had
lowered their sails, cast anchor.   The youths had
drawn their dripping skiffs on to the platform of the
clubhouse and stood in groups talking together.   The
lights of evening were coming out.   The smoke from
Vesuvius drooped dark as a funeral plume.   Why
had he not gone with Bond?   What was there for
him to do here?   Why had she not given him one
look?   How was he to find out who she was?

He went into the bedroom and switched on the
light.   He thought it was a very luxurious room.
Besides the central light there was a silk-shaded lamp
on the commode between the beds.   There were easy-
chairs, a writing table, and another French window
giving on to a balcony above a side street.   There was

a marble basin with "Caldo" and "Freddo" on the taps. There was the foot bath with more taps. There was a large screen and behind it long velours curtains leading — he wondered where.

He drew one aside and found himself facing double doors. He was going to try one when he heard voices raised on the other side.

A man's voice, cultivated, slightly pompous, said: —

"You have seemed to approve all along of going to Egypt. We have studied all these folders together. What has changed you?"

A woman's voice, musical, vibrant, answered in the precise accent of the foreigner: —

"I am bored."

"But why? Everything is the same as it has been all along."

"That is why I am bored."

"But Varvara," the man's voice broke, angrily, complainingly. "You have no right to be bored. I am always doing things for you. I am always the same."

"That is why you bore me."

"Do you mean to say that I bore you?"

"Yes, I do. You bore me to death."

His voice became fierce. "The trouble with you is that I have spoiled you. You are the kind of woman who would like to be beaten."

"Perhaps — by the right man!"

"Strange that you only discover now that I am not the right man. After three months together."

"Oh, it is not just now! You always have bored me."

"Then — " his voice vibrated — "you have deceived me! You lived with me only for what you could get out of me!"

She did not answer. Diego heard her moving about the room. Heard the opening and shutting of drawers.

"Yes, you are a deceiver! A false, deceiving woman."

She broke into a short, wild burst of song in a foreign language.

"Stop that singing and answer me!"

"I have answered you."

"You will not come to Egypt?"

"No."

"You have deceived me?"

"If you say it."

"You need not think that you have hurt me." His voice broke. "I am as glad to separate as you are. I will pay the bill here and we shall each go our own way."

The voices became blurred then. The pair were moving about the room. One of them went into the bathroom. Diego heard water running. Then, for a space, silence. He was deeply thrilled. He had never heard anything like this before. And that girl! That strangely lovely girl! She was here with that man — English, by his accent — in those relations. And tired of him. Going to break away from him. What would Josie think of a situation like this?

He stood there inside the curtains, unashamed, eavesdropping to this intimate scene.

He could not, at first, make out what the next sound was. It was a shuffling, tapping sound, just on the other side of the door. Then came the voice of the girl, on a sneering note.

"Yes. Play your old patience! You make me sick — always playing patience. You would sit there playing patience if Vesuvius erupted. Bah!"

The man talked to himself, in a cool tantalizing tone. "The black queen . . . Yes, there on the red king . . . Now the knave of hearts. . . . Good . . . He goes on her. . . ."

She crossed the room rapidly and Diego heard a prolonged trill of the bell. She rang three times before there was an answer. Then she flung open the door and poured a flood of Italian on the porter who stood there. Silence again. Diego came from behind the curtain and walked up and down the room, wary to every sound.

The porter returned and the chink of glasses sounded on a tray. The door of the bedroom was opened and he went in. Diego opened his own door and walked down the passage, hoping to have a glimpse of her, but he only saw the waiter come out. He returned to his balcony and sat there in the hope that she might come out on hers. He sat there till Bond's return. He said nothing to him of what he had heard.

The dining room was almost full when they went down. It was a mixed company, a few English,

Germans, and Americans, but the greater part Italians. Diego's eyes searched the room for a sight of the girl, but could not discover her. Bond was interested in those about. He drew Diego's attention to the occupants of the near-by tables and thought the boy was in one of his stupid moods. He barely grunted, scarcely looked at the people pointed out. Two tables distant were a fair, good-looking German, in English clothes, and his pale young wife in a rather clumsy evening gown. He talked incessantly, his face alive, full of humor. She seemed to hang adoringly on his words. At the next table sat an English couple. The man red-faced, blue-eyed, with the stamp of the army. The woman stout, fair-haired, black-gowned, with snowy shoulders. They talked both at once, appeared to be chaffing each other. Just across from them sat four Italian business men, choosing their food with exuberant pleasure, drinking a good deal of wine, and illustrating their remarks by quick gestures and shrugs of their rounded shoulders.

Diego scarcely noticed what he ate. Up and down the rows of tables his eyes moved searchingly for the girl. Then, when he had made up his mind that she was not in the dining room, he saw her and her companion enter and go to a table almost at the other end of the room. But as they moved slowly past the other tables he saw them clearly and drew Bond's attention to them.

"Look, Purley, that girl in white with the little red

bolero is in the room next ours. I saw her on the balcony."

Bond looked at the pair judicially.

"Pretty girl," he observed, "but bold-looking. I
like the looks of the man better. He does n't seem
to suit her at all."

Diego groaned inwardly. Pretty! To express
such loveliness by such a word! And to like the
looks of the man better! That tall, lean, melancholy-
looking dud with a chin that needed shaving. He
did not trouble himself to speak to Bond during the
rest of the meal. He noticed how the waiter hung
above her, seemed eager to please her. Varvara was
her name. He remembered that suddenly and said it
over to himself. How it suited her! How different
from an idiotic little name like Josie.

After dinner they sat in the little glass-ceilinged
lounge, drinking the coffee that seemed so bad to
them, and smoking Lucky Strikes. Diego kept his
eyes on the door of the dining room, watching. At
last she came, followed close by the man. They chose
a settee almost opposite, half hidden by a palm.

"There 's your couple," said Bond, in an undertone.
"They 're rather interesting. Did you hear them
speak? They don't look like Americans."

"They 're not. He spoke like an Englishman.
And I sort of think she 's a Russian."

"She has the loveliest arms I 've ever seen."

"Her eyes seem to be the color of her hair. Would
you call it bronze?"

"I don't see how you can make out the color of her eyes from here. Bronze-colored eyes certainly would be queer. I don't care about the way she sits. It is n't — well, I suppose I 'm old-fashioned — but just notice the way she slumps. As though she 'd no backbone. . . . Here comes Britannia and her husband. Now I like the way she carries herself." He looked admiringly at the English couple, who made for two chairs in the remotest corner and sat there, with her snowy chest and his snowy shirt front turned defensively toward the room.

"They don't appear to notice anyone," went on Bond, "but they saw that girl. They gave her one swift look as they passed. She 's very remarkable even in a crowd like this."

A tall American bishop, wearing a gold cross on his waistcoat, passed with his two daughters, frank-faced girls almost as tall as he. They took seats in the middle of the room and, seeing the Russian girl, gave her a stare of good-humored curiosity, then began examining the snapshots they had had printed that day.

The Russian, sitting elbows on knees, gazed moodily at her clasped hands, her companion seeming at once angered by and proud of the attention she attracted.

The four Italians had come in and were sipping their liqueurs with sidelong glances in her direction. Diego tried to make her look at him, but she seemed unconscious of his presence until she and her companion shortly rose and left the lounge. Then, as she passed, she gave him a slight smile, a pouting, perverse smile, as though she wanted him to know that the man she was with meant nothing to her.

After a little he said to Bond, "I 'm tired. I think I 'll go up. You need n't come."

Bond acquiesced, interested in all about him. He was used to being by himself and this opportunity for being alone pleased him.

He sipped a liqueur and thought how different all this was from Saltport. At thirty-six he was really beginning to see life. He wondered if his pleasure would be increased or lessened if Fay had been at his side. What was she doing now? Pouring out her thoughts, he dared say, to that Sicilian fellow.

It was some time before he went up. He tried to talk to the diminutive lift boy, but their conversation only reached the point of Bond's giving him five lire. Outside the door of the room next his own two pairs of shoes were standing, one square-toed, solemn, and black, the other high-heeled, pointed, of patent leather. Queer people, traveling together in these foreign places. It would give you something to think about if you knew their pasts. He guessed that they would think his pretty tame. . . . His solitary white house behind the hedge, his drug store. Well, his thoughts had not been tied down, tamed. They had been so adventurous that sometimes they had made him almost ashamed.

He opened the door softly and went in. The room was in darkness except for the glimmering light from a half-moon. Was Diego in bed? He could make out that the nearest bed was empty. He went around it to the other one and ran his hand gently across it. No one in that, either. He went to the balcony and found it empty. He looked out at the starry night, the glimmering bay, the black shape of Castel dell' Ovo. The hoarse whistle of a steamship told of a new arrival in port. He felt a little uneasy. It was strange that the boy should go off like that, pretending he was coming up to bed. He came back into the room and heard the sound of voices and laughter from the one adjoining. He switched on the light.

The first thing he saw was Diego's hat on the table. He had gone out bareheaded, then. He 'd better go downstairs and wait for him there. Well, that queer pair were certainly making up for their glumness now! He hated such carrying-on in a hotel bed-room. He would cough loudly, let them know he was on the other side of the door.

He went close to the velours curtain, coughing. His elbow touched something firm, yet soft, unmis-takably a human body. Startled, almost frightened, he jerked back the curtain. Diego stood disclosed, scowling and sheepish.

"Well, I 'll be damned!" said Bond. He spoke forcefully.

Diego glided out into the room.

"That fellow," he said in a low vicious tone, "makes me sick! He 's determined to keep that girl with him and she 's told him that he bores her to death."

"And you make me sick," said Bond sternly. "Listening outside other folks' bedrooms!"

" 'Pon my word I thought there was going to be a murder in there when I first came up."

"Well, they seem to be killing each other with kindness now."

"She's just pretending. I think she's just keeping him in a good humor till she can get away from him."

"You seem to know all about them," said Bond, sarcastically.

The man's voice came from the other room, cultivated and precise. "And now, Varvara, since everything is all right again, I shall get out the folders and we'll arrange our Egyptian tour."

"Yes, yes, do get out the folders!"

"You look so lovely, Varvara, in that pretty pink thing, that I — "

Bond went to the curtains and coughed. There was sudden silence on the other side of the door. Diego began to undress.

He could not sleep. Pictures floated before his eyes. Pictures erotic, willful, indescribable, culminating in voluptuous imaginings of himself and Varvara (for so he now named her in his thoughts) floating, unhampered by earthly limitations, in some divinely new dimension of existence. He had the rare gift of contemplation, of enjoying his own sensations to the utmost. And whatever form his thoughts took they seemed good and pure to him. He did not know what it was to feel embarrassed or ashamed of himself. He had received so many new impressions during the last fifteen days — they had been laid, layer upon layer, on the freshness of his young sensibility — that it seemed in no way remarkable to him that he should be lying in this foreign bed, with a fabulous volcano sleeping only a few miles away, and he feeling a magnetic relation with a Russian girl, with whom he had never exchanged a word, in the next room.

Bond slept — a deep sleep colored by extravagant dreams. He was always pursuing Montleone. He pursued him in ships, in aeroplanes, in submarines. He ran barefoot after him up and down the sides of mountains, in and out of the rooms of Montleone's villa, and at last caught him in the glassed-in corner of his own drug store. And when he caught him, they embraced and kissed.

He woke, grinning at himself.

"This is the day," said Diego, "that we go to Pompeii. I believe I'll just hang around the hotel. I don't feel up to an excursion."

"You'll spoil the day for your mother."

"Fay will be happy if the Count's there." There was malice in his lazy smile.

But Bond was imperturbable. He said good-humoredly: —

"I know why you want to hang around the hotel. And you know that I know. Now let me tell you something. I heard the gentleman on the other side of the door speak of going to Pompeii, just before you woke."

Diego was unabashed. "Did he? What did he say?"

Bond attempted to imitate the tones he had overheard. "He said, 'My love, what a perfect morning
for Pompeii!'"

Diego, in one supple movement, turned out of bed
and on to his feet.

They had engaged a car to take them. Fay, Josie,
and Montleone called for the other two. Fay's face
was darkly bright beneath the brim of a white hat.
Montleone sat beside her, his straight features and
delicately moulded lips wearing an expression both
remote and gracious. Josie sat by herself, her hands,
which had become brown during the voyage, clasped
in her lap. She gave Diego a look of invitation, but
he, after a squeeze of his mother's hand, took the seat
beside the driver. Josie fancied that he hated her,
would not sit beside her. She gave a grudging smile
to Bond as he dropped into the place next her.

"Why, Purley," said Fay, "how natural you look
after all your adventures! What have you two been
up to since you left us?"

"Trying to become cosmopolitan," answered Bond,
stiffly, aware of Montleone's questioning gaze on him.

"Do tell us about the hotel! Were there many
Americans there?"

"There were enough. And some Germans, British,
Italians, and — a Russian. Ask Diego."

Fay poked her son in the back. "What did you do
last night, Diego?"

"Nothing," he mumbled, without looking round.

Montleone's teeth gleamed. "To do nothing is so
pleasant in Napoli," he said.

"Jimmy's doing nothing is generally mischief," said Josie.

Diego put his hand behind him and felt for her. His fingers touched the nape of her neck and gave it a quick pinch. She colored angrily, yet the small pain was magnified in her mind into a fascinating torture. She desired to be hurt by him and to hate him for it.

Bond gave her a sidelong glance. He had seen the act and was annoyed at her for coloring. She was supersensitive, even morbid. And he felt irritated by the bond between them. They were in the same boat, — both loving someone who scarcely valued their love, — though he did not for a moment compare Josie's perverse feeling for Diego with his own passion for Fay.

Pompeii was not like a dead city that day, neither did it lie scorching in the sun, overflowing with tourists. The breeze was alive, running through the narrow streets full of memories of two thousand years ago. Fay walked boldly over the uneven stones, her head thrown back, feeling like a charioteer, feeling like a flower-crowned beauty of Pompeii followed by her train. When she was a girl she had read Bulwer Lytton's tale of tragic love within those walls and had not forgotten it. She knew just how she ought to feel. She was Ione. Montleone was Glaucus. Josie the blind girl, Nydia — though nothing escaped Josie's eyes. Diego the noble young gladiator, and Purley Bond nothing less terrible than the cruel Egyptian wizard. In this way the prescriptions of Saltport were connected with the alchemy of Pompeii.

Her companions, believing themselves to be themselves, followed her from house to house. At last they sat down in the garden of the house of Loreius Tiburtius to eat the lunch they had brought with them. The tinkling of fountains sounded in their ears. Diego went off to look at the paintings. Josie slipped after him. She saw him standing before "The Rape of Europa." Two other people had just come up. She saw a tall man with a bluish chin and a rather short, odd-looking girl. Josie stood tense, watching them. She knew that all three were unaware of her presence. She saw the girl looking only at the picture, the two men looking only at the girl. In the bright sunlight the colors of the picture were heightened — the blueness of the tall man's chin, the brownness of Diego's throat, the bronze of the girl's hair. There was silence except for the bubbling of water from a jet. The four people stood as though risen from the ruin of Pompeii.

Then Diego saw Josie. He gave her his lazy smile, then came to her and said, in an undertone: —

"Speak to the girl."

She stiffened. "But why?"

"Because I want to get talking with them."

"Talk to them then — and be damned!"

"I want you to start it."

"Jimmy — you can't see a pretty girl without — "

"Ask her how she likes the picture."

"No — not that picture." She was weakening and hating herself for it.

"The garden then. The whole place. Anything!"

The other two moved away.

Diego felt annoyed. But his face expressed despair. "Quick," he said, and pushed her.

"Oh, I can't — I can't — they 're strangers!" Suddenly she was in an agony of shyness.

The girl turned her head, looked earnestly at her, then smiled. Diego pushed Josie, as though she were a shy child. She said, in a gasping voice: —

"Oh, is n't it all wonderful?"

The girl answered, with a shrug: "Yes, but the Temple at Pæstum is better."

Diego said, looking at the man: "What I am interested in is how the color in these pictures has been preserved."

It was as though he had pressed an electric button loosing a concentration of energy. The man came straight to his side and began to talk learnedly, with the explicit information of the archæologist. He led Diego from place to place expounding his opinions. With one part of his brain Diego absorbed every word. With another part he was thinking: "And this is the man who was quarreling on the other side of the door . . . the one who was saying later, 'You look so lovely, Varvara, in that pretty pink thing. . . .'"

The girls sauntered on by themselves, talking.

After a little Josie glanced back and Diego threw

her an imploring look.   A moment later she turned
to the Englishman and asked: —

"Would you mind telling me about the things in
the glass case?"   Her face quivered with the effort
it cost her.

"Which?   Oh, yes!   Now those are tremendously
interesting."

Diego and Varvara were left together.   He looked
into her eyes, saw their bronze depths slanting above
the broad cheek bones.   He said: —

"I 'll never see you again, after to-day."

"Why not?"

"Because we 're going to Sicily to-night."

"To Sicily."   She smiled as she said the word.
"Yes . . . Sicily will suit you."

"No place will suit me — when you 're not there.
Say, is there any likelihood that you 'll come?"

"I have friends there."

"Then you 'll come?"

"I may."

"We 're going to Tramontana."

"I have a friend there."

"You 're Russian, are n't you?"

"Yes.   And you are American?"

"Yes.   My name is Diego Palmas.   Do say you 'll
come to Tramontana!"

"I 'll try."   Her eyes moved toward the tall figure
bending beside Josie over the glass case.

Diego put out a feeler.   "He knows a lot, does n't
he?"

"Too much.   He is a professor of archæology."

"On a holiday!"

She drew up one rounded shoulder.   "He is a child.
He knows less than you."

Diego did not know whether to be pleased or hurt.
"Perhaps I know more than you think."   A scowl
darkened his forehead.

"I think — a little later — you will be — oh, quite
wonderful. . . ."

The professor of archæology was coming toward
them.   "I think, my dear, we must be getting on."
He cast an uneasy look at Diego.

Diego whispered, "For God's sake — Varvara — "

She answered, in a low unhurried tone: "I am sure
I shall be in Tramontana."

"If you don't — " he gave her a threatening look —
"If you don't — "

He found himself alone with Josie.   He stared at
her dazed, scarcely seeing her.

"The things you make me do!" she exclaimed, bit-
ingly.   "The beastly deceit!"

"Is n't she marvelous, Josie?"

"Is that man her husband?"

"How should I know?"

"Now I do admire him!"

"You would!   But I can't understand what she
ever saw in him."

"I can't imagine what you see in her."

"Yes, you can."

"Well, then, you like her because she 's thoroughly
bad."

"And you hate her because you envy her."

"Just one thing I envy her. Her self-possession."

"Not my admiration?" He gave her a sly, side-long glance.

"I know how little it 's worth!"

"How can you? You 've never had it."

Her cheeks blazed. She remembered the day in the studio when he had held her in his arms, kissed her. What had she seen in his half-closed eyes then? Well, perhaps not admiration, but something that had made him want to stroke her arm, hold her. She gazed at him now, scarcely seeing him, thinking of that day when he had seemed so near to her.

Diego thought only of Varvara.

When he returned to the hotel that evening to collect his things he hesitated by the double door between the two bedrooms. He heard her soft contemptuous voice.

"Yes. . . . Lie down and rest yourself. . . . Sleep, and wake up a new man . . . one not so boring. . . . As for me, I go to-night to my friends in Sicily."

There came the decisive snap of a suitcase.

"I hope — " his voice sounded muffled in the pillows — "that I shall never see your deceitful face again."

"And I hope that I shall never see your boring face. . . ."

Diego smiled happily at Bond, just entering the room.

CHAPTER VI

FAY PALMAS and Josie Froward, their fingers inter-
laced, stood together looking through the open French
window of their bedroom in a hotel in Tramontana.
After the driving rain, the thunder and hail of their
arrival at Messina, their hours of shivering in an icy
station while their three escorts searched the pier for
lost luggage, the tiring train journey, this high-
ceilinged white room with its windows that opened
above an evening scene of trancelike beauty took away
all their words, left them, for once, speechless in each
other's company.

From the garden a mimosa tree, leaning above a
stone-edged pool, sent up its fragrance. Beyond the
garden wall the steep road wound its way in countless
ledges down, and ever down, till it reached the sea.
Up it an old woman was riding a donkey, almost hidden under a great mound of faggots. In front of
her she drove her goat, leaning forward now and then
to prod it with a long stick. The sea stretched still
and blue far below, binding the shore in a white brace-
let of foam.

A village lay below, its lights twinkling beside the
foam. And another village, perched on a mountain
top, twinkled through a pale cloud that hung there.

Between the village far below and the village far above little farms were scattered, half hidden among olive and almond groves.

The scene, in its compressed, extravagant beauty, affected them in accordance with their very different natures. To Josie it seemed unreal, a painted picture come to life. She herself seemed unreal — a figure from a dream, floating into this fabulous picture. Would she ever be able to paint such scenery? The very air, the shadows, were of a quality new to her. She was conscious of the classic past, terrible and beautiful, clothing the mountain peaks, sleeping on the sea.

As for Fay, she saw it all as a background for herself. It was what she had always lacked — a dramatic and suitable background. She had always felt herself an alien in Saltport, had always known that people were staring at her, talking about her. She had liked that. But such people! They were not worth the astonishment of her presence. At this moment she shook off Saltport and its inhabitants as a strong swimmer might shake off seaweed or a snake slough its old skin.

She almost wished that Josie and Bond were not with her. They were a reminder of Saltport. They could not throw it aside as she and Diego could. To Diego and to her nothing was impossible. Their strange mixed blood produced in them an inner fire that consumed what stood in their way. She saw herself married to Montleone, a Contessa, living in the ancestral home. For the present she scarcely gave a thought to how this might be accomplished. She was intoxicated by the brilliant possibilities that crowded in upon her.

In spite of her fatigue she moved lightly about the room, hanging her clothes in the cupboard, laying out fresh things for dinner.   Josie was still at the window. Fay thought she would take a hot bath and, wrapped in a flowered dressing gown, crossed a little passage to the bathroom.   She broke loudly into one of the Negro songs she loved, as the water gushed noisily into the porcelain bath, filling the air with steam.   She sang "Swing low, sweet chariot," without her voice once breaking.   But Josie began to rap on the wall that separated them and she ceased to sing.   Bother Josie!   She was always considering what people would think.

She sang under her breath as she splashed.   She stretched out in the tub, admiring the dark shimmer of her skin under the water.   She felt the hair at the back of her neck getting wet.   Then she got out and, throwing the bath towel about her shoulders, went to the window through which she could look unseen, shielded by tendrils of jasmine and wistaria that grew about it.

From this window the sea looked farther away and more blue.   Sudden hills and valleys shouldered and sank toward the shore.   To her right the main road wound upward to the town, and from it came the clatter of hoofs, the rattle of a wagon, and the sound of a motor horn.   Directly below her in the garden, a waiter, trim in his black tail coat, stood waiting for the dinner hour.   He bent, picked a small white flower, and held it to his nose. White stocks, cyclamen, in January. Fay laughed to herself with delight.

A red-tiled terrace, with a low stone balustrade, was on a level with the bathroom. The door of Bond's room opened on to the terrace. He came out on it now and strolled to the balustrade and leaned over, looking down into the garden. How strange to see him in such surroundings. How amusing to watch him, one's self unseen. He had an odd face, she thought, a good face, kind and a little sombre, in spite of the tow hair and blue eyes. . . . That other face came before her, the dark, subtle face of Montleone, the intense look that took the strength from her, made her feel faint and young and inexperienced.

She rubbed her shoulders with the towel as she stood looking out of the window. Her hair fell about her, far below her waist. A smell of burnt coffee came up to her, and a flood of Italian voices from a dark, cavelike room beneath the terrace. Fay had a glimpse of a brown old woman bent over a brazier. Shouts and the cracking of a whip came from the road above. The hiccuping, heart-rending bray of a donkey came from the road below. The waiter plucked another flower and held it to his nose. Bond passed his hand over his thick fair hair and straightened his tie. How could Fay keep from singing?

She tossed back the black mane from her shoulders, rubbed her sides with the towel, and began, in her sweetest tones: —

"I 've got a crown,
You 've got a crown,
All God's chillun got crowns — "

Josie rattled the handle of the door.

Fay opened a crack and peered through it defensively.

"You 've had a bath — " sang Josie, in a hoarse whisper — "I 'd like a bath.   All God's chillun want baths — "

Fay threw the door wide and embraced her.

"Josie, how funny you are!"

They laughed like excited children.   Then they exchanged places, Josie going into the bathroom and Fay to the bedroom.   She put on fresh silk underthings and combed her hair.   Seated in front of the mirror she began smoothing cream from a small jar over her face.   The jar was labeled "Bond's Cream."

What an excellent cream it was, she thought.   A pure, good, useful preparation — like Bond himself. It had stood by her all those years in Saltport, protected her from the rough winds of winter and the parching heat.   And she had recommended it to many of the summer visitors — done Purley a good turn when she could.   Some of the visitors had taken away a supply of it when they left Saltport.

Purley was a dear fellow, she thought, smoothing the cream between her finely marked brows.   A dear fellow, and yet she could never love him as he wanted her to, could never have married him — even if she had not met Montleone, who now possessed her mind.

Montleone had gone to stay with an old family servant who had a small farm on the mountain side. He
was to come in the morning and take her to see his
old home. They would walk together in the garden
he so often had described to her.

When she and Josie went into the lounge they found
Diego and Bond waiting for them. The two men
glanced swiftly at Fay's scarlet lips. She had never
used lipstick before. Diego was lazily pleased, but
Bond had a feeling of affront, as though she were still
further cutting herself off from him. Yet, in his
own drug store, he sold lipstick to the summer colony.

He marched beside her rather severely through the
lounge, down the wide stone steps to the dining room.
Its walls were washed white, its curtains white, its
rows of unshaded electric lights, hung from the white
ceiling, were white. There was silence among the
guests while the new arrivals were led to a table in
the middle of the room. The waiter whom Fay had
seen in the garden, and another, equally smooth-haired
and deft, glided about, gravely anxious to please. It
was delightful, Fay thought, conscious of being observed with interest. She leaned toward Bond, looking into his eyes with a flashing smile, but seeing him
not. The voices of other guests rose around her,
men talking about military stations in Malta, in
Gibraltar; women about London. The women's
voices were high-pitched, they talked in quick, throaty
gusts, slurring the words so that Fay could follow little
of what they said. But after her first glass of wine
she raised her voice and began talking that way too,

as well as she could. She looked at Diego compel-
lingly, talking at him, but he only smiled back stupidly. Bond spoke in a muttering undertone. It
was Josie who followed her lead, overtook her. She
began talking on a high note, talking Fay down, trying to make her ashamed of herself for imitating these
strangers. She succeeded in confusing her. Fay's
voice died away and she listened meekly to what Bond
was saying.

"That couple in the corner, the gray-haired people
who are not speaking, are New Yorkers," he said.
"I've been talking to the man. They're to be here
for some time. He's had a sort of nervous breakdown. Too much business strain, I gather. Lots of
money."

Fay looked enviously toward the couple. "How
lovely! If only I had!"

Josie asked teasingly, "What would you do?"

Fay looked at her, smiling across her wineglass.
"Stay in Tramontana forever."

"That man," continued Bond, "can't forget business even over here. Was talking about new invest-
ments he had in mind."

Fay's eyes lighted. "I wonder if we could interest
him in buying back Count Montleone's home for him.
You might interest him in that, Purley."

"He's not throwing money away," returned Bond.

"Oh, Montleone would pay him a large interest."

"Talk sense," put in Diego. "Where would Montleone get the interest?"

"I haven't thought that out yet."

The three others looked at her suspiciously. What had she in her mind? As a matter of fact she had nothing in her mind but seething desires, wistful longings, wild determinations which she had not the power to sort out or control. She said: —

"Well, it will do no harm to be nice to Mr. — what's his name?"

"Putnam."

"I mean to be exceptionally nice to him and I hope you'll all do the same." She tossed off another glass of wine.

Josie said sarcastically: "Fay, you drink your wine like lemonade."

But Fay was not to be offended. "Fill my glass again, Purley. I'll try to sip this one. But I do get so excited!" She passed her hand over her forehead, disarranging her hair.

The other three smiled at her with the half-irritated tolerance given to a too exuberant child.

In the lounge after dinner everyone was friendly. In this hotel the guests were like one big family. Bond and Josie marveled at the way Fay held her own as a woman of the world. But Diego marveled only at Varvara's remembered loveliness.

Fay was up early awaiting the arrival of Montleone. She moved restlessly about the terrace, flicking her cheek with a blossom from the mimosa tree. She gave him a hot, challenging look as he approached, with an aquiline fierceness in it. His face lit up with delight. He kissed her hand.

The *concierge* regarded them with beaming approval as they climbed the steep flight of stone steps to the street. He had known Montleone since he was a child. He hoped very much that Montleone would be able to marry the rich American lady and buy back his house and settle down in Tramontana where he belonged. There were so few of the nobles left in Sicily.

From the doorways of all the little shops where they sold embroideries dark faces looked out to see them pass. Significant smiles were exchanged. Il Conte was at last going to retrieve the family fortunes, and not before they needed it, for the Montleone family had been almost as poor as peasants, for generations, in spite of their big villa.

They passed the embroidery shops, the antique shops, the jewelry and tortoise-shell shops, the English tea shop and the Café Oreste, in front of which people were already seated about little tables in the sun. They passed under one of the ancient arched gateways of the town and Montleone led the way up a winding side street that mounted in irregular steps and was just wide enough for them to walk abreast. They were mounting upward, side by side, in a narrow way, as though together they entered a new life.

At the top they turned along an earth road from which they could look down on the tumbled roofs of the Corso, into gardens where oranges and lemons glowed among dark polished leaves. And, beyond the houses, the blue sea. A church bell began to clang, drowning all other sounds. A woman passed

them carrying a tall urn of water on her head. She
walked majestically, turning her sad eyes toward the
lovers. For they had become lovers. Standing there
in the glowing light, deafened by the church bell, they
passionately desired each other. Something new and
mysterious opened before them — she who had known
so little of love, he who had known so much; she to
whom the scene was so movingly new, he to whom it
was so movingly familiar.

They walked along the road, then turned again upward into a street so narrow that it was little more
than a lane, muddy, with fowls pecking in the mud.
He stopped in front of a door in a high wall and pulled
at a rusty iron bell.

Fay stood close beside him like an excited child.
He had come here, she thought, to get the key. She
stood smiling expectantly as the door opened and an
old woman, brown as a chestnut, showed herself strong
and stout in the opening.

"Benita!" exclaimed Montleone, and the old
woman caught his hand and covered it with kisses.
He and she exchanged a vehement fire of Italian and
she gave shrewd looks at the handsome lady in white.

Montleone led the way in. Fay found herself in
a garden with paved terraces rising one above the
other from stone steps. Neglected flower beds pressed
between and ran over in urgent foliage. Cyclamen
showed blue and violet and narcissus starry white.
Oranges and lemons glinted. Urns placed on the
walls overflowed in hanging flowers and tendrils.
From a gargoyle face, set in a stone niche, a jet of

water fell bubbling into a basin.   A flock of doves
that had been feeding on the terrace rose, beating their
wings, and found perches for themselves on wall and
tree.   One settled on the head of a marble figure of a
man, weather-stained and clothed in moss.

"But," she gasped, "where are we?   It's all just like
a dream."

He looked at her puzzled.   "Why, we are arrived.
This is my garden — the place I told you of."

She gave a sigh half of delight, half disappointment.
She had expected an imposing entrance.   But here
she was — alone in the garden with him — where
she had dreamed of being.

"The old woman who is here is the caretaker," he
said.   "She is leaving the door of the villa open so we
may go in."

"And this is where you played as a child?"

"Yes."

"How marvelous!   I can see you running about in
it — a beautiful little boy."

"Look — between the trees you can see Etna."

She looked and saw Etna like a white rose-tinted
pavilion.   It was all mysterious.   They were cut off,
in a world of their own.   The noises of the town came
muted to them, the church bells, the shouts of children, the braying of donkeys.   They walked along
the paved paths, he rather abstracted, as though he
felt unreal at finding himself there with her.   She
longed for him to make love to her and yet she feared
him — he was so strange and different from the men

she was used to, and yet, compared to them, he was oddly childlike.

Up and up above the garden rose a mountain with its ruined castle and its village of Bomba on the top.

"Tell me about your childhood," she said.

"There is nothing to tell. I have forgotten it. It passed like a dream."

"Tell me about your boyhood, then."

"Oh, I climbed the mountains and I bathed and I lay on these benches in the sun — imagining things. It, too, was a dream."

"Do you live only in the present, then?"

"I live in my imaginings of the future." He looked at her directly and her pulses throbbed quickly in response.

"Could we go into the house?" she asked a little timidly.

He led the way into a hall paved with squares of black and white marble, and from one chill dim room to another. The furniture standing about the stone walls was old Italian.

"The furniture," he said, "is still mine. Cardino, who owns the villa, allows me to keep it here until I find a place for it. I suppose it will happen that I shall lose it also." He stood looking about him with a puzzled air.

If only she were rich! If only she had the money to buy this place and give it back to him! She wished that she had never been so foolish as to let him think she was, so stupid as to throw money about as though it meant nothing to her.   She shivered in the chill of the house.   She said: —

"Let us go out into the garden.   It is cold here."

He did not answer, but stood tracing the outline of a marble square with his stick.   His face was so mysterious to her, his lowered lids so baffling, that she felt her hopes sink, her desire faint.

"I must tell you something," she said, in a low husky voice.   "I am a poor woman.   It does not matter to you, I know, but I must tell you."

He looked at her out of the sides of his eyes.   She saw his desire for her smouldering in them.   Her heart leaped to new life.

"It does not matter," he answered.   "I love you for yourself."

She moved so that her arm touched his.   She shivered as though with cold.   He laid his stick across a table, and his hat beside it with a punctilious air, and turned and faced her, standing close to her.   She looked into his eyes on a level with her own.   Then they boldly recognized their passion and were in each other's arms.   They clung together, their hearts beating wildly, as though calling to one another.   The doves had returned to the terrace and one of them strutted into the hall on coral-pink feet, nodding and cooing to them.   They heard the old woman moving about in a distant room.   He whispered endearments to her in Italian which she could not understand, but repeated again and again to him as terms of endearment.   He could not let her go.   He kissed her eyes, her black hair, her mouth. He had taken all her strength, she thought, feeling almost as though she were dying. He loved her for herself, he had said that, and that sweet knowledge and the passion of his kisses had taken all the strength from her. She could not let him go. She kissed his eyes and his black hair and his mouth, and he received fresh strength from her passion.

At last they returned to the garden and sat on a bench feeling suddenly shy of each other, though he held one of her hands and stroked it.

The old woman came to the door and peered out at them, asking if she might lock up the house.

"*Si, si, si,*" he answered impatiently, and turned to look into Fay's eyes. They began to talk, telling each other of all their feelings since their first meeting, not tiring of hearing the same thing over and over. They must marry. Her determination to marry him was like a candle burning brightly. Somehow she would find a way for them to come and live here. He was sorry that she was not rich, but he could not believe that she was really poor. He had confidence in her. She was so brilliant, so courageous, she could do anything she chose. They felt that they were sitting in their own garden, by their own villa, with their own doves fluttering about their heads. The great Sicilian sun rose higher and higher above the garden, magnificent in its energy, driving back the shadows till they crept under the leaves, under the stone benches, under the basin into which cool water jetted.

The three others had gone on a walk over the mountain paths.   They had carried their lunch with them and did not return till late afternoon.   Fay found Bond sitting on a deep couch in a corner of the deserted lounge, reading, pipe in mouth.   She sat down beside him.

"What are you reading?" she asked.

He showed her.   It was an article on Norway in a back number of the *Geographic*.   "I think I'll go there," he said.

She felt that she could not do without him — yet. She needed his support, if she could get it.   She discovered, too, that she loved his presence for its stability, its comfort.   But she could never have loved him. She said: —

"You were wonderful, Purley, the way you sold that old copy of *Huckleberry Finn* for me.   And got such a price.   Just think, it paid my passage over here!"

"It's a pity you hadn't more like it," he said stiffly. He rather baffled her.   She scarcely knew what to say next.   But after a moment of indecision, she murmured: —

"I'm going to marry Montleone."

A shadow, as of pain, passed over his fair, rugged face, then he answered in a polite tone: —

"Well — I hope you'll be happy.   I guess he's very congenial to you."

"Oh, Purley."   She twisted her fingers together. "I'm just crazy about him.   And he about me."

Bond looked down at a picture of a Norwegian

fiord. "I wish you 'd been crazy about me," he said.

"Oh, I wish I had!" she exclaimed impulsively.

"No, you don't." He spoke almost sternly. "Don't say anything so foolish, Mrs. Palmas. You 've never wanted to care for anyone but Montleone."

"But I 've appreciated you, Purley! I 've liked you always and I 'm in perfect earnest when I say — "

"Don't say it! I 'd rather not."

She looked at him almost appealingly out of her narrow dark eyes that glowed from her love for Montleone. He was conscious of her living body beside him, the body she was so desirous of submitting to Montleone's will.

"May I ask one question?" he proceeded.

"As many as you like."

"Then — what do you expect to live on? You have told me that Montleone has lost everything."

"All but his furniture. He has his beautiful old Italian furniture still. I saw it this morning."

"In the villa?"

"Yes."

"But he cannot live there?"

"He could only rent it. It is up for rent."

"This is a queer fix, Mrs. Palmas. Your money won't last long."

"I know. I can't see what we 're to do."

"And you must have him?"

"If we starve!"

Bond sat, elbows on knees, his clenched hands pressed into his cheeks. After a long silence, he said: —

"I suppose Montleone would be against anything like trade."

"Oh, no — he has n't any ideas like that at all. He 'd do anything.   So would I."

Bond gave a slight, ironic smile.   "That 's a good thing.   Well then — I suggest that you rent Montleone's villa and go into the antique business.   There are always plenty of tourists here in the season, and you have a stock already on hand."

It was a moment before she grasped the possibilities of his suggestion.   Then she leaned toward him and caught his hand in both of hers.   "How perfectly splendid!   Purley — you 're wonderful!   It 's the very thing.   It 's just what I 'd like to do.   Gian will know where to buy more furniture from the impoverished old families.   Josie can help me.   She might even start a tea room or something to attract the tourists.   How can I ever thank you?   I was sure you 'd help me, but this is beyond my wildest hopes — it 's just splendid!"

"Mr. Putnam has come into the lounge," said Bond, warningly.   "Perhaps you 'd better not hold my hand."

She drew away, her face sparkling with excitement. Bond introduced the tired-looking New Yorker to her.   Others came into the lounge. . . .

She told Josie of her engagement while they dressed for dinner.   Josie was thrilled for Fay.   To be an Italian Contessa — Fay, the widow of the Saltport baker!   It was fanciful — even fantastic.   She herself, the cousin of a Contessa. It was all of a piece with this Italian scenery. What were they coming to? And where would they end? She and Diego might do anything. . . . But her heart gave a sudden deep ache for Bond. He had loved Fay for years and now he was to see her marry a man she had only met a few weeks ago, a foreigner. It was like Bond to have put aside his own disappointment and suggest means by which they could marry. He could forget self because he was strong. Fay and Diego could never cease from looking inward on their own desires because they were weak.

Fay had asked Josie to break the news to Diego that evening. There was something revengeful in Josie's nature. She felt that now she would repay Diego for the times when he had hurt her. His mother was the only one he loved, and it would hurt him to give her up to Montleone. For give her up he must, Josie felt sure, if she married the Sicilian. Their lives would be irrevocably altered by the introduction of this foreign element. Josie watched him, hungrily eating his dinner, with the feeling that she was lying in wait for him. He ate with a lazy, catlike zest, taking little part in the conversation, sufficient to himself. Fay talked a great deal, using the names of Tramontana streets and squares and gates as glibly as though she had lived there for years instead of a day.

Bond talked too, telling her of the mountain paths, the farms built on ledges of rock, never that troubled, compassionate look leaving his face. Once his eyes met Josie's and they exchanged a look of understanding. They had exchanged this look before. It was becoming natural to them to seek understanding in each other. She never looked into Bond's blue eyes in this way without an inner vision of the sea at Saltport, the harbor with its lighthouse, the sharp salt smell.

It was easy to see that Fay thought, in her headstrong way, that some day Mr. Putnam, the New Yorker, might be of use to her, and that she gloried in the fact that his weary sophisticated eyes found her beautiful. After dinner she drew Bond to join him and his wife in the lounge.

In the long, whitewashed, red-carpeted passage from the dining room Josie caught Diego's arm and said: —

"Did you know that there is an outside stairway leading to the roof? Let 's go up. There 's a moon."

He pushed out his lips. "I 've had enough of climbing for one day. My legs ache." But he allowed himself to be led out of doors and propelled to the foot of the wooden stairs.

The flat roof was the size of the whole hotel. In the middle of it rose the arched skylight of amber glass which lighted the lounge. Behind and on a level with the roof, but concealed by a wall, curved the main road, and beyond it a high hill, with a villa clinging to its side, rose black against the sky. On three sides the garden lay in darkness beneath, the foliage of the orange and lemon trees, the pavement of the terrace, the water of a stone-edged pool, glimmering in the moonlight. From the garden rose the scent of mimosa. The great mounting moon silvered the clustering mountain sides and the sea far below. The stars, which seemed to tremble in a new design, swarmed in watchful brightness. The rattle of a cart came from the road, and a man's voice, hoarse yet sweet, singing a Sicilian air.

Diego sat down on the low wall surrounding the roof and lighted a cigarette. He was deep in his own thoughts and returned his cigarette case to his pocket without offering one to Josie. Frowning, she nipped his from his lips and put it between her own.

"Selfish pig," she said softly. "You think of no one but yourself."

Unperturbed, he took out another cigarette and lighted it. She looked into his face, illumined by the flare of the match, and was glad that she held the power to disturb him.

"I could live here forever," he said, kicking a heel gently against the wall.

"Well — perhaps you may — if you choose to live with your stepfather."

The tip of Diego's cigarette brightened as he drew on it deeply. But he asked in a casual tone: —

"Is Fay going to marry Montleone?"

"Yes. He asked her this morning in the garden of his villa. She 's mad about him."

"Well — I don't wonder. He 's an interesting fellow. Fay does n't care about people who are n't unusual. Neither do I."

"It will make a terrible difference to you. To me too, of course, but not quite so great."

"It won't make any difference to me at all. I 'll be

glad to see her happy just as she'd be glad to see me happy."

He was impervious. She almost hissed: "He will break her heart. Those Southern Europeans always do break American women's hearts. He's after her money. And she hasn't got any."

"What does she expect to live on?"

"Oh, she has a scheme for renting his villa and going into the antique business. It's full of old furniture belonging to him." She gave up trying to hurt him and slid up beside him on the wall, her shoulder against his.

"Does Purley know?"

"Yes. She told him before dinner. He seemed to bear up well. He couldn't have cared so terribly much for her and eat a good dinner and talk about his walk after hearing news like that."

Diego said contemptuously: "Men don't go about sobbing when they can't have what they want. But Purley's always loved Fay and he always will. She's the sort of woman men go on loving whether they get them or not."

There was insult in his tone. How Josie hated him! She would have liked to push him over the wall so that he would fall on to the stones of the terrace below and be smashed, or into the pool and be drowned. She wriggled her sharp shoulder wickedly against his.

He moved away from her a little. He slouched easily on the wall like a sleek black cat under the starry

sky. The strange big stars trembled above them in
that new design that made them feel far away from
all they had known. Diego said: —

"You see that brightest light up the mountain side.
A Russian artist and his wife live there. Varvara
Walkonsky has come to stay with them. Are n't you
glad?"

Josie peered round his shoulder, trying to see his
face. But though she could not see it, she hated its
expression. And though she hated the expression of
his unseen face, she craved the dark comfort of his
body touching hers. She leaned against him and answered in a stifled voice: —

"No, I 'm not glad. Who was that man she was
with? Not her husband, I 'm very sure. Do you expect to introduce that sort of woman to Fay?"

"Fay would have the sense to be civil to her."

"Oh, you 've got the most distorted ideas, Jimmy!
There 's no use arguing with you."

"Why do you try it, then? Why don't you accept
me just as I am and be comfortable?"

"Because you fascinate me."

"All the more reason."

"I keep wanting to know what is in your mind."

"You 'll know all right when the time comes."

"You encouraged her to follow you here. I can
fathom that out. I 'll tell Fay. See if I don't!"

"Do! And Purley, too. And Montleone. They 'll
all like to know."

"Jimmy, I believe you hate me, and yet . . . There

was that time in the studio . . . Have you forgotten it?"

"Well — you were a nice little thing that day."

He only hated her because she was not Varvara, but he could not tell her that.

She said: "I pity that girl, and I pity Purley Bond. I pity anyone who loves either of you.   You 're both as selfish as hell.   And she 's the worst because she 's so warm and affectionate on the surface.   She seems to sort of throw herself on you.   You don't give anything or ask anything."

He scarcely heard her.   He said: "The light 's out up there.   They 've gone to bed early."

"Who?"

"The Russians.   Their light 's out.   It 's like a black cave on the mountain side.   A magic cave."

CHAPTER VII

DIEGO could think of nothing but Varvara. As he lay in his little room, the windows of which looked into the garden, he was conscious of a spark burning on the mountain side — the spark of her magnetism drawing him. He gave himself up to her magnetism with a deep, indolent satisfaction. He was like a plant or an animal that is aware of a dark, powerful communion between itself and an unseen source of energy. There was no excitement, no uneasy reaching out; there was just a quiet self-pleasure in the consciousness of this spark.

To-morrow he would go up the mountain side alone. The others could do what they liked — Fay and Montleone make love, Josie and Bond wander off by themselves. He would find Varvara and she would tell him all about herself, if she chose. But it did not matter if she told nothing; he would find her, look into her bronze-colored slanting eyes — that would be enough. Enough — until he wanted more.

Just now Fay and Bond and Josie were nothing to him. They were shadows thrown on the unyielding rock of his egotism. Bond, disappointed, sombre; Josie, thin as a monkey, craving for she knew not what; Fay, absorbed by her passion for the Sicilian. There were only two realities, himself and Varvara —

he, lying in this trance-like self-satisfaction; she, asleep on the mountain side.   For he chose to think of her asleep, not even dreaming of him, not dreaming at all — just lying there unconscious, passive, exercising this effortless magnetism on him.   He thought of her as lying with her knees drawn up, her body curved in the shape of a horseshoe, charged with magnetism.

He thought he would not sleep at all that night, but would surrender it to deep, pleasurable wonderings about her.   All the dark hours of the night should remain in his remembrance forever, sensuous unpainted pictures.

Whether or not he had slept he could not tell when morning came, but he rose refreshed and stood at the open window, drinking in the smell of violets and the purple bloom of shadows in the garden.

He went to Fay's room and pushed a half-sheet of note paper under the door.   On it he had written: —

I'm off to spend the day by myself.   You know that I like to do that so I guess you won't mind.   You'll be with Montleone, won't you?   Josie told me about you and him. I'm glad because I want you to have whatever you want now.   You had a rough deal for a good many years.

Congratulations and kisses.
DIEGO.

He walked up the steps to the road, carrying a paper bag with cord handles packed with his lunch.   He had just reached the corner when the clang of the bell from the church of San Sebastiano at the corner shattered the morning quiet.   The bell was not rung, but

beaten by an iron hammer into a ferocious call for
attention. It was an early call to Mass, he supposed,
standing subdued by the noise. But then a solemn
tolling began and, turning the corner, he went down
the steep side road that led to the sea, and stared up
at the cream-colored, domed tower of the church, in
which a sturdy bush grew, pushing out its boughs
through every opening, into the air.

The bell continued its tolling and Diego saw the
door of the church open and a stout, cassocked priest
emerge, followed by half a dozen little boys in short
surplices. After the little boys came a bent man, old
before his time, and behind, following him, a thin
young man carrying the smallest coffin Diego had ever
seen, on his shoulder.

The procession passed Diego and wound joltingly
down the rough road. It turned a sharp bend and
disappeared behind a wall, reappearing again farther
down, in a peculiar swaying movement. Diego followed, not so much from curiosity as from a strange
feeling that he was one of the party, that the mourn-
ing was a part of him also. He gained on them until
he was behind the young father, keeping his eyes on
the diminutive coffin, picturing what lay enclosed
there, a weak, tiny newborn child that would never
play in the Sicilian sun.

Below, on a bend of the road, was the walled cemetery, white gravestones and statues pressing close beneath dark cypresses. He waited outside the gates,
motionless. He heard the priest's voice rise and fall,
the voices of the little boys sweet and metallic in

response.   After a short time the bent, middle-aged
man and the thin young man came out together,
passed him without a look, and began slowly to climb
the hill.   The young man was very thin.   He looked
as though he had never had enough to eat and the expression of his face was tragic.   How had it felt,
Diego wondered, to carry that little box containing
the body of one's child — that one had begot from
one's own body — down the steep road in the early
morning.   Would he himself ever have to do anything like that?   What was the mysterious life that
lay before him?   What things would he be called on
to endure?   His face, as these thoughts passed through
his brain, wore an expression even more tragic than
that of the young father.

He stood there waiting for the priest and his at-
tendants to return.   At last they came, the little boys
trotting in irregular fashion about the stout, cassocked
man.   Suddenly he caught one by the shoulder, then
another, then another, placing them on the road in
front of him.   He uttered a sharp exclamation and
struck his hands together.   He was setting them off
in a race.   They came helter-skelter towards Diego
and passed him in a clatter of thick-soled boots, their
dark hair flying, their eyes wild.   They ran up and
up and around the bend toward the church.   The
priest plodded behind, stout, benign, casting a kindly
look at Diego as he passed.   His little boys came running back to him, clustering about him.

Diego watched them disappear.   He liked them all
— the young father, the half-humorous, benign priest,

the scampering urchins. But he did not like the cemetery beneath the cypresses. He walked on, going down the fisherman's path that branched from the road toward the sea, instead of continuing his way toward the mountain.

He did not ask himself why he had taken this new direction. It was not his way to resist or question his own impulses. He followed the stony path downward, ledge after ledge, each turn discovering some new grouping of valley and hill, some new unfolding of strange loveliness.

As he neared the sea he saw three people on a grassy space beside the path. A man and a woman stood in front of easels and another woman sat at a little distance clasping her knees in her arms. There was a strong wind, and Diego saw how the short hair of the women was tossed and the man's yellow beard blown. The one clasping her knees was Varvara Walkonsky. It had been her presence that had drawn him this way, the drawing of her magnetic body, curved like a horseshoe magnet.

He stood close beside them at the edge of the path, looking at them through a hedge of wild cactus and flowering gorse. The two who painted were absorbed in their work, but Varvara looked over her shoulder and saw him. She smiled without starting, as though she were expecting him.

He clambered through the hedge and stood beside her.

"Hullo," he said. "You 've come, all right."

"You got my message?"

"Yes."

She sat with her head thrown back, her broad face, with its slanting eyes, smiling up at him.

"I was going up the mountain to find you," he said. "But something made me come here."

"You could not help to find me."   The soft huskiness of her voice, its foreign intonation, created a deeper intimacy between them than if she had spoken in a way familiar to him.   A look passed between them which carried them on the quick-moving current of its intimacy.

She turned then to the other two and introduced them.   They were much older than Varvara, Russian refugees of the upper class.   The woman's face showed what she had passed through, in the drawn though self-contained line of her lips, but the man's face was as serene as a child's.   They were Maria and Peter Narishkin.   They spoke English almost as well as Varvara.   When they found that Diego was a painter also, they accepted his presence with an added friendliness.

Maria Narishkin had barely got a bold beginning on her canvas, but Peter was putting the last touches on a picture.   This picture of rock and sea interested Diego because of its resemblance to his own work, in spite of the differences of atmosphere and treatment. There was the same appearance of disorder, the same startling freedom and intensity.   He wondered what Josie would make of it.   In his secret mind he believed that Josie could improve it, as she could always

improve his.   The Narishkins asked him to join them
the next day.   They would like to see his conception
of the scene.

He and Varvara left them and followed the path to
the beach.   They sat side by side on the sand, watching
the play of light and shadow on the sea and the rocky
island where once sirens had sung.   Varvara told him
of them.

"You 're siren enough for me," he said.

She looked at him with an expression in which he
saw a tinge of compassion.   He added, half sulkily: —

"You think I 'm only a boy.   But I 'm not."

"I think you are charming."

"A charming boy, then."

"No-o.   A man.   But you have much to learn."

"Well, I 'm willing to be taught — by you."

"Ah, I must not teach you."

"Why?"

"I know too much. . . .   You should be taught first
by someone who knows just a little more than you.
That girl — for instance — who was with you in
Pompeii.   She is not your sister?"

"No — my cousin.   But Josie does n't know anything about life. . . ."

"This Josie — does she love you?"

Diego laughed.   "You 'd call it a queer sort of love.
She 's always gibing at me.   But she hangs round me.
She paints too.   I 'll tell you what she does.   I 've
never told this to anyone — not even my teacher.
She finishes all my pictures for me.   There 's something

queer about me.   Incomplete.   It's mighty queer,
but I'm not able to finish up a single picture.   I
just can't.   But Josie does it for me.   If it were n't
for that I'd never get anywhere.   It's sort of rotten,
is n't it?"

Varvara looked at him speculatively.   "It is very
strange.   Do you like her for it?"

He frowned.   "No.   She's too conceited.   Sometimes I hate her when she stands staring at a picture of
mine.   Just staring and wondering what she will do
with it."

"Yes.   It is not good.   And this Josie, can she paint
well?"

"Oh, nothing at all remarkable.   There's a lot of
detail in what she does.   She draws well. . . . Say,
don't let's talk about Josie or me.   I want to hear
about you.   I wish you'd tell me whether you cared
about that fellow in Naples.   You know what I mean.
Say, he did n't mean much to you, did he?   He was n't
your sort.   You're not going to see any more of him,
are you?"   He looked at her imploringly, his face
showing so plainly his mixed blood.   New England,
Indian, Portuguese.

She shook her head.   "No, he was not my sort.
But he amused me — for a little while.   It amused
me to show him Paris.   He knew so little."

"Like me — eh?"

"Oh, he knew much less than you.   He knew nothing of life.   He had been a schoolmaster — shut up
in a school — all his days.   Then a little fortune was
left to him and he wanted to see life.   He went to

Paris. We met there and — I showed him a little of life."

"But" — anxiously — "you will not ever go back to him?"

"Never. He bored me."

"You got tired of him pretty soon, did n't you? You were n't with him long?"

"Oh, no, he bored me too much. I brought him to Italy to see if it would be better, but it was worse. So we parted."

"I suppose you know Paris awfully well."

"I was brought up there. I speak French better than Russian. I was a child when my people were driven from Russia. They lost everything."

"And you 're alone in the world?"

"Except for a few friends. Like these — " she nodded in the direction of the two artists.

"Say, Varvara, I 'm going to be your friend. You 'll let me, won't you? You don't think I 'll bore you in just a little while, do you?"

She turned and smiled at him, showing her small beautiful teeth. She seemed to glisten in the Sicilian sunlight. She was all warmth and seductiveness. Diego took her hand, that lay on the grass, in both his. The grass was starred by marigolds, their seeds blown over from the shore of Africa. He lay down and put his cheek against her hand. He did not kiss it. He wanted to wait for that. He wanted to advance toward that intimacy — even the kissing of her hand — without haste. He wanted to savor the sensuous pleasure of each moment with her, for, deep within himself, he knew that no intimacy with her could last, that he must resign himself, at the outset, to parting with her sooner or later.

"Your eyelashes tickle my hand," she said.

He winked extravagantly. "That is my way of kissing your hand."

"How charming you are!" she said. "Shall you stay long in Tramontana?"

His face against her hand, he spoke indistinctly. "As long as you want me."

"But your mother — the beautiful one is your mother, is n't she? What will she say?"

"She is to marry Montleone."

"She will live here, then."

He raised his head. "A Sicilian Count is not of much importance, is he?" He felt a sudden anxiety about his mother's marriage.

She shrugged. "Of what use is nobility in these days? We are all poor. But he has an interesting face. He has seen life."

He frowned. "Life, life," he said petulantly. "You 're always talking about *life!*"

"I am a worshiper of life. That is my religion."

He put her hand from him and sat up. "I worship life, too. But I have a theory different from yours. To me, anyone or anything is seeing life. That fisherman down there, pulling in his boat, is seeing life. That donkey in the field there is seeing life. You can't hear him bray without knowing that he and his ancestors have seen the very depths of life. The dead fish, lying in the bottom of that fisherman's boat, have

seen life. This flower" — he touched a marigold with
his finger — "is seeing a lot of life. You have only to
look into its dark eyes to realize that. That's my
feeling about it, Varvara."

"But why did you not pick the flower, to illus-
trate?"

"Because that would spoil everything for it. It
would n't see anything more."

"Ah, that is where you are wrong. Then it would
have begun to see — a little."

She plucked the marigold and stuck it over his ear.
"Now you look so pretty!" she exclaimed.

Peter Narishkin came down the slope toward them.

"We are going to eat something, Maria and I," he
said. "We are starving. And you too must be
hungry, Varvara. I come to ask if Mr. Palmas will
join us."

"I have brought my own lunch with me," said
Diego, "but I'm not hungry yet. At least — not
very hungry — perhaps I can eat a little — well, just
what you say — I'll do whatever you like." He
scarcely knew what he was saying. Varvara filled his
mind. He held her arm against his side as they followed Peter Narishkin up the slope.

Maria had set out some cheese, a crusty Sicilian loaf,
and a bottle of wine. Diego added his sandwiches and
cakes. They sat down together like old friends.
They talked of painting, and Diego, who had thought
he was extraordinarily advanced in his ideas of art,
felt himself to be immature in the presence of
these people. Yet their simplicity kept him from

embarrassment.   There was nothing patronizing about
them.   He found himself repeating what he had already told Varvara, that he was not able to complete
a picture without Josie's help.

"It just won't be finished," he said.   "It's as
though I was the painter and Josie the thinker.   And
the picture is a kind of battlefield between us.   But
she always wins and I always see that she is right."

"It is remarkable," said Peter Narishkin.   "Did
your teacher know of this?"

"He knew nothing of it."

"Was he not conscious of anything different —
antagonistic?"

"I don't know.   Yes — he was conscious of something strange.   He used to say I had a dual personality."

"And he had taught her, too?"

"Yes."

"Stupid! Stupid! Not to have discovered that two
people had worked on the canvas."

"I'd defy anyone," said Diego, "to discover it.   She
scarcely seems to do anything.   Yet something happens.   The picture is complete."

"I should like to meet the young lady.   Will you
bring her to see us?"

Would Josie consent, Diego wondered.   He thought
she would.   Her curiosity would be too much for her
disapproval of Varvara.   He said: "Thanks.   I guess
Josie'd like to come."

"Wait!" put in Maria.   "Let Mr. Palmas do a
painting first.   Let him show it to us, before and after

his cousin has touched it.   Then afterward let us meet her.   What do you say?"

"It would be better," agreed her husband.

Diego joined the three Russians next day in an excursion to a distant point.   They painted, had lunch together, painted again, lay on the rocks and talked. He returned with them to the half-ruined farmhouse on the mountain side, where they lived.

Maria and Varvara cooked the evening meal.   They ate it by the light of a brazier and the last daylight coming in at the open door.   Fowls perched about the doorway, and a silky, long-haired goat came into the room and was fed from Varvara's hand.   Everything that Varvara did seemed right and beautiful to Diego. There were that strange sensuousness and simplicity in her movements.   The goat went straight to her, stamping its little hoofs on the stone floor and arching its neck.

"Varvara is so funny," said Maria.   "She makes a pet of the goat already.   She has even combed its long hair that was all tangled."

The goat's hair shimmered smooth and glossy against its sides.   Varvara took a horn in each of her hands and bent and kissed it between them.   She laughed up at Diego.   Outside a turkey gobbled. . . . Challenging, clanging notes, as though a bronze gong were in its breast.   The goat pressed its horns against Varvara's hands and rolled its light eyes.   The valley lay purple below.   The lights of the village on the beach shone strangely, as though they were reflections of stars washed up by the sea.   Diego felt that he could go on living like this forever — if only Varvara would be kind to him.

He spent day after day with her and the Narishkins. She wandered over the hillsides picking purple anemones, golden marigolds, and pale asphodels while the others painted.   At first Diego could do nothing that he thought worth finishing, but one cloudy day they came upon a young almond in bloom, growing out of a cleft in dark rocks, with the dark sky above.   Diego, with a new look of purpose in his eyes, began to paint. Peter and Maria turned from their own work now and again to watch him.   They exchanged looks. He was justifying the interest they had taken in him. Varvara cared nothing for his painting.   She wandered down into a deep valley where women were washing clothes in a stream, and talked to them. Diego could forget her while he painted.

Josie was bitterly jealous of his new friendships, from which she thought herself willfully excluded, even while she disapproved of Varvara.   She was coolly critical of the picture when he showed it to her.   It was not so good, she said, as things he had done in Saltport.

He took her to the spot where he had painted it and she stood gazing a long while at the tree and the rocks and the sky that was still a wrathful gray.   She was passionately lonely standing there.   She thought she was like the young almond tree, blooming uncared for.

"Can you do anything with it?"   Diego asked her that night.

"I don't know. . . . What did those Russians think of it?"

"They did n't say. Well — they asked me if it was finished."

Josie smiled. She felt her power over him. She loved his weakness.

"I suppose you 've never told them that I finish your pictures for you?"

"Why should I?" He smiled indolently.

Two days later he carried the picture to the farm-house. Peter and Maria Narishkin looked at it in silence for a space, then, both at once, they began to talk. The picture was, in their opinion, ruined. Maria said that it had been rendered lively, coherent, that the essence of impressionism had been flattened out of it. Peter said that the emotions had been taken away — all the rhythm, the plastic relations of the forms, was rendered meaningless. They talked end-lessly. It seemed to Diego that they would never tire of talking. Varvara sat with folded hands, gravely attentive, like a child. He sat silent, wondering what Josie would say when he forbade her to touch another of his pictures. He must be pretty good, he thought, or the Russians would not go on and on talking about him. But he scarcely heard what they said. He was watching Varvara, thinking how she always detached herself from her background, became the one impor-tant object of the scene.

But he asked Josie to go to the farm with him, since they were urgent to see her. At first she refused, then her curiosity overcame her. After all, the

Narishkins were respectable. And — if Varvara were not — well, Russians were Russians. You had only to read their novels to find that out. So she put on a little gay red coat and a red beret that became her, and followed Diego up the mountain path.

It gave her the feeling of Saltport to be out with Diego. Here she saw almost nothing of him. He was always off with the Russians.

"Jimmy!" she exclaimed. "Isn't this like old times?"

"Not a bit," he answered. "We're two different people. We were kids then. Of course, you may not feel yourself very different. But I am. I couldn't possibly go back to that life. The thought of the main street and the shop sickens me."

"What about the studio and the sea? They were your real life."

"Yes. They were real."

"So were the bakeshop and the main street. They seem sort of beautiful when I think of them at this distance."

He cast a look of disgust over his shoulder. "You're a sentimental little fool, Josie. You'll be telling me next that you liked the Baptist Church and that it was good fun baking bread and doughnuts."

"Don't think I'd ever go back there," she cried. "It's just — can't you understand? — well, I was happy there."

"No, you weren't," he muttered. "You're never happy anywhere. You're an irritable, fussy, fault-finding, sentimental girl." But, though he said these

words, he felt tender toward Josie at the moment.
She was going to be hurt soon, and hurts went so deep
with her.

They had to stand back from the path to let a
peasant woman ride by on her donkey. She gave
them a quick, dark-eyed glance as she passed, urging
her donkey with hisses. Diego had clasped Josie's
fingers in his.

He still held them as they walked on. The farmhouse looked quite near, though they had to descend
into a valley and climb a rocky steep to reach it.
Now the almond trees were in full blow, as prolific of
their clouds of pinkness as a sunset sky. Urns filled
with flowering vines stood on either side of the arched
stone gateway of the farm, giving a false idea of elegance within. Within, all was poverty, but so picturesque, Josie thought.

And Peter Narishkin in his blue smock, with his
golden beard and calm childlike forehead, was touching. And Maria in her short-sleeved blue jumper,
with her wiry arms and tragic smile, was touching and
somehow beautiful.

But Varvara in her long green dress, standing in a
dark corner of the room with the silken-haired goat
peering timidly from behind her, was not touching.
Josie hated her presence there. She would have enjoyed being at the Narishkins' with Diego if only Varvara had not been there.

The Russians made much of her. They showed her
all there was to see on the farm. It was owned and
worked by an old Italian couple who lived in a room

above the stable. They showed her the donkey, the
fowls, the turkey gobbler, who wheeled and spread his
tail and gobbled at her, and the little herd of goats
of which Varvara's silken-haired pet was the head.
Then they sat down around the table and Maria gave
them tea with slices of lemon in it and sugary Sicilian
cakes.

Josie was flattered by the interest the two artists
took in her. They led the conversation almost
timidly to the subject of painting. They brought out
their pictures to show her and asked her opinion of
them. She thought the coloring was vivid, beautiful, but the pictures painted by Peter had a tumultu-
ous, chaotic look to her. Those done by Maria she
thought were excessively simple in arrangement and
lacked design. They seemed to want to hear all she
had to say about art. Her cheeks burned as she
talked.

At last Peter Narishkin said gently: "But the ideas
of each one are good only for his own work. We
must not put our hand to the work of another. That
is stifling. It is the touch of death."

Josie looked at him, startled. What was coming?

"You must never again," continued Peter gently,
"try to complete one of your cousin's pictures. They
are complete as he leaves them. As complete as a
wave of the sea. I think he is going to do very fine
work indeed — if only he is let alone."

Maria Narishkin could restrain herself no longer.
Speech, which had been dammed like a stream by some
obstacle, now rushed out in a torrent, sweeping Peter's

gentle words aside, drowning Josie's stammered self-defense. Diego would be ruined — ruined — ruined — if Josie went on interfering with his work. Let her do what she liked to her own canvas, but let her keep away from his if she valued his talent, which indeed promised to be great. When Maria hesitated for want of breath, Peter took up the tale. Josie sat rigid, listening, her hands clenched in her lap.

All the way down the mountain path she refused to speak to Diego.

"That's just their idea," he muttered once or twice. "They may be all wrong."

He felt uncomfortable and rather contrite at seeing her hurt. At the same time he had a new feeling of strength and pride. He was his own. He need depend on no one.

She went straight to her room and threw herself on the bed, sobbing. Presently Fay came in and found her.

"Josie — whatever is the matter?"

Josie's voice came stifled in the pillow. "It's those hateful Russians. They've been horrible to me."

"The Russians! Were you up there? But what did they do?"

"Oh — you wouldn't understand! It's about Diego's painting."

"But Josie — " Fay put her arms about her — "tell me all about it." Fay was so happy herself that she could not bear to see Josie unhappy. She and Diego must have been having one of their old quarrels. But she would soon fix that up. Yet she could get nothing out of Josie. She only burrowed into the pillow and said angry incoherent things about the Russians.

Fay went to Diego's room. He was sitting by the window. His last picture was held on his knees and he was looking at it with an expression she could not understand. He looked both proud and sullen. But then Diego so often wore strange expressions. She said, "What have you been doing to Josie?"

"Nothing." He pushed out his lips.

"Well, your friends then. Don't pretend you don't know what I mean!"

"They told her to keep her hands off my pictures. She's always finished them up for me. I've never told you that before, have I?" He looked up at her, pouting.

"Is that all? What a silly girl she is!"

"It's serious to her. It's been a funny sort of thing. I felt I could n't finish a picture without her help. And she thought everything I did looked crude until she'd coaxed it along a bit. The Narishkins think that's all wrong. They think I'll do far better work if I'm left alone."

Fay flung her arms about his neck and pressed his head to her breast. She pressed his face against some carved beads she wore, hurting it. He struggled, but she held him tightly. "Mamma's darling little boy!" she exclaimed. "He's going to be a wonderful artist. Mamma knows it."

"Oh, hell," said Diego, freeing himself. "I wish you would n't get sloppy, Fay."

Fay was not offended. "But I can't help it.

We're both so wonderful. We're handsome. We're talented. We've come over here — almost nobody, you might say. Yet everybody's feverishly interested in us. You take after me. And even people like Purley and Josie admit that I — " She began to laugh. "But it is fun, is n't it, darling? After all these years, you and I are going to mount up and up — getting all that we want, realizing all our most wonderful dreams. Is n't it dazzling?"

"Uh-huh," mumbled Diego, nuzzling against her.

CHAPTER VIII

MONTLEONE made application at once to the authorities for his marriage to Fay Palmas. They were equally eager to begin their new life together. All would go well. He had a childlike faith in her strength and self-assurance. She would steer them triumphantly through all difficulties — even make a fortune for them in the proposed antique business. She hid from him — and almost hid from herself — the fact that his presence robbed her of her strength, sapped her self-assurance, as the sun drinks the dew from a plant. He made her feel weak, languorous. Her boastful plans were bravado. They consisted of little more than the wild reaching out to get him what he wanted. Sometimes when she was away from him, and felt her vitality and arrogance return in the presence of Bond and Josie, she cherished a strange anger against Montleone. But once they were together again and she saw the sultry light of desire in his eyes, the fine curve of his sensitive lips as he smiled at her, she forgot all but her love for him.

It had been easy to acquire his villa at a fairly high rental. The present owner was willing enough to make something out of it. He had been unable to let it to the members of the foreign group who lived in Tramontana because of its lack of modern improvements. They would not play bridge by the light of candles or antique oil lamps. They could not bathe in a few inches of dubious water in a tub that looked as though unearthed from Pompeii. Little light came in at the high narrow windows. But to Fay it was perfect. The bitter part was having to sell the old furniture. However, she made up her mind to sell no more of that than was absolutely necessary.

Fay and Montleone were married one morning and left that same day for a honeymoon in Rome. Josie, Diego, and Bond were the only others present. Fay had met scarcely anyone in Tramontana. She did not want to mingle in its society until she burst upon it in the light of a Contessa. Montleone affirmed, with a shrug, that there was no society there worth knowing in any case — except perhaps a few of the English residents and an artist or two. At Diego's request the three Russians were invited to the wedding breakfast, which took place in the hall of the villa. It was the first time Fay had met them and she was charmed by their naturalness — by Peter's golden beard, Maria's tragic look, and Varvara's beauty. She was grateful to Diego for having brought them. Otherwise it might have been a gloomy feast. There was a chill in the hall, and a smell of must. Wild rain beat against the narrow windows, and the food cooked by Benita required the addition of the good wine to make it at all palatable.

Montleone was unusually quiet. He seemed to be in a dreamy state, his thoughts turned inward on himself except when his eyes met Fay's, and then, again, she felt that weakness — that disturbing languor. Bond sat rigid, eating and drinking little. He too had withdrawn into himself, and when his blue eyes met Fay's she thought she saw a look of reproach in them, and it hurt her. Diego was indolent, untalkative as usual. Josie was downright depressed. The presence of the Russians wrought calamitously on her nerves after the scene at the farmhouse. She was seated opposite Peter Narishkin and refused to look at him or to speak except in short jerky sentences. He drank a good deal of wine and began to talk about art. The calm beauty of his forehead was disfigured by a scowl. He leaned across the table and beat on it with the handle of his fork to attract Josie's attention. He said loudly: —

"Never again must you touch a picture painted by your cousin. I have made him promise me that he will not let you. But I do not trust him. I want you yourself to promise me!"

"I am scarcely likely to," she returned hotly.

Diego said: "Only last night I found her hanging over my new picture with a kind of ghoulish look in her eyes. I look to you to restrain her, Peter."

"By God," shouted Peter Narishkin, "I will restrain her. I will show her how wrong it is. I will prove to her how she harms you."

"Nothing on earth," returned Josie in a shaking voice, "would make me touch one of his old pictures. I 'm not even interested in them now." She gave a furious look at Diego.

Fay said: "I think you paint beautifully yourself,

Josie. I think she 'll make a name for herself too, don't you, Mr. Narishkin?"

He glared at her. "What I want to know is why was she hanging over your son's new picture?"

"Peter, Peter," put in his wife, "drink your wine and be calm."

Montleone smiled across at Bond. "These artists are difficult, are they not? It is only business men like you and me who are easy to get on with."

Bond liked Montleone. When he was with him, when Montleone smiled at him, he could not help liking him. But he envied him Fay with a bitter cruel envy that was hard to conceal. He twisted his features into what he hoped was a friendly smile and answered, "You 're right, Count."

He was angry with the Russian for his attack on Josie. He would have liked to take him by the beard and throw him out. He hated the dark blue velvet smock which Narishkin had affected for the wedding. He hated Maria Narishkin's enormous earrings and beads. He liked what was sedate and seemly and commonplace, he thought. Yet he could not get over loving Fay and she was none of these.

When they had said good-bye to her and Montleone and the three Russians and Diego had followed them to the road, throwing confetti after them, he and Josie found themselves alone in the hall with the remains of the feast. Benita's grandson, who had waited at table in a suit too large for him, had already begun to clear away. They had been delighted by the excitement of the wedding party. They talked loudly in unison as they carried out the plates. The grandson threw a handful of crusts to the doves at the door, which strutted in, bowing and chuckling, to the very centre of the room.

No one paid any attention to Bond or Josie. With a bereft feeling they sought the privacy of an ante-room.

"Here," said Josie, "I can have my little tea room. There is just space for six small round tables. I'd not need more than that. It must be very select and things served in the daintiest way. And real American coffee — not the sort of thing they give you over here and pretend it's American."

"I hope you are not tackling too much," said Bond. "It seems a big undertaking for a girl of your experience."

"My experience," repeated Josie, on an offended note. "I've had a great deal of experience."

"Not with foreign servants. You don't know a dozen words of Italian."

"I'll soon learn. Someone has got to make this thing pay or Fay's marriage won't be a success. Montleone is a perfect child."

"Perhaps — in some ways."

"Of course, in other ways, he's quite subtle."

Bond smiled grimly. "I'll make a guess," he said, "that we seem like children to Montleone."

Josie stared. "Oh, I don't think so. He's always saying how wonderfully progressive America is."

"That just proves what I guessed."

"My goodness, you're sarcastic!"

"No, I'm not.   I only think that Montleone usually talks down to us."

"Well, he's got no head for business and you and I
have.   We're the ones who must put this antique shop
on its feet."

"I can't stay much longer in Tramontana."

Josie looked aghast.   "But you must!   You won't
go off and leave us to shift for ourselves right in the
beginning!"   The thought of Tramontana without
Bond loomed rather frightening.

"What can I do?"

"Oh, you've such a good head!"

"It's your idea that my good head is to put Montleone on his feet, eh?"

"It's really Fay.   You know that, Purley."

Bond made a slight grimace, in which there were
both chagrin and tenderness.   "Well — I'll do what
I can, though it won't be much.   Fay looks on me as
a sort of wizard since I sold the books for her.   The
first thing I must do is to get a cheap hotel.   There is
one just below ours in a nice quiet place.   There are
only two guests in it now — a half-mad Englishwoman and her companion.   She stays in bed holding
an umbrella over her head — so I guess we won't get
in each other's way.   I'm an unsociable fellow, Josie,
you know that."

"I think you're wonderful!"   Tremulous admiration shone out of her eyes.   His was a comforting
presence.   She had felt the comfort of it during the
attack from the Russians.

"I'm glad someone thinks so.   I don't feel quite

so much out of it. Has Diego told you where he is going?"

"No. Diego tells me nothing."

"He's going up to the farm — with the Narishkins."

Josie's lip curled. "That's a good arrangement. He can be near his charmer." Her eyes filled with tears and she added passionately: "I'm done with Diego! He's been awfully mean to me! Letting that Peter Narishkin rave against me for trying to make something of his old pictures! He's become a perfect beast."

"Diego is just what he has always been. He does n't pretend to gratitude. Did he ever ask you to tinker at his pictures?"

"No. I did it of my own accord. I was a fool. Do you agree with Peter Narishkin?"

"I don't know anything about pictures, but I think he was mighty ill-mannered. Anyhow, if Diego turns out to be a genius it will be a good thing."

"Well, there's this to be said for me — Mr. Selby, who taught Diego, always marveled at the way Diego's pictures came on when he 'd worked on them at home. He just could n't understand it."

"He was right, I daresay. I saw a picture done by this Russian and I thought it was a mess."

Diego appeared in the doorway. He had overheard Bond's words. He smiled in his peculiar cat-like way, but said nothing. He stood looking at them, smiling, his hands in his pockets.

Josie began excitedly talking of how she would arrange the room — the kind of curtains she would have, the Italian pottery, the color of the tables and chairs. She walked about measuring spaces between windows and doors.   She moved close to Diego and withdrew from him again, like a wave that presses toward a rock and, returning, leaves it in its original dark, glossy immobility.   He watched her, smiling, but Bond frowned a little.   Josie's attitude toward the boy irritated him, and somehow hurt him.   It seemed to him that it took little in these days to hurt him — he was becoming sensitive, introspective, he thought.   He strained toward the moment when he would be free of Tramontana, would go off on his travels by himself.

During the three weeks of Fay's absence he and Josie worked hard to get the place in order for her.   Diego was unexpectedly helpful.   Already he had a smattering of Italian and he seemed able to make old Benita and her grandson understand what was wanted when Josie and Bond had failed.   Three rooms, opening one from the other, were to be used as showrooms for furniture.   Dressing tables, mirrors, and chests were carried downstairs to add to the furniture already there.   Much of it was out of repair, and Diego found a good cabinetmaker who was able to put it in order. They cleaned and polished most of it themselves, while Benita scrubbed floors and her grandson made windows and mirrors shine.

Bond hired a motor car and they drove to near-by towns, picking up now and again a piece of furniture, a picture, or a strip of embroidery to add to the collection.   It would have been impossible for them to have acquired these things at a fair price had not Diego brought Varvara to the rescue.   At first Josie refused assistance from the Russian, but Bond persuaded her to accept.   Varvara spoke Italian fluently and she had a lively talent for bargaining.   She threw herself into the project with enthusiasm.   She thought and talked of little else, it seemed to Josie, though she suspected that, underneath, Varvara had passionate thoughts for Diego.   She was at the villa in the morning almost before Josie was awake.   Josie, at last, asked her to sleep there, but Varvara refused.   She could not quite desert Maria Narishkin.   And Diego slept at the farm.

One morning Peter Narishkin appeared at the villa with his arms full of pictures.   He sought out Josie, who was putting up curtains in her tea room, and said with bland assurance: —

"Here are some pictures by Maria Feodorovna and myself.   You shall exhibit them in your antique rooms and people will come to see them and then they will buy your furniture.   And perhaps they will buy a picture also.   If you will get me a hammer and some nails I shall proceed to hang them to the best advantage."

Josie wanted to insult him, to tell him that his pictures were abominations, that she would not disfigure her walls with them, but instead she said: —

"All right.   I need something to brighten up the walls.   I 'll like some splashes of color behind the furniture."

She brought nails and hammer.   Young Giuseppe held the stepladder.   The principal wall was well cov-

ered when Diego came in carrying an old Sicilian cart
end carved in figures of saints and angels.

"Look what I 've got — " he began, then stopped
abruptly, open-mouthed, staring at the pictures.

"Your friend," said Josie, in a mildly explanatory
tone, "is going to let us show his pictures here. Is n't
it splendid? Just the brightness we lacked."

"Oh," said Diego, stupidly.

He stared at Peter Narishkin as though he saw him
for the first time. The Russian fingered his yellow
beard.

"Maria also," he said apologetically, "has sent some
of her pictures. Small little ones that do not take up
too much room. I have friends, two Englishmen, who
meet all the guests at the Grande Hotel Vittoria.
They will send the most important tourists to see our
pictures and the beauty of your furniture will then
be discovered. Much will be sold — entirely through
the inspection, invited by my two English friends, of
the pictures of Maria Feodorovna and myself."

Diego's expression of stupor changed to one of
tragedy as a sea fog dissolves and shows a frowning
rock. He looked at Josie with hate. "You have done
this," his eyes said, "to spite me." He muttered: —

"Perhaps I can find some place to hang this cart
end."

"There, in that dim corner," said Josie, pointing.
"It will help to brighten that."

Peter Narishkin snatched up the hammer and nails.
He possessed himself of the cart end. Diego watched
them put it up without further comment.

"How good you both are," said Josie. "The walls look so much brighter."

She brushed against Diego as she passed him, and he drew away. He scowled at her beneath his beret, which he ill-manneredly wore indoors as well as out.

Josie was happy. She had got the better of Diego. In a way she had a certain control over both him and Peter Narishkin. She was very busy and a prospect of interesting work stretched before her. She would even find time to do some painting herself, would hang her pictures in the best places, and possibly excite a desire to possess them in the hearts of rich tourists. She pictured a group standing in front of one of her pictures while in far corners Diego sulked and Narishkin pulled his beard. She would be the guardian angel of Fay and Montleone. If their marriage were a success it would be due in a large part to her unflagging efforts on their behalf. She would be important. But she must have Purley Bond to support her until things were flowing smoothly. She went to the door that opened on to a paved yard where he was polishing furniture. His shirt sleeves were rolled up and his tow hair hung over his forehead.

"How are you getting on?" she asked. He was rubbing the back of one of the two carved grey-hounds supporting a console table.

"Fine. You have no idea how much dirt there was on these beasts. But I've got a pretty good shine on them now. What was the hammering?"

"Peter Narishkin. Covering the south wall with

his pictures. Diego brought a cart end, too. They help to brighten the place."

Bond straightened his back. "Josie, I believe you 're being femininely spiteful."

"No, I 'm not. I can't discover anything better in them. Come and see them for yourself."

He looked at his dirty hands. "Not like this."

"Please — I want you. Diego and Peter have gone out to the front. Varvara is overseeing the hanging of the sign. I don't want to go tagging after them alone."

She led him through the rooms where the antiques were displayed. He, too, felt proud of the way the place looked, and he agreed with her about the pictures. There was a comforting sense of intimacy between them.

In the road they found four workmen hanging a wrought-iron sign above the arching gate. Between them and Varvara a vehement discussion raged in which Peter Narishkin joined whenever there was an opening. Diego was repeating monotonously, *"Più alto — più alto."*

Two strangers joined the group as Bond and Josie appeared and were greeted with delight by Peter Narishkin. They were the two friends of whom he had told Josie. The taller was Valentine Consaul, a Montrealer, who for some years had lived in Tramontana. He was a great traveler, a big-game hunter, and his villa was the social centre of the town. He had the chin of a fighter, a smile with something feminine in it, and the blue eyes of a startled seraph. His friend, a Londoner named Field, was suave, good-looking, with an expression of boyish eagerness.

"I am going to make a properly formal call when the Conte and Contessa return," said Consaul. "I have known Montleone for years. But, in the meantime, I have come to ask you if there is anything I can do to help. Field and I are at your disposal."

Josie's color came and went. She felt suddenly awkward. She stammered: "No — I don't think so — at least — what do you think, Mr. Bond?"

"I think we 'll soon have things in order," returned Bond, stiffly.

Varvara turned from her work and said to Consaul: "Have you any Italian oaths to spare? I so badly need a few."

He smiled down at her. "I have an unlimited number. And, as I always swear in the infinitive, they 're twice as effective."

"Come, let us waste no time," she answered, and led him on one side by a pinch of his sleeve.

Josie looked after them. "Had they met before?" she asked Field.

He shrugged. "I don't think so. But she has an appraising eye, it appears. I say, Miss Froward, I wonder if you 'll help me. I 'm frightfully keen about amateur theatricals. Valentine has a private theatre, you know, and I produce a group of one-act plays for him each season. I feel sure that you can act. I 've been watching you."

"I have acted a little," she admitted. She had, in truth, taken part in the amateur theatricals of the high school of Saltport. "But I 'd be terribly nervous trying to act here. It would be so terribly different."

"I have the very part for you. I should train you. I am pretty severe, you know. Where have you acted?"

"Almost in Boston," she answered, hesitatingly.

"Oh," he said, and stared. "Well, that sounds promising. When I 've finished with you you 'll be ready to act in the very heart of Boston."

Life was moving almost too swiftly for Josie. She felt her spirit panting in the effort to keep from being submerged. Here she was in Tramontana, associating with all sorts of interesting people. She was first cousin to an Italian Contessa. She was arranging an antique shop for her titled cousin. She was opening a tea room. She was going to act in a play produced by a London actor. And she must have an eye to Purley Bond and Diego. Men were so strange and weak.

Valentine Consaul came to her side.

"May I see the antiques?" he asked.

She felt less at ease with him than with Captain Field, but she led the way indoors with pride in the way the rooms were arranged.

"Splendid!" he said, walking about with a preoccupied air. "You must come and see my things. You 'd be interested, I think. I have cabinets that belonged to a murdered Empress of Korea. I brought

them from there in a Chinese junk, myself.   And I
have some Buddhas you 'll like.   Have you met a New
Yorker named Putnam?"

"Oh, yes.   He 's very rich, is n't he?"

"Rather.   What do you suppose he did?   I had him
to a cocktail party and he admired two ebony disciples
of Confucius I have.   They 're pets of mine and I
talked quite a bit about them.   The next day he sent
me a blank check — signed by himself — and a note
bidding me fill out the check for whatever amount I
chose.   He wanted the two disciples.   Now, what do
you think of that?"   He glared at her.

Josie thought it was the most generous act she had
ever heard of, but something in Consaul's glare warned
her not to express this thought.   She said: "It was
queer, was n't it?"

"Queer!   It was beastly cheek."

"I don't think a Bostonian would have done that."

"Oh, no.   You 're quite different, I 'm sure."

He stared through the doorway at Bond who had returned to the paved yard and his polishing.   He said:
"I like the looks of your man.   The Contessa brought
him with her, did n't she?"

"He 's not a man! He 's a — "   What was it that
Fay had been calling Purley?   Oh, yes!   "He 's a scientist," she finished.

"A scientist, eh?   What particular branch?"

"Chemicals — I think."

"I 'm afraid I can't talk science to him.   Don't
know a thing about it."

"He won't mind that.   He hates talking shop."

"I'd like to be introduced."

Bond straightened his back and shook hands. "I wish," he said, "that I had some of my own furniture-cleaning mixture here. It can knock the spots off this stuff. I wonder if I could get it made up here?"

Josie looked at him forbiddingly, but Mr. Consaul seemed not to think it strange that a scientist should be interested in furniture polish.

"I have a most remarkable cleaner and polisher," he said. "Let me send you some of it."

Captain Field came up and was introduced. He at once asked Bond if he could act, and took his word for it that he could not, without question.

"Though it's easy enough to act here," he said. "It's a theatrical background. We begin to act a part as soon as we settle down in the country."

Valentine Consaul asked: "Will the Conte and Contessa be back in time for the *carnevale?*"

It was the first the newcomers had heard of a carnival. Bond disliked dressing up, and said so.

"All you need do is to throw confetti and make one of the crowd. The people of the place will provide the fun. It's really very picturesque."

Consaul put in, "We shall give a cocktail party first and start things off in the right spirit."

When they were alone again Bond observed, as he filled his pipe with a pensive air: "I like Tramontana. But I don't like — what d' you call 'em — the *forestieri*. If I could just meet the natives, I'd feel comfortable here."

"But those men are so friendly," said Josie, anxiously.

"I know. They 're real nice fellows." His tone was doleful. "But they 're just not my sort."

"Yet Mr. Consaul has traveled all over the world and you 're so interested in traveling."

"That 's so. But he 's not my sort."

"Well — do you like Captain Field?"

"Yes. He seems an agreeable young fellow. But I could n't get on with him."

Diego and Josie sat side by side on the edge of a table looking at this new, pensive, rather doleful Bond.

Diego said, "You like Mr. Putnam, don't you?"

"Well, he 's not exactly objectionable to me."

Josie said, "After all, there 's Diego and me."

"Yes," agreed Bond, regarding them pessimistically, "there 's you."

"Fay will soon be back."

"*And* Montleone." A jeering note came into Bond's voice.

"Well, I 'm absolutely happy here," said Diego, "but I don't like the way Peter Narishkin has plastered the walls with his pictures. That 's your fault, Josie."

The two began to quarrel.

CHAPTER IX

FAY and Montleone moved slowly through the crowded Corso toward the open space where those who were taking part in the procession, on this last day of the *carnevale,* were collected. She was eager to find Diego. Never before had she been separated from him for more than a day or two. Into all the passion, the dramatic change of her honeymoon in Rome, her longing for Diego had been woven like a dark thread in a bright tapestry. Her desire for him was scarcely maternal. It was highly emotional, fiercely possessive. His person held some essence from which the avid flame of her egotism was fed. Alone with Montleone she found herself weak and femininely clinging. She longed for the feeling of power that she was able to draw from the dark impervious presence of her son. She liked to think of him as her child, her little boy, her dependent, but in reality he was a well of strength to her. Her eyes searched the moving figures in the square for a sight of him.

They had arrived at lunch time from Rome and had driven straight to the Villa Benedittino. Josie had had everything prepared. Flowers in every vase. A hot luncheon, cooked by Benita, on the table. Josie had looked excited, very important. She had displayed the arrangement of antique shop and tea room with girlish pride. She had pointed out what a desirable background the pictures of Peter Narishkin made. Bond had not been there.

Montleone had been delighted with the changes worked by Josie in his old home. No thought of desecration marred his pleasure. The antique shop and the bright tea room seemed to him a vast improvement on the chill dignity of the old arrangement. Josie was a wonder of ingenuity and taste, he thought. As a woman she did not exist for him. Her clear gray eyes, her changing color, her sensitive thin body, no more attracted him than a slender palm tree holds the gaze of a panther.

But he was courteous to her. He was deferential, for he perceived that she was to be valued. She would be eager, this strange young woman, he thought, to spend the rest of her days in striving for the welfare of himself and Fay.

Fay embraced her — hugged her so that it hurt. She thought Josie nothing short of a marvel, and told her so. She was relieved that Bond did not appear at the villa. But she longed for Diego.

They pressed forward through the throng of peasants down from the hills, and the German, English, and American tourists. Shouts, laughter, passionate outbursts of expostulation and the brays of donkeys came from the square. Those in command ran here and there trying to set the procession in order. They dragged the donkeys forward, then back. They all but tore the riders from their seats. The riders were devil-may-care, but they were obedient.   They went where they were bid, and when someone gave the word to start, though having no right to do so, half the cavalcade urged their donkeys forward and disappeared into the throng on the Corso, leaving the remaining half in a sea of bewilderment.   A large blue bird in a wicker cage above a doorway burst into a loud piping which rose even above the tumult.

The donkeys were decorated with tassels, ribbons, flowers, and even vegetables.   The men wore Sicilian costumes with tasseled caps, white linen showing at the knees of their short breeches, and some had pipes in their mouths.   Some carried scythes or rakes and bundles of hay behind them.   One had great white geese tied on either side of the panniers, their wings stretched, their bills gaping in terror.   One carried behind him a pen, in which two little pigs, washed and decorated with ribbons, jostled each other and squealed plaintively.   Another carried a crate in which a flaming red-gold rooster shook his hackle, triumphant, unabashed by the confusion.   A young boy on a frisky donkey galloped here and there, while the rabbits on one pannier and the doves on the other gazed timidly through the bars of their cages.   The gay-colored skirts and kerchiefs of girls in Sicilian costume were bright in the sunshine.   The girls were anxious to look their best, smiling gravely.   Some carried distaffs and skeins of wool.   Others had their arms full of flowers or held baskets of fruit.   A small girl, with flowers above her ears, rode a diminutive donkey half-hidden in his tasseled harness.   Boys ran beside her, teasing the frightened guinea pigs in the cage in front of her. On the skirts of the crowd a donkey boy was belaboring his donkey across the face because it would not join the procession.

Fay's eyes sparkled with excitement. She could scarcely contain herself. Looking on did not satisfy her. She longed to be riding a donkey, to be in Sicilian costume herself. She almost wished, for a moment, that she had married a peasant, so that she might have taken part in the procession. Montleone's face was lighted by a smile. He pointed out this costume and that. He went to the man who had the white geese tied to his panniers and stroked their spread wings.

"Oh, but it's cruel — it's cruel!" cried Fay, suddenly. "They are suffering!"

"It will soon be over," answered Montleone, still smiling.

Her eyes sought Diego in vain. They turned back to the Corso and met the impulsive first half of the procession returning at full gallop. Men, girls, animals, and birds bounced on the backs of the galloping donkeys. Small hoofs clattered on the sunny pavement. Among the last she discovered Diego and, riding beside him, Varvara Walkonsky. They rode the sleekest, best-fed donkeys in Tramontana. They had been provided with gala Sicilian costumes in silk and velvet by Valentine Consaul, who had a store of such things. Diego's shirt, open at the throat, was snowy white, his short coat was of black

velvet. He wore the pointed Sicilian cap and held
a short pipe clenched between his white teeth. He
looked so smooth, so nonchalant and lazy, that Fay's
heart went out to him in a passion of possessive love.
She would have liked to run forward and embrace
him as he sat his donkey — let all the throng know
that he was hers.

Then she saw that Varvara, in brilliant colors,
with flowers in her bronze hair, rode beside him.

"Gian," she said, pressing his arm, "there is that
Russian girl. Does n't she look beautiful?"

Montleone had no more than a glimpse of her. He
said: "Your son looks beautiful. I scarcely saw the
girl. They will be returning. But you cannot expect me to see any other woman when you are here,
carissima."

Valentine Consaul and Captain Field were working
their way through the crowd toward them. They
shook hands with Montleone and he introduced them
to Fay. Surrounded by these three distinguished-
looking men, Fay felt herself observed by all who
waited for the procession. She saw women lean over
balconies to look at her. She saw a blonde German
family across the street fix every tranquil eye on her.
She heard an American voice behind her wonder what
countrywoman she was.

She felt intoxicated by the brilliance of her situation. All the people of Tramontana must recog-
nize her as the wife of Montleone — a Contessa. She
smiled up at the women peering over the balconies.

The peasants trooping in procession were her vassals, enjoying themselves in carnival. Every shout, every handful of confetti thrown in glittering spray above the heads of the crowd, became to her an act of homage. She was so proud and so happy that she infected all those who stood near her. Three pipers, down from the hills, drew up near by, inflating their bagpipes with wild and wistful airs.

Now the procession was passing in real earnest. Tripping, beribboned donkeys, ready to break into a gallop, grave-faced girls in brilliant skirts, smiling young men clutching their turkeys, pigs, geese, or scythes, dancing children dressed to imitate their elders or in the costume of Pierrots. Last of the riders, Diego and Varvara. A little black pig, tucked under the arm of a youth, shrieked high above the pipes as he twisted its curly tail. One of the white geese had got its wing loose and hung head down by the feet, a whirlwind of flapping. A week-old kid, white as milk, with a collar of blue ribbon, cried loudly as its tender ears were tweaked. The air was charged with cries and laughter and the music of the pipes. Flowers were flung down from balconies. Confetti rose to greet the flowers.

"There she is," said Fay, pointing to Varvara. "Is n't she striking in that costume? It just suits her. No wonder Diego admires her!"

Montleone followed the figure of Varvara with eyes shadowed by a look Fay could not understand. She had never seen that look in his eyes before. It troubled her, for she had the credulity to believe that she understood him. But her mind, even if he had confided all his thoughts to her, was unable to understand the complexities of a nature like his.

But the shadow in his eyes and the trouble in hers were soon past, driven away by the approach of the great rumbling floats that brought up the rear of the procession. The crowd broke into frenzied shouts, confetti swirled in a storm, as the first of these, decked with flowers and bearing a group of girls, their faces smiling fixedly through gilded cardboard cut in the shapes of moon and stars, came into view. It was not possible to think in the din.

Last came King Carnevale, an enormous swaying figure in grotesque trappings. Half a dozen lithe Sicilians writhed inside his inflated form. At each corner of his dais mummers kept up a ceaseless jigging and ogling of the crowd. They whirled and stamped, their eyes blank and dazed. From the float fireworks were sent up which broke, sending up rockets and filling the nostrils with the smell of powder.

A ragged old man with the face of an imbecile satyr and a trickle of saliva running over his beard danced and whirled about the float. He broke into steps of the tarantella and was all but knocked down by the ponderously moving wheels. Someone dragged him away, but he escaped and struggled back, resuming his crazy dance. The crowd closed in behind him and moved in a dense mass with the procession.

A young woman with bold eyes flung a handful of

confetti squarely in Fay's face. Valentine Consaul frowned.

"I'm so sorry," he said. "Did you mind very much?"

"Not at all," she laughed, "I'm just one of them to-day."

They too followed along the Corso, and soon they met members of the now disorganized procession galloping up and down on donkeys which seemed to have forgotten that their life was one of heavy toil. Their little hoofs clattered, red tassels bounced between their ears. The little black pig squealed frantically as his tail was twisted. The tail-twister's white teeth gleamed. The week-old kid, decked with ribbons, lay in the curve of a handsome youth's arm, crying loudly when he tweaked its ears.

Bond appeared out of the crowd and stood at Fay's side. She started. It was as though the main street of Saltport had opened up before her — the drug store, the bakery. He could not know that the forced smile she gave him was made rigid by the harsh air of Saltport. Her heart really warmed at the sight of his blunt features, his sagacious, kind look.

"Are you enjoying it?" he asked, thinking how the hard bright sunlight became her.

"With every bit of me! Isn't it gorgeous, Purley, the way these simple folks throw themselves into fêtes? Just think — they've been doing this every year for thousands of years!"

"How many twisted tails and ears in all those centuries!"

"Oh, they don't really hurt them," she declared.
"I think the birds and animals enjoy the fun as much
as the peasants."

"Just the way I enjoyed your honeymoon."

She colored. "Purley, you are a silly boy!"

But she liked his being silly. Pity him as she might,
she could not have wished him happy at this moment.

He said: "I suppose you 've seen all Josie has done.
I think she 's made a mighty fine antique shop for you
out of that old villa." He found himself desiring
praise for Josie, determined that Josie should be
valued.

Fay did not quite like his tone, but she said lightly:
"I think Josie 's wonderful." Then she added seriously: "She has told me how you have worked.
Polishing all that furniture. Helping to shift those
heavy pieces from one room to another."

"I liked working with Josie. We enjoyed ourselves — in our own way."

"I 'm so glad!" But she felt rebuffed.

Montleone, who had gone ahead with Consaul and
Field, so that Fay and Bond might talk undisturbed,
now came back to them. The Corso was becoming
deserted as the people collected in the Piazza del
Duomo. The shouts of venders of confetti and
roasted beans rose above the noise and laughter.
Now and again an explosion of fireworks subdued all
else.

Montleone shook hands with Bond. He said: "Mr.
Consaul asks us to go to his house and drink a cocktail. You will like that, Fay?"

"Purley too?"

"Yes.   He must come also."

"But I must find Diego.   I have not spoken to him yet."

"You cannot find him in that crowd without disarranging yourself."

"I'd like terribly to have just one little word with my boy."   Her tone was petulant.

Montleone shrugged.   When Fay was maternal she was a different person.   She irritated him.   He said: —

"Diego and the Russians are to come in later.   Let us join the others."   He took her arm.

She gave herself up to the pleasure of being overruled by him, but her eyes, with appeal in them, rested on Bond.

Farther along the Corso, Bond saw Diego descending a flight of stone steps on his donkey, for the admiration of a group of tourists.   He strolled forward and took the donkey by the bridle.

"Come and see your mother," he said.

Diego jogged up, smiling.

"Say, Mamma, what do you suppose Purley has called you?"

"What?"

"Mother to a donkey!"

"And so I am . . . My own precious *asinello!*" She took him in her arms and held him, kissing him on either cheek.   She must kiss him in the proper Italian way.   Women on the balcony above smiled

their approval. One flung down a handful of flowers.

Fay was supremely happy.

Valentine owned a beautiful villa and gardens in
a secluded part of the town. Here he lived with
Captain Field and a secretary, though one might have
wondered why he needed a secretary. But he collected people as he collected furniture, treasures from
Chinese temples, and rare tulips for his garden.

When Fay, Montleone, and Bond entered, Consaul
was showing a snow-white cockatoo to a group of
guests from the Grande Hotel Vittoria.

He bowed to the bird, and said courteously:
"Good morning, Connie."

The cockatoo returned the bow with a supple dip
of its crested head.

"Connie," it repeated. "Connie Consuella." Its
voice was gasping, sibilant.

Consaul bowed lower, his strange blue eyes fixed
on the bird's.

"You're very handsome," he said. "What is your
name?"

The cockatoo dipped deeply, swiftly, with a sinister flash of the eyes.

"Connie," it hissed, "Connie Consuella."

Consaul straightened himself, his face flushed, and
came to meet the three.

"I am so glad you were able to come," he said.
"Did you find your son, Contessa?"

Oh, the sweetness of that title in her ears!

"Yes. Mr. Bond found him for me. I guess you 've met Mr. Bond?"

"He and I are old friends. He and Miss Josie have been doing wonderful things with your antiques. Look here." He led her on one side. "I have a prospective customer or two for you. Of course, it 's hideously materialistic of me to thrust them on you the instant you return from your honeymoon, but — in times like these — it 's not safe to let them escape."

Fay's face became eager and businesslike.

"I should think not! We'll be real grateful for anyone you can bring round to us. I guess it won't be easy with so many rivals."

"You will have no rivals. None of the other places have such a background — such atmosphere. Then — there 's yourself. You 'll appear occasionally, I suppose, to give an air to the business."

"Oh, I intend to work all the time. I'm not afraid of work." A vision of herself drawing forth a great pan of blazing buns from the oven of the bakery blurred her eyes for a moment, made her face burn.

Consaul went on, "Then the tea room will be a great attraction. I suppose Miss Josie and Mr. Bond will stay with you."

"I 'm afraid we can't keep Purley. I wish we could. He 's just the most reliable person you can imagine."

They both looked across at Bond, who was in conversation with Mr. Putnam, the New Yorker.

"I have great hopes of Putnam," said Consaul. "He has any amount of money and he's at a loose end since his health has broken down. His only excitement is in buying things. Their room at the hotel is like a curio shop — simply crammed. How soon do you think I might take him to see your things?"

"Any time. The sooner the better. Everything is arranged. All we lack is customers. Josie is opening her tea room this afternoon. Won't you all come and take tea with me there? Then Mr. Putnam and the others could walk about and look at the things just in an informal way."

"That would be perfect. Tea suits his digestion better than cocktails. Field has ours ready now. Here comes Giovanni with the tray."

Bond looked across the room at Fay drinking with Valentine Consaul. He gave only a part of his mind to what his companion was saying. The other part brooded on Fay and the change that had come over her fortunes. She was changing into a different woman before his very eyes. He could do nothing to stop the process; she was becoming worldly — sophisticated would be the right word, he supposed. And with each gain in that, something of her old ingenuous self was lost. Something fresh and free and rather tragic, that he loved.

He listened to Mr. Putnam talking about his poor digestion. He told him that he had a formula which he believed might help him. He could have it made up at the chemist's if it were possible. Mr. Putnam was delighted and took another sip of his cocktail on the strength of this hope. Could Mr. Bond have the prescription ready for him at the tea room that afternoon? Bond promised to try, his mind all the while on Fay.

He saw her deep in conversation with Consaul. He saw Montleone, that handsome smile curving his lips, talking with two intense ladies from Washington. He heard Captain Field and a German-looking young man discussing the drama. He heard a British Vice-Consul and an elderly Scottish spinster growing heated over politics. He saw Peter Narishkin finishing the anchovy sandwiches. The Italian servant glided about, carrying a tray.

The cockatoo nodded and hissed her name for her own pleasure. The naked ebony figures, for which Mr. Putnam had sent a blank check, looked respectively credulous and doubting. Firelight twinkled on the intricate brass locks of the treasure chests of a murdered Empress of Korea. Fay talked to Consaul in clear-cut, slightly foreign accents.

"All this," thought Bond, "is as unreal to me as hell. What am I doing here? I don't belong. I 'm absolutely myself when I 'm out on the mountains or poking about the back streets, but here I 'm as unnatural as a soda fountain in a drug store." His mind dwelt, for a space, in hatred of the soda fountain in his own drug store.

As soon as possible he made his escape. He remembered a tall carved chair that he had promised Josie to polish.

There was no one in the small room at the villa
where he did his work. But he could hear Josie's
voice raised in a dreadful attempt at Italian, giving
orders to Benita.

"*Il latte non e buono. Portare* — I mean —
prego de portare freddo — no — no — not *freddo* —
fresco latte per — "

"*Si, si, si, si*" — Benita's intelligent assent rushed
forth.

Bond hung his coat on a hook, rolled up his sleeves,
and looked long at the tall chair. He did not like
the look of it at all. There was too much carving
on it. It was pretentious, theatrical. It made him
tired.

He took it by one arm, as one might take a refrac-
tory boy, and yanked it into another position. He
felt packed with spite, as Mr. Putnam was packed
with indigestion. He took the chair by the other
arm and yanked it back into its first position. He
glared at it, scratching his chin. An explosion of
fireworks rose from the Corso.

He walked up and down the little room, bristling
with spite, like a caged tiger. He looked out of a
deep window and saw the sharp mountain peaks bristling together. He looked out of another window
and saw the blue sea far below, level, sapphire blue,
flat as a carpet on the floor of the deep. Again he
felt the surge of jealous spite. He thought he should
like to knock the heads of the mountains together —
knock them into a cocked hat — leave them in a
disheveled pointless heap. He should like to gather up

the blue sea — roll it up like a flexible Chinese carpet and stuff it down the gaping throat of Etna.

If he were an artist, now he could paint a picture
worth seeing. Splash over the canvas all the longing
and spite that hurt him. He envied those young
creatures, Diego and Josie, who could translate their
emotions into trees and clouds.

Josie had not painted anything since her discred-
ited attempt to finish Diego's picture. She had been
too hurt and angry. But now she had a canvas prepared and it stood waiting her rare leisure, propped
against the wall. On a chair lay her palette, her
brushes, and a box of paints.

Bond picked up the palette and thrust his thumb
through it. He selected the largest brush and, as-
suming a fervent pose, surveyed his reflection in a
tall Venetian mirror. He felt pleased with his reflection. He could not have believed that the accoutre-
ments of art would so well become him. He rum-
pled his thick tow-colored hair and scowled. Portrait
of the Artist — by Himself! If he were to grow a
beard and wear a smock he would look as much an
artist as Peter Narishkin. What would life have been
to him if he had been an artist? Perhaps Fay would
have loved him.

He turned to the tubes of paint and began to
squeeze brilliant blobs on to the palette. He felt as
though he were back in his drug store mixing a prescription. He dragged Josie's easel from a corner
and set the bare canvas on it.

On the left he plastered a flaming spot of vermilion.

That was his love for Fay. Above the vermilion spot he stroked long gray and purple arches. These represented life in Saltport. A frenzy of blue and green and ochre symbolized the cruise from New York to Naples. These, the bristling mountains of Sicily. That round dark hole the smouldering crater of Etna. This sulphurous, hateful spot of yellow the passion of Fay for Montleone. These swirling, chaotic curves his own troubled emotions. He worked long and fervently, oblivious of the sounds in the villa, the echoes of carnival from the street.

He had a good deal of paint on himself. He stood back from the painting, at gaze. Surely this was a picture! It meant more to him than any of Peter Narishkin's. It had more sense than some of Diego's. He understood every bit of it. He liked the looks of it. So this was what it was to be an artist! He stood on his strong legs, as though he would never tire, admiring his first artistic effort.

He was disturbed by a loud laugh from Josie. She had come up behind him and was staring at the canvas.

"Well, I never!" she exclaimed.

"What do you think of it?" he asked. He was not hurt by her laughter, for it had more of the quality of hysteria in it than derision.

She stopped laughing and looked at him.

"How handsome you look with your hair like that," she said. "I'd no idea you had so much of it."

"If I grew a beard I'd be a passable-looking artist, don't you think so?"

"I like you as you are." She examined the picture again. "Is it symbolic?"

"Yes. It represents ten years in the life of a druggist."

"It 's very interesting. I 'm in earnest. I heard of an artist who used to give children his brushes and paints to play with just to see what they would do. Sometimes he would get ideas from them. I believe I 'll have to do that with you. We might work together, eh?"

Abstractedly she took the brush and palette from his hand and gazed intently at the canvas. She began to make little dabs at it. She began to draw it out of chaos into some sort of form. He stood watching her passively for a moment, then he took the brush from her hand.

"No," he said, firmly. "No, no, no."

She laughed and turned red, annoyed at repeating herself. She returned the palette to him.

"I 'll tell you what we 'll do," she said. "We 'll put it in a conspicuous place in the showroom and see what happens."

He carried the easel and she his picture, and placed them in a corner of the principal room. The light was not too bright. There were no other pictures near it, for Peter Narishkin's hung on the opposite wall. Josie smiled a little savage smile as she considered the insult she was doing the Russian. She and Bond stood together looking at the rooms they had arranged, with deep satisfaction. Surely money could be wrung from the prosperous travelers with such a display as this.

"Those pictures of Peter Narishkin's make a nice bright background for the furniture," she said maliciously.

"Yes," agreed Bond. "And mine looks first-rate too. Painting is sort of like putting up prescriptions, anyway. You find out what's wrong with your subject and mix him up a dose."

Josie danced through the arched doorway into the tea room.

"This is where I shine," she said. "I've got delicious little cakes made. And sugar cookies. And doughnuts. They'd melt in your mouth."

"I wish you'd give me one. It would seem like Saltport again."

"Stay and have tea with us. Our first afternoon! Fay is bringing some people. Benita's grandson distributed our little notice cards all over the place. I'm so excited that I curl right up inside."

"And you saw nothing of the carnival?"

"This is carnival enough for me."

"Josie, I must paint a picture symbolic of your life."

"Not yet — wait till it's more beautiful."

"I think it's beautiful now."

He was so embarrassed after saying this that he hurried back to the little workroom and began to scrape the chair, keeping out of sight when he heard a babble of voices in the tea room.

Josie looked in at him. "Are n't you coming to tea?" She spoke severely, with an odd, possessive air.

"I hate tea. Just bring me a couple of doughnuts here."

"But you ought to come out. It's good fun. They're making a great fuss over the rooms."

But he went on scraping the chair.

"No. I don't get on with those folks. Besides, I'm dirty."

She brought him a tray with a medley of cakes and a pot of coffee to himself. She set it before him brusquely. Again she had that possessive air.

"Coffee!" he exclaimed. "Now I call that kind of you, Miss Froward."

"Miss Froward! Why not Josie?"

"Well — Josie."

She looked at him curiously. "Why did you say my life was beautiful?"

He bit into the succulent circle of a doughnut. He wished she would leave him alone with it. He answered: —

"I suppose because you're always doing things for others."

The brightness left her face. "Oh . . . Is that all? I don't think there is any beauty in that. I do it to please myself."

She flew back to the showroom, eager to hear what was being said of the arrangement there. It and the tea room were both nearly full of people. The announcement cards handed about by Benita's younger grandson had been effective. Fay had drawn up her party, with Mr. Putnam as the central figure. He stood there, a sick man, looking rather vacantly about the room, wondering if there might be something to please his fancy.

They stood before an inlaid cabinet which was the most expensive piece of furniture in the room.

"Isn't this a wonderful old piece?" Fay said. "It breaks my heart to part with it. It has been in the family for generations."

"Sell all the other things first, then," he drawled. "Fix things so you won't have to sell it. I believe in being sentimental. I built up a fortune on sentiment."

"Oh, but I can't afford to be sentimental!" Suddenly he seemed rather sinister to her. She did not like him. "This piece must be sold — and soon, too."

He turned toward the pictures.

"Who painted them?" he asked.

"Our Russian friend — Peter Narishkin. They make a lovely colorful background for the furniture, don't they?" Now she echoed Josie, as she echoed everyone with whom she came in contact, but all the while she was inexorably herself.

Peter Narishkin, who had been standing in a corner stroking his beard, now came eagerly forward.

Mr. Putnam said: "I like this new impressionistic art. I don't know what they're driving at and I don't try to find out. It's a real rest."

"That one," cried Peter Narishkin, pointing passionately to the largest picture, "is a young girl bathing at dawn, in the sea."

"I 'm glad you told me," returned Mr. Putnam. "I sort of thought it was an old lighthouse on the New England coast. But I 'm easy to convince. I can make out her two legs now and I suppose that globular object is her left breast. But where is the right one?"

"Behind her!" shouted Narishkin.

"I daresay. Anything seems possible to that young lady." He turned toward the picture on the easel. "Did you paint that one, too?"

"No, no, I have not seen it before. It is too terrible!"

Fay looked at it dubiously. "It must be one of Diego's. How very remarkable it is — "

"Is it symbolic?" asked Valentine Consaul.

"I will find Diego and ask him."

"I like it," said Mr. Putnam. "I like it better than any of the others. I see that it is still wet, but perhaps it is finished. I may look at it again. However, I 'm not wanting any pictures just now, but I 'm shipping some furniture to New York and I would n't mind picking up another chair or two."

He went over to a carved, child's chair.

"This is a comical little chair. It would just suit my small granddaughter. What do you ask for it?"

Montleone laughed. "That was mine when I was a little boy. It was given to me after I had an illness. I was set in it when I was too weak to walk. Ah, how I loved it! I remember sitting in it while my old nurse knelt in front of me feeding me *zabaione*."

Fay could just see him with his beautiful little face pale from suffering. She could see his little hands on the carved arms of the sturdy chair. At that time she had been in the young ladies' seminary, growing toward the day of her marriage with Palmas. She could not bear to part with the chair. She laid her hand caressingly on it.

"I'm sorry, Mr. Putnam," she said, with sad dignity, "but I cannot part with this chair. I — I had not known that it was Gian's."

Montleone said angrily: "Of course we will sell it! It is a very good little chair and would greatly become your small granddaughter. We should be glad to take five hundred lire for it."

"Never — never!" Fay stood before the chair guarding it.

Mr. Putnam looked from one to the other. "Well — what are you going to do about it?"

Mrs. Putnam put in: "I don't think the Contessa should be asked to part with the chair, Calvin. I can see how much it means to her. I'd feel just the same way if you'd been sick in it, as a little boy."

Her husband gave her a tender look. "Very well, very well. I guess we can find something for Nancy Anne she'll like just as well."

"I saw a fine old chair here the other day," said Consaul. "I am sure it would interest Mr. Putnam. I wonder what has become of it."

"Purley is scraping it in the workroom," answered

Josie. "I'll get him to bring it in." She hurried away, afraid that they might miss a sale.

Bond appeared almost immediately, carrying the chair. He set it down in their midst and looked at the prospective purchasers with a defiant air. With his tow-colored hair on end, his blue overalls, his rugged face and bare forearms smudged, he looked a hardy workman indeed.

"Now isn't that a beauty?" cried Fay.

"If you mean Mr. Bond, I agree with you," answered the New Yorker. "To my mind he's the most attractive article in this room. If I could just purchase his digestion and his nerves, you might ask me any price you like, Contessa."

The Conte and Contessa and their supporters were all smiles. They closed in about Mr. Putnam, and before he was released he had bought not only the chair but the cabinet, and, because of something in the way Peter Narishkin pulled at his beard, one of his pictures.

Diego and Varvara entered the room just in time to see this purchase effected. Diego's brow became black.

"This is Josie's doing," he thought. "If it hadn't been for her, one of my pictures would have been sold." He had painted three since coming to Tramontana, all of them free from the controlling touch of Josie. He only cared about selling them because he wanted to buy something beautiful for Varvara.

They stood together, in their Sicilian costumes, framed in the stone doorway. They were a haughty, half-sullen pair, holding themselves aloof from the people in the room, feeling a cool dislike of the chattering voices that filled the tea shop. They stood in the doorway motionless, wanting to be admired for their beauty, paid homage for their aloofness. But all those inside had already seen them on the donkeys. They had only a passing glance for them — all but Montleone.

His shadowed gaze rested on Varvara, as though something in her laconic acceptance of life pleased him. She was experienced in life, he felt. The only person in the room who was experienced, except himself and Valentine Consaul. All the rest were children.

A weight was on his chest. He felt suddenly stifled. He would have liked to sweep all these people out of his house — all these pawing, appraising, tea-guzzling people. He had a sudden hideous vision of his future. . . . Always standing by, always watching, smiling encouragement, while loathsome tourists pawed his furniture, bargained for it, took it away, until every bit of it was gone, and his house was filled again with the furniture of some other broken-down nobleman. It was not even his house. It belonged to a swine whom he could not have brought himself to touch. He himself was only here on sufferance — the husband of a strange American woman. For, in this moment, Fay seemed strange to him. Strange and overpowering in her height, her vitality, her savage, childlike delight in new experiences. Varvara's acquiescence, the slumberous indolence in her eyes, drew his unease as a wave draws the scattered shells and driftwood.

She was like a wave, he thought, in her softness and her indolent power. He wondered if young Diego loved her. . . .

"So you are going?" he said, a smile curving his lips, as the Putnams advanced toward him to say good-bye. "I am very glad that you are interested in what we have. You will come again some day?"

He bent and kissed Mrs. Putnam's short, manicured fingers. Her rings would have paid for his house and all that was in it.

CHAPTER X

THE spring advanced and with it the sunburned tide of tourists. Yellow-haired, red-faced Germans climbed the mountain paths or talked fluently in guttural Italian to the guide who conducted them over the ruins of the Teatro Greco. They bargained for elaborate tablecloths in the little embroidery shops and bought German newspapers. Americans, the female sex predominant, found out more about Tramontana in a week than its inhabitants in a lifetime. They bought embroidered bags and walking sticks and American magazines. British tourists, the men with a clean-cut, well-bred air of wearing their tweeds not to be achieved by males of any other country; their women, without style, but with the air of good pals, strode in the direction of the sea and filled the tea shops at four o'clock. Honeymooning Italian couples from Northern cities took snaps of each other astride donkeys or broke off branches of almond blooms or picked anemones and scattered them again. Here and there a French provincial family might be seen, the husband declaiming in precise tones, one arm extended towards Etna, the wraps of his wife and daughter hanging on the other and the women on his words. Bareheaded Tramontana youths, traces of Saracen or Greek showing in the sombre dignity of

their profiles, lounged everywhere, eager to pick
acquaintance with rich American girls. They did no
work at all, being provided for by the embroidery
making of their mothers and sisters.

Every day the sun on the Piazza del Duomo became brighter. Sicilian youths lounging on the stone
seats faced its reflection unblinkingly, but dark gog-
gles began to adorn the faces of the tourists. The
man outside the door of the marionette theatre
shouted to passers-by to enter and see the exploits
of the great Orlando. Every afternoon on the roof
of the Hotel Flora, a dancer in Sicilian costume
whirled and bounded in the tarantella for the delight
of those who drank tea. Tourists who were explor-
ing the Teatro Greco left the ruin and gathered in little groups on the road, overlooking the roof of the
Flora to watch the agile leaping.

As the weeks passed and the season reached its
height, the four travelers from Saltport were drawn
into the life of Tramontana, as drops of water into a
sponge. The antique shop and the tea room were
successes above all hope. The romance of Fay's marriage to Montleone, his romantic and dignified presence, her peculiar beauty, attracted many people out
of curiosity. The Putnams, Valentine Consaul, and
Captain Field were all good friends. Among them
they met everyone of importance who came to the
town, and they were sure to mention the delightful
antique shop of the Montleones and the delicious
teas offered by Miss Froward. There was no im-
portunity to buy. The Conte or the Contessa

walked about with one — he talking, with an air of
gentle reminiscence, about the pieces; she, in a tone
of almost passionate reluctance to part with them.
The effect was to imbue the casual loiterer with a determination to possess one of these treasures. Before the season was half over, every piece of furniture in the villa worth selling (with the exception of
the child's chair, to which Fay still clung) had been
sold and had by degrees been replaced by other furniture. The newly acquired pieces were so skillfully
introduced that they had the appearance of having
been there for many years. A motor car — as antique
as some of the furniture — was bought, and Montleone
and Diego journeyed to quite distant places — any
place where they heard there was a chance of buying
a piece of furniture, embroidery, old church candle-
sticks, miniatures, snuffboxes, fans, or antique jewelry.
Varvara often went with them on these trips. She
had a gift for buying things at the lowest possible
figure.

Fay did not altogether like Varvara's going off in
this intimate way with her husband and her son, but
she soon discovered that better bargains were made,
and these she could not resist. Once she accom-
panied them herself, but the very exuberance and
force of her person, the gleam in her strange eyes, sent
the price up as certainly as water boils over fire.

Sometimes when she woke in the early morning,
lying in the great carved bed with Montleone's dark
head against her breast, hearing the shouts and songs
of men going to work, the laughter of women and

boys, the braying of donkeys, and thought of the
new day before her, she could scarcely believe that
she was she.   The old life in Saltport seemed remote
as a dream, and yet there was a strange unreality about
the new life, as though she were a figure in a painted
picture or a marionette in a play.   The bristling
mountain peaks, the painted pavilion of Etna, were
the scene on the drop curtain, the staring tourists
her audiences.   She told herself that she was extravagantly happy, but sometimes at these moments of
early morning she felt extravagantly unreal.

When she was up and dressed, all was reality and
action.   There was no sloth in her.   The others were
swept along by her without either desire or will to resist.

Josie's tea room kept her almost constantly busy.
She became proficient in the Italian of the kitchen;
she baked as much or more than she had ever done
in Saltport.   Sometimes, when she was heated and
tired, she grew angry and told herself that she had
escaped from one kind of slavery into another.   In
the evening she was too tired to enjoy anything that
required energy.   It was still too cold to sit in the
garden at night.   She would stroll along the Corso by
herself at twilight and watch the goats being milked
in the little square before the Church of San Giovanni.   Diego liked fresh goat's milk, and sometimes
she carried a small jug with her and had it filled for
him.

She saw a good deal of Bond.   He had always had

a liking for old furniture and had kept the Colonial pieces belonging to his mother in good order. He got a book on cleaning and polishing and spent a large part of his time in the paved yard outside the kitchen and in his workroom. Josie would come to the window of the kitchen and hand him out hot sugar cookies or doughnuts, which he would devour hungrily. Sometimes he would make her feed them to him so that they should not be contaminated by his oily fingers. Josie rather liked doing that. It pleased her to see his coarse yellow hair and the blue of his eyes at close quarters. She liked the way he snapped at the food like a jocular dog. There was something fine and unquestioning in his fidelity, she thought, rather like that of a faithful animal.

He had sold his business and had come forth to see the world, and here he was polishing furniture for Fay (the wife of another man) in the yard behind a shabby Sicilian villa. Yet he questioned his position less than any of the others. It was his desire to see Fay happy. To see her established in whatever fabulous form of life she chose. When he had done his part toward the accomplishment of this, then he would set out.

He had made one firm friend, and that was Mr. Putnam. He liked Bond so well that a day seldom passed that he did not come and sit awhile with him and watch him work. He talked to him about his ailments, and Bond listened with sympathetic concentration as he rubbed and polished. He told Mr.

Putnam of all the cases of distressed digestions he could remember in his drug business and of the various remedies which had proved efficacious.

Mr. Putnam, clasping a thin knee in his thin hands, would watch Bond's muscular body bent double and wonder how he would ever straighten himself after being so long in this posture. But Bond would straighten himself and stand erect, oily and nonchalant, gazing down at the New Yorker with his kind expression.

"You should have been a doctor, Mr. Bond," he said. "You 're just wasted in the life you lead. I never have a talk with you but I feel better for it. Why, as far as I can make out, you 're doctoring this old furniture. You 're a born medical man."

Bond grunted acquiescence. "My father was a doctor. And his father before him. The Bonds have mostly been doctors. I could n't stick it out."

Fay's gratitude lapped him about like a summer sea. She introduced him to everyone as "our dearest friend, Purley Bond." Behind his back she spoke of him as a scientist, and he was so shy that he rarely gave her away. She was not ashamed of his being a druggist, but truth was congenitally distasteful to her. Montleone was friendly towards him, almost too demonstratively grateful for what he did. But Bond liked him, though he was uncomfortable when left alone with him. He would have liked to hear of the strange adventures he was sure Montleone had had, but they just could not talk together. Yet Bond could talk with Mr. Putnam about his dyspepsia (which greatly bored him) by the hour. He was often puzzled by the complexities of his life.

There was much beside business to engage their attention that spring. There was a lively social interest in the newcomers, and one after another those who lived in the principal villas gave entertainments for them. Teas, musical evenings, with frequent dinners at the Hotel Santa Lucia with the Putnams, and a dance afterwards to the music of the hotel orchestra. Fay found herself clasped in the embrace of Sicilian youths no older than Diego. Her eyes glowed with a becoming exhilaration. But she never neglected her prosperous countrymen, and many a dance resulted in the sale of a piece of furniture or an amber necklet.

She remembered faces, she was sympathetic. She appeared self-forgetful, but she never forgot herself. She had a deep, mysterious, almost barbarous look. Her thoughts were egotistically childlike. She learned Italian with more ease than either Josie or Diego and was soon able to make herself understood by those members of Tramontana society who had no English. She imitated Montleone's accent and his supple impassioned gestures so well that an observer might have taken her for an Italian.

She was tireless, with the bottled-up energy of half a lifetime. She would stand and talk to visitors to the antique gallery until her late lunch, which she would often snatch, still standing, in a corner of Bond's workroom. The afternoons would be still busier, for tourists took no siesta. She would rush to

her room and dress, — painting her mouth the color
of a pomegranate, — and hurry to a tea in the villa
of some new acquaintance. She and Montleone
would go out to dinner and then dance at one of the
hotels till nearly morning. But she was dressed and
arranging her showrooms at nine, while he still slept.

She sought out a visiting Neapolitan singing master
and had him test her voice. He said that what it
needed was exercise, not rest. She might accomplish wonders under his tuition. He would be two
months in Tramontana.

She took three lessons a week from him, and rose
an hour earlier to practise. Montleone, hearing these
early morning scales, drew the bedclothes over his
head, his fine lips curled petulantly.

One evening Consaul heard her sing some Negro
spirituals. He begged her to sing between two of
the one-act plays which Captain Field was producing
in his private theatre. She agreed, and from that
time the sound of "All God's Chillun" or "Swing
Low, Sweet Chariot" was heard in the Villa Benedittino at every moment when she could escape from
her customers.

The night of the entertainment she put on so much
dark powder that she was of a mulatto hue. She
wore a flame-colored dress and stood facing the cosmopolitan audience with the self-assurance with
which she had faced a Baptist Church social in Saltport. She was a success and got so much applause
that Captain Field's next play opened on a flat feeling and he cursed Consaul for the innovation.

Josie took part in the Irish play. She could not
act well even for an amateur, but there was an intensity, a girlish wistfulness, about her that pleased
the uncritical audience, and, with her American accent, gave a better imitation of Irish than most English
amateurs.

From the moment of this success Fay considered
herself the leader of Tramontana society — the most
important woman in it, in any case. She had beauty.
She could sing. She danced beautifully. She could
attract attention anywhere. She was the Contessa
di Montleone.

There were other titled people in Tramontana.
There was an elderly Duca, but he was conservative,
seldom moving outside his own dull little circle.
There was a titled Englishwoman, but she was a semi-
invalid and she too belonged to the Duca's circle.
Fay openly ignored them, but secretly she resented
them.

Up and up she soared. She had neither the staff
nor the social knowledge necessary for giving dinner
parties, but her care-free musical evenings became a
feature of Tramontana society. No visitor had been
many days in the town before hearing of them, and
invitations were eagerly sought for. It was easy to
get an invitation. She asked everyone, so that the
rooms were thronged. The evening began with a
programme in the preparation of which she was as-
sisted by Valentine Consaul. He had a shrewder
knowledge of her former background than any other
of her new acquaintances. She interested and

amused him.   There was a flirtatious passage between
them.   Guests of the hotels who were musical were
asked to perform at her evenings.   She panted after
any visiting celebrity.

She patronized an orchestra composed of young
men, whose principal meal of the day was often the
substantial supper she provided.   They played clas-
sical music.   They played for the dancing.   One of
them sang like an angel and one of them danced the
tarantella.   Their instruments were mandolins and
guitars.

In May, before the close of the season, she gave a
fancy-dress dance, the largest affair of the kind ever
given in Tramontana.   The house and garden seethed
with people in extravagant and grotesque costumes.
She herself appeared in the dress of a red Indian princess, with two black braids reaching to her waist and
embroidered moccasins on her feet.   She looked so
startlingly natural in this costume that people, to
whom she was a mystery, began to believe that she
was pure Indian.

It was at this dance that Mr. Putnam fell on the
polished floor and broke his leg, which made it necessary for him to extend his stay at the Santa Lucia.

The tourist season was now over, except for cheap
excursions from Germany.   British owners of villas
were closing them and returning home.   It was a
good thing that a time of rest had come, for Fay had
grown suddenly tired and was extraordinarily thin.
She began to realize that she had been living under a
continued strain.

The sudden access of heat at the end of May, the retreat of visitors, the half-mad flowering in the garden, as though flowers, in a delirium of desire, struggled against the threat of advancing drought, presented Tramontana in a new light to Fay. She felt half afraid of it, yet languorously surrendered herself to it. This was the Tramontana of which she was to become a part.

She realized that she and Montleone had of late seen less and less of each other. He had several times shown irritation at the crowding of strangers into the villa. He had twice hurried past customers, in the very act of buying, with a scowl instead of a smile. He had stood, his fine lips curved ironically, while two ladies from Michigan had held the brocaded hangings of his mother's bed toward the light to look for moth holes. Yet, when Fay had whispered to him, "Would you sooner not sell it? I can easily put them on to something else?" his face had quivered with resentment, and he had muttered, "Sell it certainly. I shall be glad when all is sold. I hate the things."

He hated the things to be sold. And he hated the buyers. He sneered at the grossness of the Germans, the stupidity of the Britons, the greed of the Americans. Sometimes his face assumed the wild and restless expression it had had when she first saw him at Teneriffe. Then she turned from him with a baffled feeling. She realized that he had depths which her direct and uncomplex nature could not fathom.

An Irishman named Darragh lived in a dilapidated

villa far up the mountain side beyond the Narishkins.
He drank a good deal, but never lost his head. His
one pleasure was gambling. He hated the society of
women and none, except his Italian servant, entered
the house. Montleone went more and more often
there. Darragh belonged in spirit to Paris, where he
longed to return — away from the dullness of this
Tramontana where he was stuck. He and Montleone
talked of Paris. They were usually joined by the
Mayor of Tramontana and a young German count,
who, for some reason, seemed reluctant to return to
either Germany or France. They played, and sometimes Montleone won, but more often he lost.

Now Fay went to a garden seat and stretched herself out on it. The Villa Benedittino had retired
into the somnolent state out of which she had roused
it. Looking through the branches of trees and the
feverish rush of bloom, Fay saw its bulk rise, dark
with old memories, unchanged by all the peering, chattering tourists that had thronged it in the
past months. The doves, coral-footed, hovered or
strutted about the open space by the door. Great
bunches of cyclamen and scarlet geraniums flamed
against the sunlight. Honeysuckle, clambering
everywhere, made the air heavy with its scent. Over
the trellis, above the seat where she lay, white and
purple wistaria hung its generous plumes. An almond
tree that grew at one end of the seat, pushing its
branches up through the wistaria, was itself a subject
of the amorous advances of a climbing red rose, that

twisted about its branches, pressed its way into every crook, and flung out the passion of its dusky flowers to the topmost twig.

Fay reached up and took an almond from the tree, pulled off its soft green sheath, and met her strong teeth in the sweet bitterness of the kernel. Her sleeveless dress exposed her arms of an Indian brownness. She wore no stockings, and her blouse was so thin as to show the warm brown flesh beneath. She lay with the almond kernel in her mouth, watching the lizards dart in and out of a dark crack in the pavement. A flowerpot, turned upside down, had become the citadel of an army of ants. In and out from under it they scrambled in excursions and raids. tottering under loads of provisions or spoil, sometimes emerging from the hole at the top to survey the surrounding landscape. It was like the tourist season in Tramontana, Fay thought. "Time to close up shop," she thought, and she stretched out her sandaled foot to upset the flowerpot.

But Josie was coming through the garden at that moment and exclaimed: "Oh, Fay, don't! I call it mean to upset all their work."

Fay hesitated, her foot dangling. "I don't want to see anything being busy," she said.

"Don't look at them, then." She took Fay's ankle in her hand and replaced the long narrow foot beside its fellow. She stood looking down at Fay, thinking that happiness and the new life had not been kind to her looks. Her cheeks were hollow and fine lines

Josie had never seen before gathered at the corners of her eyes. Her mouth looked tired, as though the lips had been forced to speak and to smile when they should have been folded together in repose. But perhaps it was the hardness of the light that accentuated the lines.

Josie, on the contrary, had improved in appearance. Her weariness had been physical. Since Diego had cast aside her dominance over his work, as a snake sloughs its undesired skin, her interest in him had gradually faded. He no longer fascinated her by his mere cat-like, indifferent presence. Yet absorption in another was necessary to her, and her thoughts now turned to Bond.

She sat down on the garden path cross-legged, and picked up one of the small oranges that lay scattered about. She tore it apart, exposing its purplish-red insides, and began to eat it. She tried to eat it delicately, but the juice would run over her hands.

Fay thought: "What an awkward girl Josie is! She never thinks of how she is doing things — how she is appearing to others. She never tries to attract a man. Strange that women should be so different."

Josie said, "There is something I have been wanting to ask you, Fay."

"Yes? What is it?" She hoped Josie was not going to ask for a salary. It would be rather unfair to her, she thought, because it had all been a wonderful experience for Josie, who would never have got out of Saltport but for her.

Josie asked slowly: "Have you really made much

money? Is this going to be a paying concern? I hear that bad times are coming."

"Oh, I'm not worrying about bad times."

"Do you know how much you've made?"

"I've paid the rent, and all expenses, and I've given the rest to Gian to put into the bank. I have n't seen the books lately. Italian figures are so hard to make out."

Josie looked startled. She had done the bookkeeping for the bakery, done it efficiently, but Fay had taken the new business into her own hands.

"Have you kept any books?" she asked.

"No." Fay spoke haughtily, but she was embarrassed. "Well, I kept books in a kind of way. I jotted down sales, and of course I know pretty well what the expenses have been. But Gian has attended to the business of banking. It was impossible for me to do that, not knowing much Italian."

"Oh, well, I suppose it's all right. But it's not the way Uncle Richard looked after his business."

"Gian is perfectly capable. He's as anxious as we are for things to succeed. I'll tell you what, Josie — you just run up to our room and you'll find the pass book in the upper left-hand corner of the small chest of drawers. It's pushed under the paper at the bottom of the drawer."

"But what would Montleone think of me touching his things?"

Fay gave a shrug and spread the fingers of her left hand. "Oh, he's up at that Irishman's house. I don't know what he sees in him. I dislike the man, myself. I suppose he 's the kind of man other men find amusing. One thing about Gian — he never drinks a drop too much."

Josie threw the orange peel among some bushes and wiped her fingers on the hem of her cotton skirt. In a few minutes she returned with the bank book.

Fay took it and frowned over the figures.

"Their sevens and their threes are a crime," she muttered. "Let 's see. Just where are we? Oh, I 'm looking at the wrong date. No — why, Josie — " she stared at Josie, startled. "Gian has n't been to the bank for nearly two weeks — "

"Did you give him money to deposit?"

"Certainly. Last Saturday morning there was four thousand lire. And at the beginning of the week — almost as much. Say, Josie, what do you suppose it means?" Her tired eyes looked anxiously into Josie's. They had been intimate too long for Fay to attempt to hide anything from Josie now.

"Well," said Josie slowly, "he must just have forgotten to go to the bank. I suppose he 's put the money out of sight some place in his room. But it 's very careless of him, is n't it?"

"Careless! It 's perfectly terrible." Her tone was tragic. "Josie — do you suppose Gian 's been gambling with the money? I know perfectly well that they play for money at that Darragh's, but I never thought it amounted to anything. Darragh is as poor as a church mouse."

Josie was quivering with anger. She saw it all.

They had worked, they had slaved, and Montleone squandered what they earned. What a fool Fay was! A vain, egotistical, silly woman. Josie would like to see the man who would hoodwink her like that. She clenched her hands and looked fixedly at Fay. Fay suddenly remembered a night when Josie had sat in the room behind the bakery, her cheeks grotesquely painted by Diego. She had worn the same fixed stare then. Fay burst out laughing.

"It's a good thing you can laugh," said Josie savagely.

Fay snatched up the pass book and again perused it. She turned pale when she saw the irregularity and the small amounts of the later deposits. Montleone had begun by being conscientious, but he had soon desisted and was now apparently making no pretense of banking what she gave him. What did he expect her to say to that? Did he think she would take that sort of thing lying down? She, an American woman, brought up as the equal, even the superior, of man. All that beautiful furniture! What she had gone through to dispose of it to the best advantage! And now this paltry sum in the bank. . . .

She rose from the seat, in her hurry knocking over the inverted flowerpot, sending a thousand ants scattering in all directions. The lizards, which had been basking in the sun, slid in one darting movement into their crannies. She strode the full length of the garden, scattering the doves at the other end. Her eyes blazed. She walked feverishly up and down the paved walk between the bright beds of cyclamen

and campanula, under the scented plumes of the wistaria, as she had raged up and down the little sitting
room in Saltport that had smelled of hot bread and
pastry.

Josie sat looking at her, saying nothing, thinking
of how hard Fay had worked in the past months, of
how Bond had scraped, rubbed, and polished one
piece of furniture after another, of the innumerable
tea cakes, doughnuts, and scones she had made.   The
icing — enough to have whitened the villa, she
thought.   And the proceeds were to go into Darragh
pockets.

She heard the bell above the door in the wall clang.
She saw Benita hobbling to open it.   Montleone came
into the garden.   She ran softly to the other end of
the terrace and hid herself in a little garden house
that seemed to be sinking beneath its weight of wistaria.

Fay stood where she was, her hands clenched, facing Montleone as he approached her smiling.   He
was bareheaded.   The alternate sunlight and leaf
shadows flickered over his face, curiously changing
his expression at every step, as though his thoughts,
bright and dark, were suddenly made palpable.   He
had a complete, a finished look.   He was like a fine
piece of sculpture, definite, eloquent in all its lines.

Watching him draw near, Fay was startled by the
consciousness that she was afraid of him.   At that
moment he looked like a stranger to her.   And what
was he, after all, but a stranger?   She had first met

him only a few months before. The dark inter-
course of their passion had not revealed him to her.
He was of another world. She had no equipment
with which to face him.

In another illuminating flash she remembered that
she had been afraid of her first husband, Richard
Palmas. She remembered the shrinking with which
the sallow-faced baker could inspire her when he
was angered, which had indeed been seldom. She
had been so young when he married her — a big
child. She had feared him partly because he was so
much older. Was she afraid of Montleone partly because of his youth? This view of herself filled her
with distaste — a tall, lithe, high-tempered woman,
afraid of those two men who had possessed her, she
taller than either, fiercer, more greedy for power.

Her hands unclenched. She felt tired all over.
She looked at him piteously and said: —

"Gian, what have you been doing with all the
money I have given you? I 've looked in the pass
book and you 've scarcely deposited anything lately.
It 's perfectly awful. I don't know what to say."

The smile faded from his lips.

"You look in my private book?" he exclaimed. "I
do not care to have you do that. Never fear, I shall
put plenty of money in the bank."

"But what have you done with all the money I
have given you?"

"I have put much of it into the bank. You have
seen the book?" He spoke laconically, half turning
away from her.

She went swiftly to where the pass book lay on the bench. She opened it, with a feverish fluttering of the leaves, and held the page, on which the last entries were made, under his nose. He looked at its whiteness, glaring at him in the sun, with a blinking of his black eyelashes. Then he pointed to one of the entries.

"You see — on the eighth — seven hundred lire. On the fifteenth one thousand lire — "

"One thousand! When I gave you two thousand, three hundred!"

"Then on the sixteenth" — he proceeded coolly — "another deposit. This time — I cannot see the figures. The sun dazzles me. Let us sit on the bench in the shade and talk quietly, *carissima*."

They sat down, she hunched in one corner, her hands clasped between her knees, he in the other, his head bent over the book.

"It 's no use," she said brokenly. "You 've been deceiving me, Gian. I know exactly what you 've been doing. You 've been taking the money I 've made and you 've been gambling with it up at that perfectly detestable Irishman's villa. Oh, it 's too cruel! I could n't have believed it of you!" She broke into loud sobs.

He made no attempt to pacify her. He sat with the book in his hand studying the figures. When she had become quieter he said: —

"You are not reasonable. You have not looked in the other column. Here, you see, are entries for our expenses. Here is the check for the rent. Here is

another for the car. And a little later — repairs to
the car."

"Yes," she returned in a choking voice, "and what
do they amount to compared to what I gave you to
deposit? You 've gambled with that money, Gian,
and there 's no use in denying it. Oh, I 've never
been up against anything like this before! None of
the menfolks of my family have ever gambled. The
very word made my family shudder."

He looked at her curiously, trying to imagine what
her family — her "menfolks" — had been.

"My first husband," she went on, "deposited every
cent he could spare as regularly as Saturday came
round."

"He did?" Montleone spoke politely. He was
glad she had ceased her noisy crying, but he wished she
would not look so disheveled, so unlike herself.

"Yes, and when my father found out that my
brother had won two dollars on a bet, he made him
give it back to the boy he had won it from."

Montleone shrugged. "I was not taught to believe
that it is so wrong to gamble a little."

"It 's not only the gambling! It 's the thought
that all my work has gone for nothing. I 'd built up
such hopes. Just getting started. Our first season.
What is to become of us if you go on like this?"

"I shall get it back. Never fear."

"We 'll never get it back, Gian! That brute of an
Irishman will see to that."

Montleone laughed. "He did not get so much of
it as Peter Narishkin."

"Peter Narishkin! That deceitful Russian — with his meek-as-Moses look and his yellow beard!"

"But things like this will happen in life." Suddenly he laid his hand caressingly on her thigh. His eyes smiled into hers.

She pushed his hand away.

"Oh, you Italians!" she exclaimed. "You think a woman will endure anything if only you make a little love to her!"

"Only the Americans," he observed, his lip curving, "are high-minded and honorable."

"Well, at least," she flashed, "American men don't gamble with money earned by their wives."

His left hand flew up in a gesture expressing his inability to endure more of this sort of thing.

"You forget," — he spoke suavely — "that the furniture was mine."

She had forgotten it. She stammered for a moment. She did not know what to answer. Everything in the Villa Benedittino, including Montleone, had seemed so absolutely hers.

"Oh — well," she stammered, "it may have been — to begin with — but — "

"But when did it become yours?" He still spoke suavely.

She flashed, "You never would have done anything with it."

"That did not make it yours."

"Think of the way I have slaved to sell it."

"Think of the way your friend Meestair Bond has worked to prepare it. Did that make it his?"

"He helped me because he loved me." She looked defiant as she said this, yet half afraid of what the words might bring forth.

He returned with composure: "Naturally. One needs no cleverness to discover that. But — we are talking of business — not love. And what of Mees Josie? She, too, has worked. And what belongs to her from it all? Nothing. Is not that so?"

"I don't care what you say," Fay answered sullenly. "You hadn't any right to gamble away my money."

"It was not your money. It was mine."

She felt the sudden astonished rage against him that one feels when confronted by a new and antagonistic attitude in a loved and hitherto complaisant companion.

She began to go over the whole affair from her point of view. She became incoherent. She talked so fast and used so many American idioms that he scarcely understood anything of what she said.

He understood her meaning, however, and he too began to talk. He talked a mixture of Italian and English, his voice raised so that its vibrant Southern tones filled the garden. He looked wild and uncontrollable, as he had looked when she first saw him in the bumboat off Teneriffe.

Their voices attracted the attention of urchins playing outside the wall. They stopped their play, listened rapturously for a moment, then ran off to tell their mothers. Their mothers came, hurrying from their cooking and washing or the doorsteps where they sat suckling their babes. One carried a frying pan, one a half-plucked fowl, one a wet petticoat wrung into a club-like formation. An infant clung desperately to the bobbing breast of another. A young man came riding a diminutive thin donkey, his feet almost touching the ground. Two beggars joined the group, and a clay-stained mason with his trowel. They were all glowing with happiness. It was as good as a fair, this quarrel between il Conte and la Contessa.

Josie, crouching in the garden house, on the floor of which three tangerines lay rotting, listened wide-eyed, her heart throbbing against her ribs. When at last there was silence, she crept, a little blue-frocked figure, between the blazing flower beds into the kitchen. She stayed there talking to old Benita until the time of the *colazione*. "It is all over," she kept thinking. "They will separate. We shall leave here. It is all over."

But when she went to the table she found Fay and Montleone waiting for her, all smiles and solicitude toward each other. They had made up their quarrel.

CHAPTER XI

DIEGO and Varvara were sauntering along the road that led to Guardia, one of the villages on the shore below Tramontana. He had been painting and he carried his canvas and easel. He wore the same beret he had worn when he had sauntered along Main Street in Saltport, but the expression of his face was very different. Then he had passed through the deserted street with a look of sulky suspicion. Now, with Varvara at his side, he smiled as she talked, lazily acquiescent to his surroundings. All that was here seemed good to him — the olive-cheeked women in the doorways; the traveling merchants loaded with the wares they were to spread out on the open space before the church; the ragged boy who slept beside a well, his curly head resting on his arm; the donkey loaded with the tender bodies of newly killed kids. More and more Diego felt that he belonged here, that he could never find another place he should like so well.

"There are a great many people about," said Varvara.

"Some *festa*, I guess. Up there on the mountain we never know what is going on."

"I shall ask this man. One can see that he is dressed for an occasion."

She went up to a thin young man who wore a black band on his arm and carried a fat baby.

"*Di che si tratta ?*"

Diego could not follow the answer. A tumult of emotion appeared to be unloosed in the young man. He stretched his hands toward the ground and again toward the heavens. He all but dropped his child, who never let go the finger it was sucking.

"He says," explained Varvara, "that he is on his way to the ceremony of carrying San Filippo down from his church on the hill. Rain is needed for the vines, and San Filippo — if he is pleased — can bring it."

They walked along beside the young man. Varvara took the infant's hand that dangled over the father's shoulder. The fat fingers curled resolutely about one of hers. The father threw her an approving smile.

All that she did, thought Diego, was so right and natural. She lived her life as naturally and with no more ostentation or pretense than a deer in a forest.

As they entered the village they saw that the one street was crowded. From every lane, from every bypath, men, women, and children came to increase the eager throng. They moved close together. They touched each other's breasts with eloquent fingertips. Brothers, meeting after a separation, saluted each other on the cheeks.

Diego raised his eyes and saw a triumphal arch. He saw bright paper lanterns from the windows, girls laughing in balconies. Boys passed, munching roasted

beans from paper bags. For a fortnight neither he
nor the Russians had left their mountain side. They
did not know what was going on in the villages about.
Peter Narishkin and Maria Feodorovna were absorbed
in their work, but Diego was divided between work
and Varvara.

He did not much care what went on about him.
He had little curiosity outside art and a sombre indolent curiosity about sex. As the crowd increased and
he was pressed against the wall of a wine shop, he was
content to lounge there staring up at the colors of the
roofs against the sky. But Varvara saw the head and
shoulders of Consaul towering over the crowd. He
pressed his way toward them. He nodded to the
young father and touched the baby's cheek with his
finger. Room was made for him and Captain Field,
who followed him. Consaul said: —

"So you 've come to see our San Filippo. He is on
his way down from his mountain fastness to give his
blessing to the crops. The vines need rain and, if
he does not deliver the goods, I pity him." He turned
to the Italian and spoke for a moment to him. The
Italian dandled his baby and laughed, showing his
white teeth.

The crowd became quiet, turning their eyes expectantly to where a deep murmur rose from the far
end of the street.

"Here he comes," said Consaul, and took off his hat.
His face was alight.

Shouts now vibrated against the walls. They died,
and rose again like waves gaining strength from the

subsiding and merging of their onward sweep. San Filippo was now advancing. The mountain path, as it dipped to the street, was steep and rocky. One of the bearers of the heavy gilded canopy stumbled. It swayed perilously. For a moment it seemed that San Filippo was to plunge headfirst among his people. There were cries of foreboding and terror. Then, by a surprising effort of strength, the catastrophe was averted, and amid shouts of thanksgiving the saint began his journey through the forward-pressing throng.

He was carried aloft on the strong shoulders of young men. Serene and black as any Ethiopian, he sat under his gilded canopy, his right hand raised in blessing, his left holding a silver missal. He was in white silk embroidered in gold. He looked like an Eastern king in his swarthiness, his silver crown, his fine chasuble and dalmatica. But he was San Filippo come down from his church to bless the crops.

"*Nero come il carbone*," murmured Diego, and gazed reverently at the benign countenance.

The air was filled with shouting. The young father lifted his child high above his head that he might see the saint. The child's one garment was drawn to his armpits and his baby form, mottled with cold, exposed to view. Finger in mouth, he gazed in awe at the overpowering canopy as it swept by, at the noble figure of the saint on his way to sit among the tapers on the high altar.

Consaul replaced his soft hat slightly over one eye. "Last year," he said, "San Filippo was not in such

high favor. There had been a drought the year before that ruined the vines. In effect he was hissed,
and old women shook their fists at him. I felt posi-
tively enraged myself." He gave his rather wistful
smile that was in such contrast to the contours of his
face.

Crowds poured into the church to kiss the hem of
San Filippo's silken robe.

Valentine Consaul looked curiously into the faces
of the boy and girl. "We never see you now," he
said. "You spend all your time at the Narishkins'.
Always at work, eh?"

"I work most of the time," agreed Diego.

"Are you going to spend the summer in Tramontana?"

"Yes."

"My dear children, you'll suffer! We tried it once,
but could not hold out. Better come to the Riviera
with us. I rent a place there and there's a cottage
on it that I'd like to lend to you two."

Diego looked at him stupidly; it was his way of
leaving the answer to Varvara.

"We have promised Peter and Maria Feodorovna to
remain with them," she answered.

"Well, my blessing on you," said Consaul. "And
if you change your minds, just let me know."

They were stretched on the warm sand in a cove
on the far side of the little rocky island that lay a
short distance out from Guardia. The boat in which
Diego had rowed them there lay drawn up on the

sand. The tall jagged rock behind them threw a cool shadow. On this shadow their eyes rested while the sun blazed on their brown glistening backs. The water lapping near their feet made sweet liquid sounds, speaking, it seemed, in the language of these shores. Sometimes the shadow of a gull lay for an instant on one of their bodies like a fallen leaf.

"I'm not afraid of the heat," said Diego. "I am glad you told Mr. Consaul that we're going to stay here."

Varvara made a little mound of sand into the form of a pillow and laid her cheek on it.

"It is not difficult to tell," she said, "what he thinks."

"About us, you mean?"

"Yes." She turned her eyes toward him. Her gaze caressed the bronze curve of his shoulder.

"You need n't care, when it is not so."

"But I do care."

"Why?"

"Because it is not so."

"It will be so — in time."

"But — why wait?"

"Oh, I don't know. Perhaps — I guess it's because I'm afraid."

"Afraid! Of me? But no, Diego, surely you are not afraid?" Her voice was as sweet as the sound of the lapping water that would so gladly have drawn them into its deep embrace, as it had many lovers before them.

"No — not you — just the idea. We won't be so free again — after that. I like to feel free."

"That will not change anything. Only to make us more free."

"You 're wrong. Each one of us will have been possessed. We can't take back what we 've given. There 's a spark in you that 's been drawing me ever since I first saw you. It draws me closer and closer, but — if I touch you — the spark will go out. It 'll leave just blackness."

He closed his eyes and pressed his fingers into the fine sand. His breath came quickly.

She moved closer, so that her thigh lay against his.

"I know why you are afraid. It is because of your painting. You never painted in your life as you paint now. You feel that you are under some spell. You are afraid to break it. Is that so?"

"Perhaps." His words were scarcely audible.

"But you are wrong." The husky sweetness of her voice increased. "You are so very wrong. Peter and Maria Feodorovna both say there is still a lack in your work. Josie felt it and did what she could. But she was silly. She only spoiled what was beautiful in your pictures. I shall not touch your pictures. Yet how complete, how wonderful they will be!"

She slid her arm about him. They were looking each into the eyes of the other. In the velvet darkness of his, she pursued the search for sexual excitement which was her life. In the bronze mystery of hers, he sank and almost lost the instinct to keep

himself to himself, to exercise a power beyond that of
flesh. But not for long. Colors, shapes, began to
move in a sublime procession before his eyes. They
blotted out her lovely form. He rolled over, turning
away from her embrace, picked up a curly pink shell
and held it to his ear.

She laughed softly. She could wait for his surrender. She said: "If I were an artist, I should paint
you so. With one hand holding an empty shell to
your ear. Imagining you hear music. With the
other hand, grasping the shadow of a gull. Imagining you hold life."

He pouted out his lips, threw the shell from him,
rose and strode into the sea. He swam far out and
lay there floating.

So it was with them throughout the summer. As
long as she was tranquil, exercising her power over
him without activity, he drew nearer to her, but as
soon as he felt her arms about him he felt trapped, an
angry light came into his eyes, and he withdrew.
While he was with her, his mind was stimulated
toward his painting. When he was painting, his
mind pressed, through dark alleys of thought, toward
her.

The hay on the hillside fields was cut. The gardens
of the villas became brown and flowerless. Goldfish
sank panting to the murky bottoms of their pools.
The heat week by week relentlessly increased. Now
it was tropic.

The pavement of the Corso burned the feet of the
few stragglers who passed there in the daytime. The

shopkeepers drowsed inside their doorways, only rousing themselves to beat off the flies. The ground became hard and opened in parched cracks. A donkey's foot, striking one of the loose stones on the mountain paths, would send it rattling down the burning hardness of the decline with a fierce arid clatter. There was no peace for the eyes until sundown. Even at night the stars never ceased their burning shine. The birds migrated to the North and the island was songless.

Fay, like Diego, bore the heat as few from a Northern climate could have borne it. She was in a kind of trance during the day, scarcely moving or even thinking. At night she was all alive. She and Montleone, Josie, the Russians and Diego, would go to the shore and cool their bodies in the sea. They would form a circle on the sand and Peter Narishkin would talk, his sonorous voice and the lapping of the waves making an orchestral accompaniment to the play of emotion that passed among others of the group.

Fay feasted her eyes on Montleone's Grecian beauty, while her mind, alive as fire, sought ways of controlling him; ways of keeping him from losing what she had gained; ways of keeping her hands on the Villa Benedittino, which she was mortally afraid might be sold over her head by the owner. Already the question of where the next quarter's rent was to come from troubled her mind.

Montleone gazed into her eyes, but his dark hand slid across the sand behind him to hold Varvara's ankle.

Between Varvara and Diego the old struggle went on.

Josie watched all four fascinated. More than any of the others she felt the heat. During the day it gave her a half-crazed feeling. She could not lie in a waking dream as the others did, letting the hours slip by uncounted. She prowled from room to room in the villa, from seat to seat in the garden. She almost had a sunstroke from going down the fishermen's path in the noonday to bathe. At night she was too worn out to speak, but a fiery unrest made her acutely aware of all that went on about her. Her mind magnified every look and gesture into a monstrous significance. When she perceived how Montleone's hand slid behind him to grasp Varvara's ankle, she stared at him with a look of open horror. He was being false to Fay under her very eyes. Poor, credulous Fay, who saw nothing! But surely Diego must see what was going on! No — for he lay with his head on Fay's lap gazing up at the stars. Perhaps the Narishkins saw. Not Peter. He was looking straight in front of him as though contemplating the palpable essence of his own talk as it flowed through his golden beard. Not Maria Feodorovna. She was looking admiringly at Peter.

Josie burned with pity for Fay, with resentment toward the rest. . . . The gray New England coast, the fogs, the temperate sunshine, the white flurry of snow — these were what Josie was made for.

Here she could not paint at all. Her gift seemed to

have left her. Had she had any real talent? She wondered.

She would have liked to talk to Bond, get some comfort from the stability of his presence, but Mr. Putnam had begged him to go to Northern Italy with him. He was going to the lakes to recuperate after his accident. He had said to Bond: —

"Yes, sir, I get more help from you than I get from any of the doctors I know. There's just something about you that makes my gastric juices function. This Italian diet will be the end of me if you cast me off."

Bond had not been unwilling. He had done what he could for Fay. He was no longer needed, and the thought of a summer in Tramontana was distasteful to him. He wanted to travel. From his income he had enough to live on in Europe if he stayed in the cheaper hotels. This he insisted on doing wherever they went, though Mr. Putnam grew angry each time he saw him in poor quarters. He would have liked to pay Bond's way at the luxurious hotels where he and his wife stayed, for the sake of his company. But a few hours of the Putnams' society each day was enough for Bond.

After a month he separated from them and set off on a walking tour through the hill towns. He made a point of keeping off the weary track of tourists. He had worked hard at Italian and by now had enough to carry him along. He went from place to place, enjoying himself as never before in his life.

When he rejoined the Putnams in October at Lake
Garda, his face was the color of copper and his hair
bleached to a silvery fairness.

"You certainly look good to me," said Mr. Putnam,
eyeing him. "I have n't seen a darned picture in this
darned country that looks as good to me as you do.
How did you get that way?"

"Well, I walked a good deal — and I swam sometimes. I saw a lot of things that interested me."

"You would!" Mr. Putnam grinned at him ca-
daverously and paternally. "You 're the sort that
always finds things pleasant. What 're you going to
do now? Going home?"

Bond hesitated. Then he said: "I think I 'll go
to the East and poke around there for a while. I 've
always wanted to see the East. But — before I do
anything else, I 've got to go back to Tramontana.
I 've business there."

Mr. Putnam's pale eyes flickered. He said casu-
ally, "How 's your handsome friend getting on? The
one that married the dago — Montleone, was that his
name?"

"They are very happy, I think," answered Bond,
stiffly.

"Oh, I did n't mean their marital relations. The
women say those fellows make wonderful husbands.
What I meant was — how 's the antique business
coming on?"

"Everything is dead in that line now," answered
Bond guardedly. He was not going to give Fay
away. He had had a letter from her, in which she

had, with her usual impulsiveness, poured out the whole truth to him. He was angry and troubled. He must go and see what could be done.

Mr. Putnam continued, "She did pretty well in the season, did n't she?"

"Yes. Most of Montleone's furniture was sold. And a good deal more. But they had pretty heavy expenses — starting up, you know."

"Well, I can't see what heavy expenses they had. You and Miss Froward and young Diego and that Russian girl were all working for them — gratis, so far as I could see." He saw the shadow of annoyance on Bond's face and added, "I 'm not trying to butt in. I 'm just interested — I admire the Contessa and I 'd like to see her succeed. But I think more of you than of the whole bunch of them put together, and what I 'm afraid is that you 're going to be let in for a lot of expense that you can't afford. I know what I 'm talking about. I met that Irishman, Darragh, just after you left me and he told me that he 'd won a lot off Montleone. He as much as said that he 'd cleaned him out — that he 'd never have got away from Tramontana if it had n't been for that antique business. It sort of made me mad the way he chuckled over it."

Bond's face was red. His teeth clenched on his pipe. He did not speak, for he did not know what to say. How could he say before Mr. Putnam what he thought of Fay's husband?

Mr. Putnam was too shrewd, too good a reader of character, not to have discovered that Bond's interest

in Fay was something more than friendly.   His own
interest in Bond was such that he longed above all
things, at the present moment, to be in the same boat
with him.   If Bond were going to be greatly concerned over Fay's fortunes, he also would concern
himself.   He said: —

"I'm going back to Tramontana myself.   I've
rented the villa beside the Grande Hotel Vittoria.
It's convenient, because you can get all your meals
at the hotel."   Although he was able to eat so little,
the idea of meals was of great importance to him.
"Now a letter has just come from my daughter in
Brooklyn saying she isn't well.   She's expecting another child.   Mrs. Putnam wants to go to her right
away.   I never hinder my womenfolks in anything
they want to do.   She's going to sail next week.
Now it'd be a great favor to me if you'd stay with
me while you're in Tramontana.   I wouldn't feel
nearly so lonesome, and, if you didn't want to take
your meals at the Grande Hotel Vittoria, you could
get them wherever you wanted.   What do you say?"

Bond would have preferred to go back to his own
little hotel, but he could not very well refuse, with
Mr. Putnam's appealing eyes on his.   He agreed, and,
as soon as Mrs. Putnam had been started on her journey, they set out for Tramontana.

CHAPTER XII

"WELL, Mrs. Palmas, I must say that you and Montleone have got things into a mess." Bond spoke severely, but his eyes, looking into hers through the smoke from his pipe, offered her the same homage which had enriched the barrenness of her life in Saltport.

"Purley, when will you remember that I 'm not Mrs. Palmas any more?" She gave an intimate little laugh, half-coaxing, that had the effect of softening the stern line of his lips. He said: —

"It 's pretty hard for me to remember that. You look so exactly the same."

"Do I?" She was both pleased and disappointed, for she feared she looked older and hoped more sophisticated.

"Yes, at this moment. But, of course, you 've changed some in your outlook. Life has broadened a lot for you, eh?"

Her face lighted. "Oh, it 's wonderful! I feel that I 've never really lived till this year."

"You would n't undo anything you 've done?"

"Never! I adore Gian. But — oh, I 'm so terribly worried! It 's just as you say, Purley, we 've got into deep waters. . . ."

"I said a mess."

Fay raised one shoulder in a very foreign shrug. "Well, call it anything you like. . . . I don't see how we're to get out of it. That hateful old Cardino wants his rent and, if I pay it, there'll be little left to buy new stock."

"Tch, have your funds come so low as that? It is a pity you have not another library of your father's for me to sell."

"Oh, if only I had! But there's nothing. I'm up against it, in earnest, Purley."

"Why did you let Montleone get his hands on the money? You knew he was not a business man."

"Well, you see, I did n't know the language. We thought it would be better for him to do the banking. You must not blame him too much. He's just a child when it comes to money."

"I'm blaming you — Contessa."

That word *contessa* was balm to her. Her eyes glowed pridefully. "I know I'm to blame. But I certainly told him what I thought of him. We had an awful quarrel." Her face hardened. "He said that, after all, the antiques were his and therefore the money was his."

Bond grinned. "That does n't sound so childlike." He added, puffing at his pipe, "It's true too, is n't it?"

She explained tragically: "Oh, Purley, if only I were independent! I've never known what it is to be free to live as I like. I'm in terror now that I may lose Villa Benedittino. I can't possibly tell you what it means to me. I feel as though I absolutely belonged here. I love it far more than Gian does."

Her earnestness was not to be doubted.   She rose
and began to pace the floor, as she always did when
overwrought.   Her heart was indeed set on living in
the Villa Benedittino, thought Bond, even more than
on being the wife of Montleone! This thought
brought him a sense of wry satisfaction.   He watched
the lithe strong movements of her long body, her
arched nose, her Indian eyes, and the doubt which had
before now assailed him rose again.   Could they have
been happy together?   Were they not in spirit as distant as the poles?   She had perhaps always realized
this.

But how his stubborn heart yearned over her!
How he longed to help her!

She came to him suddenly and knelt by his chair.
"I won't have you look like that!" she cried.   "You
are worrying over me, and I'm not worth it.   I get
myself all worked up and I work other people up.
After all, I have my own row to hoe and I've no business to drag my friends into my troubles."   She
pressed her hands against her cheeks.   "Say, Purley,
I wish I had some of your face cream.   I brought a
supply with me, but it's gone and I can't find anything that agrees with my skin half so well.   Just feel
how hot and dry it is!"

He touched her flushed cheek rather gingerly.
Continued excitement and strain had more to do with
its burning, he guessed, than the lack of Bond's
Cream.   He said: —

"Perhaps I could make some up for you, if I could
get the ingredients here."

She sat back on her heels, looking up at him eagerly. "Oh, I'd be so glad! It'd just be splendid. I can't tell you what a difference having that cream makes to me. All the difference between feeling smoothed out and fresh, and feeling haggard and tired." She exaggerated, as she always did, but she wanted so much to say something nice to him.

As he walked from the Villa Benedittino to the chemist, his thoughts were all for Fay — how he might help her. He had had a moment's conversation with Montleone inside the gate before leaving. He had liked him, he never could help liking him, but he had been glad to separate from him. What had they in common? Nothing — save that they cared for the same woman. He had not even a glimpse of Josie.

In the dark chemist's shop, he and the thick-set *farmacista* with his broad face, his smile half sardonic, half appealing, talked earnestly together. But he could not provide Bond with all the necessary ingredients for the cream without sending to Naples. Ten days passed before Bond sat mixing them one night in his room in Mr. Putnam's villa.

He had waited till his host was safe in bed before he began his preparations. Mr. Putnam had been unusually talkative, for the night was not one for sleep. The air was alive and sweet and heavy with moonlight.

Now it was one o'clock and Bond sat at a little table by the open window, the sleeves of his shirt rolled up, blending the thick smooth ingredients of the face cream in a small basin. He had an odd unreal feeling. Here he was, going through the motions of his old life, but in an environment so alien. All his life had been turned topsy-turvy, and that by the woman for whom he now mixed the cream. It was an intimate thing he was doing for her, and it gave him a certain pleasure. He liked to think that she clung to this preparation of his, and — in a sense — to him.

This night the air was fresh, a temperate breeze stirred the creeper that clung about the balcony outside the open French window. The sky no longer burned in oppressive brilliance. Purple bunches of grapes hung on the vines ready to be garnered. Birds, returned from the Northern countries, stirred among the olive trees. Bond was conscious of the swift movements of lizards on the balcony.

He became conscious, too, that he was watched. He looked over his shoulder and saw Mr. Putnam standing in the doorway in his dressing gown. Bond was chagrined at being discovered. If he could have no privacy in that villa, he was damned if he would stay there. With an inhospitable grunt he returned to the stirring of his mixture.

"Pardon me," said Mr. Putnam humbly, "I won't come in if you 'd sooner be alone, but I 'm darned if I can stay in bed. I don't know whether it 's the moonlight or something I 've eaten, but I feel sort of keyed up. I saw your light burning and I thought perhaps you felt restless, too. I guess I 'm bothering you." He made as if to withdraw, but Bond said, as cordially as he could: —

"Come in. I'm just putting up a formula for a friend."

Mr. Putnam, interested at once in anything in the nature of a prescription, came forward inquisitively. "Why, I did n't know you did that sort of thing here."

"It 's not medicine," answered Bond, a good deal embarrassed. "It 's — a face cream — the sort women massage into the skin to smooth it out."

Mr. Putnam peered into the various small pots. Jutting from the heavy material of his dressing gown, his neck looked old and withered. He drew up a chair and sat watching the mixing process with interest. Everything Bond did interested him. He liked the capable movements of Bond's well-shaped hands, the lean strength of his bare forearms, on which short bright hairs glistened in the electric light. He had a singular pleasure in Bond's plain, kind face, in which business shrewdness was so singularly lacking. Here was a man who would never get on in the world, never stand out for his own interests. And, instead of despising him for this lack, Mr. Putnam admired him. But he would not have admired him had there not been something strong in his face, — a strength that he himself lacked, — a sturdy power of taking life as it came, without fear, or irritation, or self-assertion. Here was a man who could wake in the night and find a world spacious for thought, not an antagonistic void which made one cower. He was twenty-five years older than Bond. He had never had a son. His feeling toward him was developing into a paternal affection. He longed to keep Bond by his side. He longed to direct and help him. Bond would have been surprised had he seen the almost tender look Mr. Putnam bent on him.

He had a very good idea for whom the face cream was being prepared. He admired the Contessa Montleone, but he wished that Bond would not be so concerned about her. He said: —

"I guess that's a good face cream all right. I've often noticed what a fine skin the Contessa has."

"She has used it for twelve years."

"Well, she is certainly a living advertisement for it."

Bond looked gratified at the double compliment. He wrote a label — "Bond's Cream" — licked it, and stuck it on the large porcelain pot he had just filled.

"There," he said, with an ironic smile. "I take the lines out of her face that Montleone puts in."

"I doubt if you can keep neck and neck with him in the race," returned Mr. Putnam grimly.

Bond sat back and rubbed his eyes. He asked, "Do you mind if I turn out this light? The moonlight is enough to see by."

They sat smoking their cigars in the blue-white brilliance that came in at the two French windows. A lizard darted halfway across the balcony, hesitated, then darted the rest of the way. A bird with a clear sharp note uttered it twice. Mr. Putnam's soul burned with a deep fatherly longing to do something for Bond.

"Would you mind telling me," he asked, "just how things are at the Villa Benedittino?"

"About as bad as they can be." Bond spoke of Fay's affairs with a candor that he had not before used. He was, in truth, deeply worried for her. "It was perfectly true what Darragh told you. He won a lot of money from Montleone. Others did, too. I don't see how the Contessa is to carry on with the business. A fresh season is coming on and no capital, you may say, to meet it with."

"It's a pity she ever married him."

"Well, perhaps it is. But she thinks a lot of him. And she thinks a lot of the villa. I just could n't tell you how much living in that villa means to Mrs. — the Contessa. Her environment, even in America, was n't what you 'd call congenial. She 's been up against a good deal in her life that has n't suited her. But living in the Villa Benedittino and being called 'Contessa' and having Montleone for a husband just suits her. But I don't see how she 's to keep it up. I really don't. I lie awake at nights trying to think of some way to help her." A sudden huskiness came into his voice.

"I gather that you 're a real friend to her."

"Yes. We 've been friends ever since Diego was a little fellow."

"I admire her. I think she 's a wonderful-looking woman. But I don't think she 's your style — if you 'll excuse me saying so."

"Oh, no, she 's not my style at all. She 's much too

vivid and elegant to be my style. Why, even in a
cosmopolitan crowd like you see here in the height of
the season, she 's always the centre of any gathering
she 's in."

"Now I 'd say — " Mr. Putnam pulled hard at his
cigar — "that Miss Froward was far more your style."

Bond looked startled, then laughed a little. "She 's
a funny little thing. She has lots of character, too.
She 's made a success of the tea room."

"I suppose the proceeds from that went into the
general fund?"

"Yes," answered Bond, glumly.

There was a long silence. The moon sank behind
the upper branches of a cypress. Its shadow darkened the room. But it was still bright on the balcony
and quick lizard shapes could be seen darting with a
new confidence.

Mr. Putnam said at last: "It 's a wonder that
you 've never tried to do anything with that face
cream of yours. It seems to be a specially good one.
Have you ever advertised it much?"

"Just little ads in the *Saltport News*. They
brought results, too. It was surprising how many of
the summer visitors took away supplies of it. Mrs.
Palmas used to recommend it to all her — friends."

"I suppose it 's a secret formula?"

"I got it from the old fellow who sold out to me.
He 'd got it from a relation of his who was a chemist
in Bavaria. It 's a real good thing. As a matter of
fact, there 's one ingredient missing in this lot." He

tapped the labeled pot with his fingers. "I could n't get it here. But the Contessa won't know that, and the cream will still be very good."

Kindness and a fatherly, protective love were now not just simmering in Mr. Putnam's brain. They were ramping there, demanding that he do something to help Bond, something to clamp this desirable being to his side forever, in gratitude. But his shrewdness did not altogether fail him. There was a possibility that he might make something out of this philanthropy for himself. The thought of having more money rather nauseated him, but the thought of making it was exhilarating. He snatched at exhilaration, held out both hands for love.

"Mr. Bond," he said, in his tired voice, "I hope you won't mind me making the statement that you 're a very loyal man."

Bond grunted an embarrassed acquiescence.

"You 're a very unusual man," continued Mr. Putnam. "I 've got an idea that if you once give your affection to anyone — woman or man — you 're ready to stick by them through everything — sickness or health, eh? — till death do you part."

"Well," returned Bond. "I value the few friends I have."

Mr. Putnam stretched out his hand and laid it on Bond's knee. "Are we friends?" he asked. Then added, hurriedly, "No, don't answer yet. I know that I care much more for you than you possibly can for me. But — sometime — I am in hopes that you 'll number me among those few."

Bond was touched. He said, "I like you very much already. You 've been mighty kind to me."

"No, I have n't! The kindness has been on your side. . . . But, I 'm wondering — I am just wondering if we could n't — between us — make something pretty good out of that cream of yours. . . . If it was properly put on the market, there might be a small fortune in it. Even a big one — as most people count fortunes. What do you say to trying it out?"

"Gosh, I don't know." Bond was almost too surprised for words. The thought of making money in large amounts had never presented itself to him. But — if only he could!

"You 'd be willing?"

"I 'd certainly be delighted. But I 've no capital. I 've just barely enough to live on."

Mr. Putnam regarded him pityingly and enviously. He said: —

"Leave that to me. All I need is the formula for the cream."

CHAPTER XIII

BEFORE the opening of the next tourist season, Bond's Cream was on the market. A flamboyant advertising campaign was inaugurated which, if it did not actually push the cream down the throat of the public, at least plastered it on the face. Full-page advertisements appeared in the leading American magazines. The most striking of these showed a really remarkable picture of Fay seated by a window in the Villa Benedittino. It was from a photograph taken by a German friend of Consaul's, and displayed to advantage the splendid lines of her shoulders and neck, as she bent her head to look at the spray of camellias lying across her lap. Beneath the picture the advertisement declared that "the beautiful Contessa Montleone, leader of one of Italy's most patrician circles, in whom is blended the regal dignity of the old *noblesse* with the exquisite graciousness of the modern society woman, attributes the fragrant delicacy of her skin — lovely as the petals of the camellia — to the constant use of Bond's Face Cream."

Bond winced when he saw this advertisement. It hurt his sense of sober seemliness, yet — he was oddly pleased. It seemed — by one telling stroke — to place Fay, in the eyes of the world, on the pedestal she occupied in his thoughts. After all, print was print, and, even though there was some exaggeration in the advertisement, there was sound truth in it — the truth of Fay's beauty.

But it made her seem very remote — even though he was Bond of the cream that kept her beautiful. She was now of a different world — Montleone's world, Consaul's world, the world of the guests of the Grande Hotel Vittoria.

He had taken the page from the magazine and tacked it on the wall of his cabin, on the return voyage from America. The placing of the cream on the market had necessitated a trip there by Mr. Putnam and him. They were in New York for six weeks during which Bond stayed at the Putnams' mansion just off Fifth Avenue. He became inured to high living. In truth he was not only as sound as a nut himself, but he was, by some telepathic power, able to transmit some semblance of soundness to Mr. Putnam, who clung to him with more and more determination.

He had insisted on paying Bond a handsome sum, as soon as the cream was put on the market.

On their return to Tramontana, Bond handed it over to Fay in order that she might buy the Villa Benedittino, just as Mr. Putnam had foreseen. It was not a gift. He knew she would refuse that. She was to pay him a fair interest which would amount to less than the rent she paid to Cardino, and, until the next season was over and the business well established, she was to pay just what she could afford.

The seventh heaven is a colorless lodging for the spirit compared to the plane to which Fay's soared when the deeds of the villa were hers and she knew that she might live there for the rest of her days.   She had a new and strong position.   She stood in a fresh relation to Montleone.

She feared him.   She feared what he would do if he had the power.   What she wanted was to keep him powerless and pour out the bounty of her love upon him.   She wanted him to be her master sexually, but subservient to her in will.

This season there was no talk of a mutual bank account.   Fay did the banking herself, but she was as generous with Montleone as she dared be, remembering the interest she owed Bond and the slack months pending.   But she was too happy at the beginning of the season to give a second thought to what was not full of color and promise.

The antique galleries were almost never empty.   A steady trickle of people passed through them from morning to night.   Fay had a talent for knowing just how much she could charge.   She knew just when to speak sentimentally (and not actually untruthfully) of a cabinet or a snuffbox.   With the help of books and the talk of Valentine Consaul, she had learned a great deal about her work in the past year.   Consaul was a good friend.   He met everyone who was worth meeting and he never failed to bring the well-off visitors to call on the Contessa.   Some of them came to see if she were really as handsome as she appeared to be in the advertisements of Bond's Cream, but they usually remained to buy.   She gave many parties, at which the Tramontana orchestra, which she now thought of as playing under her patronage entirely, provided the music. Sometimes she sang Negro spirituals with an abandon that delighted her audience, but as time went on these gave way to Sicilian folk songs. Her voice never failed her now, though she was conscious that she must not put it under a great strain.

The Irishman, Darragh, had unfortunately returned to Tramontana. Hate it though he did, he could not stay away. There was no other place in the world where he could sit in his own doorway on a mountain side and look down over such a view, where he could have such isolation and such companionship. He could (through his binoculars) see his guests ascending the winding path out of the valley half an hour before they crossed his lintel. He could watch them disappear at night carrying a lantern, pass down into the valley out of sight, and leave him free.

Montleone went often to his villa. A restlessness, a resentment, was growing in him. He went, not so much to play at cards, — for he had not the wherewithal, — as for the sake of Darragh's company. They were both resentful of the way life had treated them. They were both sensitive, isolated in themselves, rebellious. Montleone, in spite of his occasional childish gayety, was of a naturally melancholy turn of mind. He magnified a grievance till it possessed him.

Now he saw himself gradually being pushed to a position of nothingness in his own house. Worse still — it was not his own house. Nothing that was in it

was his.   If he interfered in any way, he saw that Fay
resented it, and he magnified her resentment, though
she had shown it by nothing more than a fleeting
shadow on her happy face.   He began to resent the
completeness of her happiness.   The brightness of her
eyes became to him, in moments of melancholy, a
predatory gleam.   She had taken to herself his house,
his garden, his title, his very intonations and gestures
(he was quick to see how she imitated him), and she
expected from him a never-failing demonstration of
love.   She absorbed his caresses as a greedy plant the
sun, never dreaming that her inexperience often
struck a jarring note on his sensitive nerves.

Fay urged him to show himself about the galleries.
His presence lent an air to the place.   He prowled in
the background looking darkly at the customers, curl-
ing his lips in an ironic smile.   Once one of them ap-
pealed to him: "Say, Count, don't you think you
could take a little less for this?   I have bought a good
deal from the Contessa, but she holds out for the top
price."

"Yes," he had said.   "I will take less," and he had
reduced the price appreciably.

Fay had not complained.   She had borne it well,
but she was angry enough when she missed a silver
candelabra and found that he had sold it unknown to
her.   "I needed the money," he had said coolly.   He
did not even tell her what he had got for it.   She had
looked into his eyes and had fancied that he would like
to quarrel with her.   But she shrank from that.   She

must not quarrel with him, for his very presence weakened her.

The paintings by Peter Narishkin had been sold or removed from the wall. Pictures by Diego now covered the space. Several of these had gone very well. The largest one had almost always a group around it. It was the picture of a goat girl, squatting nude among her goats. The face was hidden, but Josie was sure that the body was that of Varvara Walkonsky. She stood beside it in the early morning, before the galleries were open, studying it, the wild and beautiful background, the horned, strange-eyed goats, clustering about the girl as though to hide her. She belonged, it seemed, to them, and they resented the stare of the public for that lovely flesh. Josie was suspicious of Varvara. There was nothing, she thought, that that girl would not do. Josie hated her with the envious hatred of the convention-bound for those for whom conventions do not exist. She suspected her of making up to Montleone, though why she could not have told, for Varvara and Diego were always together. He still lived at the farm with the Narishkins.

The season was over much earlier than they had expected. Tramontana was emptied of the *forestieri* — with startling suddenness. Times were growing more depressed, and the hotels showed it by closing early in May. Still, Fay was not discouraged. She had done moderately well and — above all — she owned the Villa Benedittino.

Soon the heat was intense. The sirocco blew day after day, taking away the power of action, almost of thought. Then it was gone, and the glittering heat of summer was there.

Only in the evenings, under the close brilliance of the stars, the drooping, orange-colored moon, did they rouse themselves.

Josie walked barefoot through the garden, longing for love, and it seemed impossible that love should come to her. She envied Fay, who had so much romance in her life. It seemed unfair for one woman to have so much and another so little. There was nothing for Josie to do but to run a tea room and to answer the questions of tourists about the Contessa Montleone. Josie, with uncanny wisdom, had seen through the affair of Bond's Cream. It had been put on the market by Mr. Putnam in order to make it possible for Bond to buy the villa for Fay. Now he was losing money on it. Soon it would no longer be heard of.

She heard a movement in the tiled garden house, a low, excited laugh. It could not be mistaken for the laugh of anyone but Montleone. Then there was complete silence save for the rustling of a bird on a bough. Josie drew close, her bare feet silent as the moonlight. The garden house was half hidden by foliage. Between the leaves she could see Varvara in Montleone's arms, her beautiful arms, looking white as marble in that light, about his neck. They were kissing, with an abandon at once so sensual and so captious that Josie, wide-eyed, felt her heart pound-

ing so wildly that she feared they might hear it. She
had not known that people kissed like that. There
stretched before her a dark sea of knowledge of which
she had seen only the pale spray. These two were of
one world. Not her world. She hated them —
Montleone, for Fay's sake; Varvara, for Diego's.
Both, for her own.

Diego had come in at moonrise and he and Fay had
hired donkeys to take them to the beach to bathe.
Several times of late they had shown a disposition to
go off together. They had asked the others, in a half-
hearted way, to go too, but Montleone had been absorbed in a novel, reading by the light of a small brass
lamp placed on a window sill. Josie had looked at
him with admiration, as he sat reading with bent head.
She had felt herself not wanted by Fay and Diego.

Soon after they had gone, Montleone had finished
his book, recommended it to Josie, and, lighting a
cigarette, strolled into the garden. Then Varvara
had appeared, in search of Diego. The two girls had
talked together for a short while, and Josie had supposed that Varvara, who was carrying a bathing suit,
had also gone to the beach.

But here she was in Montleone's arms, in the garden
house. How long a time had elapsed Josie did not
know. She had picked up the book and had read a
chapter, but it was in Italian and was slow going for
her. She had wished that she could absorb the book
all at once — find out what there was in it so to hold
Montleone. Even in the first chapter there had been
implications that had teased her curiosity — but

struggling with the Italian words had made her head ache, after the heat of the day. She had wished she had gone to the beach with Varvara — how lovely she had looked in that short-sleeved, wide-trousered suit with its pattern of yellow chrysanthemums on ground the color of Chianti. And a sapphire had been shining on her hand. She managed to have jewels, that girl, though her people had lost everything in Russia.

Josie, torn between fear of discovery and a desire to disclose her presence, turned back into the garden and stood motionless twisting her fingers together. She felt terribly alone — lost, abandoned, in the sweet-scented night.

She heard the sound of donkeys' hoofs. They stopped at the gate. There was the murmur of voices. Fay and Diego had returned. They had returned fresh, cool, happy.

Josie glided to meet them, her eyes bright as a night bird's.

"Fay!" She spoke in a whisper, catching Fay's firm cool arm in her burning fingers. "Fay, don't speak! Don't make a sound. Sh, Diego, don't speak! Can you both hear me? I want you to come with me. . . . Take off your shoes. . . . I want to show you something."

She bent and drew the beach shoes from Fay's feet. Fay extended her feet, one after the other, docilely, like a large child. She thought it was some surprise, some joke prepared by Josie and Montleone. Diego stood like a statue, his face dark, unfathomable in the moonlight.

But he too was docile. There was something childlike and docile about them both. They allowed themselves to be led, one by each hand of Josie's, along the narrow walk close to the wall, their six bare feet making not a sound.

The donkeys' feet were clattering down stone steps in the distance, going to their short night's rest. They heard the sound of the boy's voice shouting as he urged them down the steps.

When they reached the end of the garden, Josie drew them cautiously toward the garden house. There was silence in it. The three linked figures passed from behind it to the open space in front. The moon, lowering its splendors behind them, shone straight into the faces of Montleone and Varvara.

They were clasped in each other's arms, cheek to cheek, staring with wide-open, tranced eyes into the moonlight. They were framed as in a picture, in the vine-clad doorway. The full light of the moon was turned on them. They were a picture of eternal lovers. There was no joy in their faces, no sorrow — just acceptance of the night's bliss.

For a moment after they knew they were discovered, they made no sign. They remained clasped together like actors, after a supreme demonstration of their art, waiting for the applause of the audience. The audience of three stood there transfixed, their merged shadow lying on the mosaic before them like the map of a strange land.

Josie felt that she could have stood gazing in silence

forever. But the other two broke into exclamations simultaneously.

"So that," said Diego, "is the way the land lies!"

"Gian! Oh, Gian!" from Fay.

Montleone and Varvara moved apart. They looked searchingly into the faces that fronted them, the expressions of which they could not see. Then Montleone passed his hand over his hair from forehead to nape, gave a little laugh of chagrin, and stepped down from the stage to join the audience. Varvara remained where she was a moment longer. She stretched her white arms to their utmost, as though they were weary with the clasping of Montleone. She stretched herself and yawned, as though all her body were pleasantly weary. Josie even saw a quick movement of her tongue, like a snake's.

Montleone laid a hand on Fay's arm and sought to draw her away. "It is nothing," he said, smiling. "A moment's — what do you say? — forgetfulness. . . . The night . . . Please, come."

Fay, however, pushed his hand violently away. He was startled by the look of furious outrage she gave him.

"But," he persisted, "it is really nothing. It is impossible that you should think it serious."

"Don't touch me!" she exclaimed. "You have deceived me! You and she, to think that you would do such a thing!"

Montleone, in despair, turned to Diego. "You understand that there is nothing wrong? You know how it is."

But Diego only looked stupid. "I see how it is," he muttered.

"I could forgive a kiss," Fay cried, "but that — that — look on your face — well, it 's over, Gian — I can't forgive you!"

"Not forgive me," he echoed, blankly. "But you must understand that there is nothing between Varvara and me. We have never before — "

Josie's eyes were blazing into his. What did she know? He hesitated. Varvara came down the steps of the garden house to his side. She looked like a gorgeous-plumaged tropic bird. She smiled possessively at him.

Diego took her by the wrist and gave her a jerk. He muttered: "I was going to marry you — when I had made some more money. . . . That 's why I did n't want . . ."

She interrupted him with a scornful laugh.

"Marry you? Never! You — bore me too much."

They were the very words she had used to the Englishman in Naples. "Bore you?" he repeated, unbelievingly. "*Me* bore you?" He remembered their bathing on the beach, their wandering in lonely mountain paths; how, like two children, they had played with her pet goat, gathered flowers together, lain on the cliffs eating *mandarini;* how she had posed for his picture. He thought the girl must be losing her wits. He drew her close and looked into her eyes. In them he saw resentment and — yes — the cold flicker of intense boredom.

He threw her hand away, and scowled. He said: —

"There's not a man living who would not soon bore you. You're as fickle as hell. Gian will soon bore you." He took their coming together for granted.

Montleone did not. He said to Fay, "Only let me explain, my darling." She had always loved the way his Southern tongue had tripped on that word. Now she hated it.

"Don't darling me!" she screamed.

"Sh," admonished Diego. "We'll soon have a crowd around if you do that."

"It won't be the first time," she retorted, and, picking a great red geranium from the urn beside her, began to tear it to pieces. She looked magnificent standing there in the moonlight with the petals dropping like blood before her.

Varvara said: "Yes, you look very wonderful, but — you are a child. You know nothing, really. Neither you nor Diego. You have learned a little — yes — since Gian and I have had you in hand, but — " she spread out her fingers and her sapphire flashed — "you are still — very boring. You are many centuries behind us. It is only for us to tolerate you while we must — while there is nothing better. No — no — do not be angry! You have much to make up for what you lack. Your strength — your newness — your aggressiveness. . . . See, you have taken all that Montleone had — his house — his garden — his name — even, as well as you can, you have imitated

his way of speaking. He has nothing left but his
spirit, his knowledge, come down to him from
Romans and Greeks and Saracens and Moors. You
cannot take that. You cannot understand that.
. . . That is left for me."

"You are welcome to each other," said Diego.
"Are n't they, Mamma? We 'll be well rid of
you."

Montleone's eyes flashed, but he did not answer.
He stood aloof, his lips curled, his arms folded somewhat theatrically, waiting for Fay to speak.

Her mind wavered. She looked at Diego for
strength.

She found strength in him — the warm, dark, secret, egotistical strength of mother-son love. As
long as she could keep Diego beside her, she would be
strong and free — she would be able to exult in her
femaleness.

But with Montleone — all was different. She became not so much female as feminine. Those eyes of
his, that smile, those supple strong hands, took the
strength from her. She could pretend to domineer,
but she was his slave. And for what? For scenes
like this? These moonlight — embraces with a girl?
Ah, she herself was a dozen years older than he!

Diego and she had in them — in spite of their love
of color, their ability to shed their old life and put on
the garment of a new — an ineradicable vein of Puritanism. They shrank from what they saw — what
they suspected — with abhorrence. The Puritanism
of their ancestors rose up in them; like a Northern

tree it spread its chill shadow across the exotic flowers of modern life. They would have disclaimed its existence in them, but there it was.

Montleone stood waiting. Diego said in an undertone to Varvara: "I wish you'd tell me how long it is since I began to bore you."

She put one arm around Montleone's neck, thrusting her other hand into the pocket of her flowered trousers. She gave a little laugh.

"You have always bored me."

"Like that man in Naples?"

"Yes. Only worse."

"You're a little liar," he said, between his teeth. "I'm glad I kept myself — to myself."

Montleone tried to take Varvara's arm from around his neck, but it clung there tightly. He knew that it was impossible for Fay to forgive him with Varvara hanging on his neck. The worst was — or was it the best? — he did not much care whether or not Fay did forgive him. He did not want to part with Varvara. The moonlight was too brilliant. It made one forget that there was an equally important world of sunshine. Nothing seemed to matter but the things that were important under its white fire. The flowers of the garden were giving themselves to it, color and scent, as they never did to the sun. Under the sun their color was merged into one hot splash of brilliance. Now each separate petal held its banner aloft, each stamened pistil bristled with meaning. The leaves spread themselves to show their silver veinings.

Fay said, feeling that ache in her throat that made her afraid for her voice: —

"I want to ask a question. . . . Josie — Diego — go away — I want to ask these two . . ." When she was alone with them she asked, "Is there — anything between you?"

Before Montleone could utter a denial, Varvara answered, "Yes, I am his mistress."

Montleone threw up his hand in a gesture of allowing a bird to escape from it.

Diego, straining his ears, had overheard. "Little liar," he growled under his breath.

"It is all over," said Fay, and she swept away from them, back to the villa.

Josie spent the rest of the night in the garden, alone. She sat on the end of a seat, hugging her knees, enacting over and over in her mind the various scenes that had led to the scene of to-night. She forgot her own life in her fascinated watching of the lives of others. Those unconscious egoists who scarcely believed in anything that did not directly affect themselves had laid their inner lives open for her inspection. How theatric they had looked standing there in the moonlight — thinking only of themselves, how this or that move of the others was for or against them — never thinking how they were laying bare their souls for her to peer into. . . . She had watched Montleone, standing with folded arms, torn between Fay and Varvara, whom he passionately desired. She had watched Fay, tearing the scarlet geranium to pieces, herself torn between Diego and Gian, her egotistic passion for whom was dead. She had watched Diego, his face drawn in the tragic mask that signified so little, angrily giving up Varvara, whom he had never possessed. She had watched Varvara, in her brilliant beach suit — taking what she wanted.

One after another they had left the garden, leaving it to her and the sliding lizards. Fay had swept to the villa, throwing one last look over her shoulder at Montleone. Diego, in pretended nonchalance, had filled his pockets with *mandarini* and slouched to his room. A light still burned up there. Before the other two had left by the garden gate Varvara had come to Josie and given her a quick embrace.

"I like you," she had said. "You are different from those others. Listen. You and Mr. Purley Bond must marry. Do not let him leave Tramontana again without you. You two were made for each other. You have been wasting time, as Gian and I have wasted time."

"Do you really love him?" Josie had asked, clutching her.

"Never before have I loved."

"Was what you told Fay the truth?"

Varvara pouted and shrugged.

"But where will you and Gian go? What will you live on?"

"To Paris. One can always live there. Besides, I have friends. I have jewels which can be sold. . . . Remember what I have said. Don't waste any more time."

She had kissed Josie and run to the door in the wall, where Montleone was waiting. He had not said good-bye to Josie.

The night had passed, warm and secret and balmy. The moon had sunk into the arms of the sun. The sun gilded first the towers and tree tops, then the terraces and tree trunks. By the time it reached the garden seat where Josie had sat, she had left the garden and had crept like a shadow through the streets, following to the Teatro Greco a tall dark figure that had emerged from the Villa Benedittino and glided through the gate in the wall. Josie had seen that it was Fay and she had felt a sudden fear. What if Fay were going to do something desperate? She had lost Montleone. Perhaps she would attempt to take her life.

Josie followed her through the narrow streets in which the people were not yet beginning to stir, though voices already sounded inside the houses and the light from a brazier occasionally illuminated the intent face of a woman. She followed her, keeping in the shadows of doorways for fear Fay would look back, to the gates of the theatre, up the steep steps, under the frowning arches, to the very top. Josie began to be frightened. She could hear the pounding of her own heart. If Fay had it in her mind to fling herself to the stones below, could she dart forward in time to save her? She had a horrid vision of the two of them swaying for a moment together and then plunging headlong to their death. She crept closer so that she almost touched the swift-moving black-shawled figure as it glided through the narrow passage that led to the parapeted space on the top.

Fay stepped out there and seated herself on the parapet. She threw back the black lace scarf from her head. Then Josie saw her face and all fear left her. Fay's face wore what Josie called its play-acting expression. It was both rapt and self-conscious. Her eyes were wide-open in a hallucinated fixity. Her dilated nostrils showed her exaltation. Only her self-consciously smiling lips gave her away.

She sat motionless for a little staring at the splendid scene before her, the newly flaming sun, the blue-white volcano, rose-tinted on its eastern side, the town scattered against the mountain side like a box of colored crayons upset, the sea in its wide encircling blueness. Her lips parted and she spoke. Josie could not make out the words, but she could make out that they were Italian. Beautiful soft-flowing Italian words that Fay loved.

After she had thus spoken, she fell into a dreamlike stillness. So, Josie thought, might some Greek actor have sat in this theatre waiting the time of entry to the stage. Was Fay rehearsing in that strange mind of hers what her new part in life was to be?

Again she smiled, and took from a velvet bag she carried a reed pipe of the kind sold by the Sicilian pipers in the streets. She put it to her lips, pouting them to meet it as if she would suck from it the very fullness of life. A high note, shrill and tremulous, issued from the pipe. It was followed by one of the wild tunes, charged with passion and vitality, that had been played among these mountains in the pagan days. Fay played it with exuberance and not unskill-fully. Josie listened admiringly. She had tried to play on a native pipe herself and had succeeded only in producing a few discordant notes, and Varvara, who had really practised for a time, could accomplish just a hesitating bar or two. And here was Fay sway-ing her lithe body, playing strains ever wilder and more volatile. When had she learned to play the pipe? Or was music so natural to her that she played as she breathed or laughed?

As Josie descended the cool dim passages of the ruin, her mind turned from Fay to Purley Bond. How would he be affected by the news? Would he feel that there was now a chance of Fay's turning to him? And how would she herself feel if those two came to-gether? Varvara's words returned to her. "You and Mr. Purley Bond must marry. . . . Don't waste any more time." How strange that Varvara should say that to her! She had always seemed so entirely ab-sorbed in herself. Yet apparently she had seen all that went on about her. And why had she thought that Bond and she were wasting time unmarried to each other? She had certainly never seen a look of love pass between them. She could not see what had never passed. Yet she might easily have intercepted looks of understanding. They often exchanged these. Tolerant or satirical or troubled looks, usually born of the vagaries of Fay, they had no passion in them. Yet, recalling them, Josie felt a strange new exhilara-tion. There was a lightness in all her body as she

went down the sunny street toward the Corso. Shopkeepers were standing in their doorways. They
smiled at her, seeing something a little different about
her, less restrained, gayer.

"Buon giorno, signorina."

"Buon giorno." She tilted her chin, threw back
the hair from her forehead, and, instead of turning
towards the Villa Benedittino, passed through the
Porto Vittorio Emanuele and went along the little
street that led to Bond's hotel.

She could not have told — that is, truthfully told
— why she was going there. If she had been asked
she would have said, "I am going to tell him about
Montleone and Varvara." But he would have found
that out very soon, without her pushing forward.
No — she was not going for the purpose of telling
him anything. She was going because she wanted to
see him, to look in his face and see whether any change
had come over it. Since Varvara had said those words
to her she could not recall Bond's face distinctly.
She saw it as though in a light so bright that it dazzled
her. His features were almost obliterated by this
strange brightness. She had never thought of Bond's
face as particularly interesting. Ever since she was
fourteen Diego's face had fascinated her. She had
watched its extravagant changes of expression, that
so belied his indolence, with the very eyes of her
spirit. She had striven, and always failed, to capture
its dark beauty on canvas. But Bond — she had seen
him without seeing him — excepting that one eve-

ning in his drug store. Perhaps, even then, the germ of this new feeling was living in her.

The morning was all alive. Flowers peered over the walls at her. Donkeys, starting out under their morning loads, peered sideways at her, then sent forth vibrant, expectant brays and jogged the faster for a yard or two.

She wished she had tidied her hair and put on a little powder before leaving the villa. She had been up all night and could imagine how far from pretty she looked. But it was too late for that now, and she remembered Diego's saying once that she looked her best in the morning.

The little hotel of pink stucco where Bond was staying stood on a long slope and had a terrace beneath almond trees on which tables were set for breakfast. He was the earliest arrival. The air was fresher this morning than it had been of late. The sight of his pile of crusty bread, his allowance of honey, thickly holding the sunshine, was appetizing to him. He filled his cup with coffee of a quality he would have rejected at home, and sipped it with a feeling of exhilaration. He had the sensation of something agreeable about to happen to him.

Perhaps this sensation originated in the fact that he was soon to leave Tramontana. He had had enough of it to last his lifetime. He would leave Fay established here, in a life that seemed to suit her, with a husband who seemed to love her, a business that seemed to be surviving in spite of the bad times, a villa which, thanks to Bond's Cream, was her very own. Diego was evidently settled down here to paint for some time. The thought of Josie came to him — that elusive, oddly fragrant essence that was Josie. Somehow he did not feel quite happy in the thought of Josie staying on in Tramontana, devoting her young energy to the running of a tea room for Fay. It was not good enough for her. She should either have her own house, her own husband, or be in a position to devote herself to art. Was her talent sufficient to justify it? The idea of Josie spending her days painting mediocre pictures was somehow repugnant to him. She was a being designed by nature to do what she did well. She must be in her right niche or never would she find content. And he believed she had never yet found it. He had no doubts of Diego. He had a great talent, perhaps a touch of genius, and he was as content as a cat. But Josie — what was to be the future of Josie? He pondered on the future of Josie, his last crust poised in mid-air, and, when she turned in at the gate and came across the terrace to him, he was scarcely surprised. He rose and went to meet her, still holding the crust in his fingers.

"Josie!" he exclaimed, "I 'm mighty glad to see you! Won't you come and have breakfast with me?"

"You are early," she answered, avoiding his eyes. "I scarcely expected to find you up."

Now he was a little puzzled by her. Why had she sought him out at this hour?

"Were you on your way to bathe?" he asked.

"No. I wanted to find you."

He led the way back to his table, looked doubtfully at the crust, wondering whether or not to put it in his mouth, then tossed it to a cat that sat under the next table. He called the waiter and ordered another pot of coffee and a supply of bread.

"Was there — is there — " his mind, from habit, flew instantly to Fay — "anything wrong?"

Now she looked into his face, suddenly aware, as with a swift pain, that it was the most fascinating and beautiful face in the world to her, and answered: —

"Yes — well — I 'm not sure. Perhaps it will turn out all right — even better so — "

"What is it?" he demanded, impatiently.

She took a quick gasping breath before she answered.

"Montleone and Varvara have gone off together."

He stared at her uncomprehendingly.

"I discovered them," she went on, "in the garden house. And I took Fay to see. They were clasped in each other's arms in the bright moonlight."

"Well, I never!" He ran his fingers through his tow hair, standing it on end. "And what then?"

"She was terribly upset. Diego was there, too. They were both upset. You 'd think they had never been out of Saltport — never seen anything of the world."

"You 'd have been the same in Fay's place, would n't you?"

"It would have depended upon who my husband was. If he were Montleone, I should n't have been surprised or shocked. I 'd have expected nothing better — especially with a girl like Varvara playing about. But — if he were you — " she looked straight into his eyes, and the uncontrollable color rose and flamed in her cheeks — "I'd have been distracted."

The waiter brought the food and set it before them with a look of friendly inquisitiveness into Josie's face. Bond was startled, not only by her words but by her expression.

"Will you have more bread?" she asked in a matter-of-fact tone.

"No, thanks. That's for you." But he poured himself another cup of coffee. He said, to cover his embarrassment: "Not much like our breakfast in Saltport, Josie. Ham and eggs, buckwheat cakes, and maple syrup."

"My tongue hangs out for American food sometimes," she answered.

"What about going back? Would you like to?"

"I'd love to."

Again there was something in her manner that disturbed him, but his mind reverted at once to Fay.

"This is terrible for her," he said. He suddenly felt surprised at himself, that he could sit here drinking coffee, with Fay in such trouble. He felt angry with Josie that she could sit there consuming bread and honey with obvious zest at such a time. Yet — even to himself his voice sounded flat. Like a hungry plant, Fay had absorbed all his depths of solicitude. He could only repeat flatly, while his eyes rested on the fair brown curl that dangled over Josie's brow,

"This is terrible for her." He thought: "She has not combed her hair this morning. It is the same lovely golden brown as her skin. And her color flows through the tan just like the pink in some of those gold-colored roses." He asked: —

"Was there a scene?"

"Yes. Montleone could scarcely believe she was going to take it so seriously. But he's tired of his life here. And Varvara's tired of Diego. He has been a disappointment to her." Josie's lips curled in a little malicious smile. "She wants a lover who would rather possess her body than paint it."

Bond was rather shocked by her words. Yet they stirred something in him that was akin to the rising heat of the day. A sultry breeze whispered in the leaves of the almond trees and flapped against his face like unseen wings.

"Where is Fay now?" he asked, rather thickly.

Her face broke into sudden laughter.

"Where do you suppose?"

He looked inquiring.

"She's on the very top of the Teatro Greco, playing a Sicilian pipe. She came out of the villa early. I followed because I was sort of frightened of what she might do. But I needn't have worried. She went straight up there. She sat a while with that look she has when she's pretending — you know what I mean — "

He gave a shamefaced assent.

"Then she took out the pipe and began to play. Not silly croaking sounds like the rest of us make

when we try to play, but real music — better than
old Sensa Gamba makes.   I guess she's learned the
airs from the shepherds.   She often goes off to the
hills for hours by herself.   She's full of music, really.
If you'd seen her play — and heard her — you'd not
worry about her.   You'd say she is having the time
of her life.   I think myself that she snatched at the
chance of getting rid of Montleone in such a dramatic
way.   She owns the Villa Benedittino, she's a Contessa.   She's been advertised as a beauty in every
American magazine.   I think she's perfectly happy."

"Do you think she'll divorce Montleone?"

Josie shook her head so hard that her uncombed
curls fell into her eyes.   She placed her palms on her
forehead and dragged her hair back from it.   Her
face, thus baldly presented, stared candidly at him.

"No!   She'll never divorce him.   She'll like to
feel that she's still his wife.   She'll like to think that
the day may come when they'll make it up.   I understand Fay, if anyone does."

She took out a tortoise-shell cigarette case.   The
dark young waiter sprang forward with a match.
Bond watched the play of the tiny flame in her eyes.
They got up, and Bond said stiffly: "Will you come
for a walk?   There's still a breath of coolness near
the sea."

They followed the windings of the path, stopping,
where it overhung the valley, to look down at the
terraced farms below, to absorb the faint freshness
that was not yet pressed down by the heat.

Bond took a pair of colored spectacles from a case

and put them on. Josie watched the movement of his hands. She had always liked to watch him do things with his hands, from making up prescriptions in Saltport to polishing furniture in Tramontana.

"These are a great help," he said. "I wonder you don't try them."

"I could n't bear anything that would spoil color for me."

"There 's no color, that I can see, in the glare of this sun. The colored lenses make the scenery pret.-tier. Just try them."

"No, no. I could n't possibly."

"Just to please me."

She stopped and held up her face resignedly. "Very well, if you want me to."

He removed the shell sides from behind his ears and began to adjust them behind hers. But her hair clung with ridiculous fervor about his fingers. It was not easy to place the sides properly. His fingers touched the cool pinkness of her ears. Her body seemed to him like the freshness of early morning, before the heat of the day.

She looked at the valley and the shining mountains through the amber-tinted lenses.

"Well," he asked, "how does it look?"

She looked at him, examining his features critically.

"I don't believe I like the landscape through them. But I like you. You 're not quite so — so — "

"So tow-colored?"

"It 's not that. It 's because you 're not quite so frightening, somehow."

"Me frightening!   Well, I like that!"

"You know what I mean."

"No, I don't."

"Frightening because — Oh, I can't explain."

He took the glasses from her and laid them precariously in the crumbling top of the wall.   He looked into her eyes.

"You must explain, Josie," he said quietly.

"Well, because — " her cheeks blazed, then paled till she was whiter than he had ever seen her.   "Because — Purley, I think you 're mean!"

"Because you love me, Josie?"

"Yes."   She clutched the front of his striped shirt. Her elbow struck the glasses and knocked them off the wall, hurtling from stone to stone, halfway down the valley, unseen by either of them.

Now her hair tried to interfere with his kisses, but he pushed it aside.

"Damn!" he exclaimed after a little.

"Why?"

"I was thinking of all the time we have wasted."

CHAPTER XIV

DIEGO PALMAS was sauntering down a precipitous path in the direction of the town. He carried his painting things and a completed canvas. In his heart was a deep content. He had just finished what he knew to be the best picture he had done. It would be years before he would weary of painting on this island. He would never really weary of it. He might go to other places later on — yet always to return to Tramontana. He pictured himself walking those mountain paths as a heavy old man — always finding some new mystery, some new beauty, for his brush.

He glanced up at the light which marked the farmhouse where the Narishkins lived. His mind dwelt for a space on his affair with Varvara. It dwelt there tranquilly. He had had just what he wanted from Varvara, no less, and no more. He was glad that she and Montleone had gone off together. Their going left him and Fay in possession of the Villa Benedittino, and in undisputed possession of each other's love. Now the hands of his spirit were reaching out toward her. She was down there where the lights were strewn like stars against the night of the sea. They were necessary to each other, but no one else was necessary to them.

He was glad that Josie and Purley Bond were out of the way, too.   Josie could not paint, never would paint, and it annoyed him to see her efforts.   Still more it annoyed him that she should criticize his work.   He liked Purley, but he did not want him about.   It was pleasant to think of the two of them married and off on a cruise in Mr. Putnam's yacht. Later they were to return to Saltport.   Just the place for them.

He ceased to think consciously of anything.   His mind lay indolently happy while his body slowly descended the darkening path.

The dusk was thick, palpable, of the velvet deepness that comes just before the night.   It brought a breeze with it, a breeze from the Ionian, and the first glimmer of distant stars.   The extravagant heat of the summer was over.   The grass lifted parched blades toward the dew.

He heard a sound behind him and stopped to listen. No, it was not actually a sound — just the echo, the shadow of the sound of little hoofs.   It gradually increased, drew nearer with the insistence of an advancing wave.   He felt rather than heard the quick breath through scores of eager nostrils.   He stepped aside, pressing close against the rock that towered above the path.

He scowled, peering into the dusk.   He strained his eyes toward the bend in the path above him.

Then they became visible, moving close together, their sides touching, their horns arching above their fairy heads. . . . All the goats that had ever grazed upon these mountain sides. Down and down they descended the path, like a gray river going down to the sea. Diego saw the pale glimmer of their eyes. . . . He heard faint music.

They swept in their mysterious trance-like trot around the bend below him and out of sight. The glimmer of their eyes was not unfriendly toward him.

Behind them he made out a figure with rounded back and elbows crooked as though a pipe were held to the lips. He saw horns, and brighter eyes beneath the horns — a figure that moved with animal grace and careless strength. It moved to the rhythm of an air that was like the breathing of the earth, the turn of the leaves in the sleep. . . .

Should he tell Fay, he wondered, continuing his way alone. No, he decided — she would be high-flown about it. She would put some ruthless interpretation of her own upon it. What had passed had been for him and no one else. He was made one with the past of these mountains. . . . His present and his future he would give to them.

CHAPTER XV

MORE than two years later two librarians from Massachusetts were walking along the Corso. They were women of nearly fifty and they had been saving up for many years for this holiday in Europe which they were now enjoying. They were enjoying it even though the weather was being unkind to them. Everywhere they went, their plump bodies were buffeted by gales, wet by driving rains. Yet they were as happy, as exhilarated, as two people well could be. They were romantic women and now they found themselves on the very Throne of Romance.

They had come from Naples by the little steamer, had been seasick most of the night, but now at evening they felt able to take a little walk. The lights from shop windows glistened on the streaming pavement, the gale had fallen, and the rain amounted to nothing more than a few fierce drops.

Electricity was cheap in Tramontana. The interiors of the little shops were discovered in a blaze of light. Embroidered table linen, lingerie, shawls, pottery, inlaid boxes, miniatures, old jewelry, carved ivory, iced cakes, French wines and British whiskey, were magnified in the brightness. But the sparkling eyes of the shopkeepers looked in vain for customers that evening. The season had scarcely begun and the only people on the Corso were a few home-faring workmen, a little boy with his arm thrust through a ring-shaped loaf of bread, and a tall woman in black. She walked steadily past the brightly lighted shops, but stopped in front of one dimly lit by an oil lamp and hung with bunches of herbs and strings of onions.

The librarians lingered outside, for they were full of curiosity and the bearing and walk of the tall woman were remarkable enough to hold the gaze of anyone who saw her. They saw that she was buying eggs, and, as she came out of the door, her face was turned full towards theirs.

She seemed to see them from a great distance, though there was nothing unfriendly in her proud, melancholy face. Her large dark eyes even rested on them for a moment in a look of flickering interest, as though the sight of them recalled something to her.

The owner of the shop followed her to the door.

"*Buona notte*, Contessa," he said genially.

"*Buona notte*, Roberto," she returned, in a deep, rather husky voice.

Contessa! The librarians exchanged a look. With one impulse they hurried after her, squeezing each other's arm, laughing secretly like two young girls.

"I dare you," whispered one, "to speak to her."

"All right. I will."

"Oh, Mary, it would be exciting!"

"I'll ask her the way to our pension. I have gotten sort of turned round."

She took a few quick steps and stood beside the Contessa.

"Pardon," she said, "but do you speak English?"

The Contessa stopped.   She looked at them a moment hesitatingly, then answered in the precise tones of a foreigner: —

"Yes.   I speak English — a little."

"Could you tell us the way to the Pension Faber? I have just forgotten which turn to take."

"Pensione Faber," she repeated, making the name sound quite different.   "Oh, yes.   I remember!   If you will walk with me I can show you exactly where it is.   Myself, I go in that direction."

They walked by her side, turning from the Corso into a narrow street between dark houses that was lighted only by a single lamp at the top of its steep steps.   She mounted swiftly, lightly, while they were panting when they reached the top.

"What a wonderful place to live in," ventured the one called Mary.

"Yes.   It is very beautiful.   You come only to-day?"

"Just this morning."

"You stay for a little while?"

"A month."

"Ah, that is too little.   Tramontana will not give herself in a month."

"Perhaps we could make it a little longer."

"But not too long!   If you stay too long you may never get away."   She gave a sudden little warm laugh.   "You are Americans?"

"Yes.   From Massachusetts.   I guess you have never been over there?"

"But I have! Once long ago — for a little visit." She stopped before a deep door in a wall. "This is where I live. You must go straight on. Then turn where there is a niche in the wall and a statue of Our Lady. Beyond there is the Pensione Faber." She raised her hand and pulled a chain attached to a bell inside the garden, and it gave a hollow mysterious clang.

The librarians, looking up, saw a wrought-iron sign bearing the word "Antiques."

"Oh," one of them exclaimed, involuntarily, and looked half-questioningly at the Contessa.

She inclined her head with a sombre smile. "Yes. We of the old families are obliged to sell some of our cherished belongings in order to live."

The librarian called Mary impulsively laid a hand on her arm. "Oh, I am so grieved for you," she said.

"*Grazie*. You are very kind." The Contessa quickly pressed the hand on her arm, then, again inclining her head, passed through the gate, which had been opened by a brown old woman.

"What a tragic figure!" exclaimed the one who was not called Mary. "I am so glad you had the courage to speak to her. If only we could know what her life has been!"

They hurried on, through the rain that was again becoming violent, to the Pension Faber.